WOVEN SERIES : BOOK TWO

embrace me

M.C. PAYNE

Embrace Me (Woven Series: Book Two)
Copyright © 2017 by Mercedes Payne
All Rights Reserved
ISBN: 978-0-9956799-5-5

Editing: Editing by C. Marie
Cover Photography © 2017 by C. E Payne
Cover Design by Marisa Shor of Cover Me Darling
Interior Formatting by Cover Me Darling and Athena Interior Book
Design

To any woman who thinks she might be hard to love, you're not you just need to learn to love yourself!!!

chapter
ONE

Knox

The music pouring from the speakers was almost deafening as I rolled the glass tumbler between my hands. There had been no reprieve in the thumping bass and club tunes spilling over the revellers encased in these walls since I arrived, but unlike the countless other songs that had played while my arse had been glued to this chair, I recognised the one that currently seemed to be on a loop. I had heard Asher play it while he got ready for a night out and beneath all the auto-tune and electronics, the lyrics were about a party girl who wanted to have a good time and ignore the consequences. It was strangely apt that this song was playing as I sat there trying not to break every bone in the body of the man currently in Freya Anson's personal space.

I fought the urge to growl as I let my eyes close. The temptation to sip on some of the amber liquid currently residing in the glass nestled between my hands was riding me harder than it usually did, so I released my hold on it and slid it just a little away from me on the bar top. I had ordered it to blend in. I hadn't touched a drop of the poison in years, but knowing places like this hovel the way I did, I was aware that ordering water would attract more attention than I wanted. The barmaid had shoved her fake tits in my face the second my arse had hit the stool, and the sudden gleam in her almost dead brown eyes had made my stomach tighten. She was no Joelle, that was for certain, and I knew that was only half the reason Freya had chosen a place like this tonight. She was upping the ante in ways I hadn't anticipated, and I was fast losing my patience.

The sound of her familiar, throaty laugh met my ears and dragged my eyes her way instinctively. To anyone else, she looked like a woman out to have a good time but I knew better. I knew things about that woman that she didn't want me to, but I couldn't erase them. I could see she didn't like the guy in the corduroy trousers who was currently stepping between her spread thighs. I could see the way her slender throat worked hard to swallow the whiskey she had just sucked into her mouth, and I noticed the almost imperceptible way her fingers tightened around the glass in her hand. I hated that she did this. I hated that she felt as though she needed to do this just to get through the night, because it was painfully obvious that doing it made her hate herself that much more.

I inhaled some of the heavy air that surrounded us and switched my attention to the woman standing beside her. Hannah Baker was a good girl, a sweet girl, definitely not the kind who should find herself in a shit hole like this. Hannah was a wine-bar-and-nibbles kind of woman, and it made me even more furious that Freya had completely disregarded that to continue the mission she had set herself—the mission I knew without a shadow of a doubt would end in tears. Whose tears they would be was still up for debate. Hannah's body language alone was telling me a story that her loyal mouth never would. She was more than just uncomfortable in this run-down dive bar; she was nearly creeping out of her skin at the attention Corduroy was showing Freya. I couldn't disagree with her there; every time his sweaty-looking paw reached out to smooth over the navy blue fall of Freya's hair—which had replaced the bright orange fire that warmed parts of me I had believed were long dead—I wanted to break something, preferably his face, with my bare fists. I knew I was capable of it, but I also knew I was better than that.

Hannah's eyes flickered around the room for what felt like the thousandth time, but I couldn't tell if she was looking for something or merely memorising it so she could relay it all to the cops later if necessary. She was the kind of girl to think like that, and I felt my mouth kick up at the corner at the thought of how innocent and naïve she seemed to be. I had no doubt that hiding beneath the pastels and A-line dresses was someone else altogether, someone she hadn't yet shown the rest of us. I was almost willing to bet she hadn't shown herself that girl either. I rubbed my thumb along my jaw as her slim shoulders became increasingly more rigid, and I could only assume it had something to do with whatever that creep was whispering to Freya as he pressed his pelvis into hers.

Red-hot fire started to tingle at the base of my spine, but before I could move, an ice-cold hand curled around my bicep. I tensed at the unexpected contact and felt warm air gust over my cheek as a female voice purred in my ear.

"Excuse me." I had learnt during my time in Acerbus that women so often had double standards when it came to physical contact. If a man ever dreamt of putting his hands on a woman the way they did to us without consent, he would be strung up and hung out to dry. As it was, society seemed to deem it perfectly acceptable for women to be as rough and handsy as they wanted without any fear of retribution.

I clenched my back teeth harder than I should have; from the sound of those words alone, I knew what I was going to find when I turned my head to look at the woman responsible for the black-tipped fingers that were currently clenching and releasing on the rigid muscle of my arm. She would most likely be young and would have smudged makeup and glazed eyes. There would be thin, straggly hair or else some really terrible extensions, and there would more than likely be a pout on her lips that wouldn't be the least bit seductive. I could already smell the desperation in the air, so instead of turning all my bulk the way a gentleman might have done, I merely cranked my neck to the side. As soon as my eyes found her, I saw that I had been spot on with my mental image—she couldn't have been more than twenty, but she looked as though she had lived a thousand lives. She looked haggard and drawn in a way only someone hooked on something nasty could.

"You're the drummer from that band aren't you." The tone of her voice was almost accusatory, and even though I knew it was probably due to the amount of cocaine she had ingested—a safe assumption if the small, dried patch of blood beneath her left nostril was anything to go by—it still sent my defences shooting up. I narrowed my eyes at her but she didn't seem to notice and continued. "That rock band that broke up, the one where the lead singer almost bawled on stage at the last concert." Her dry, cracked lips split slightly as she tried to grin at the pain two of my best friends had gone through. I had already wanted out of this conversation, but now it was a necessity. "Lacie says no way would someone like that be in Shandy's, but you are aren't you."

"You should listen to your mate or maybe do a little less coke." I tried to keep my tone even but it came out a little jagged and I saw her nostrils flare. "Drummer's my cousin, family resemblance, happens all the time."

I pushed to my feet knowing I needed to get away before I let the lecture about all the ways in which she was fucking her life up trip off my tongue. She wobbled slightly on her too-high heels but caught herself on the sticky counter of the bar, tipping her head back to gaze up at me.

"Oh." She moved a little closer, clearly not getting the hint that I was trying to get away from her, and ran the tip of her finger down the centre of my chest. The smell of rancid beer and stale cigarette smoke clung to her and my nose wrinkled involuntarily. "Well you know, I could still show you a good time. You're kind of hot. You look a lot like him." Her stained teeth sunk into her bottom lip and that was enough for me. I took a step back and her hand fell uselessly to her side.

"I'd tell you to get out of this life but I highly doubt you'd listen to me, so I'm going to wish you good luck instead. You're going to need it." With that, I turned away

9

from her. I hadn't moved more than three steps before the sound of smashing glass caught my attention. I groaned inwardly because I already knew where it had come from.

I towered over most of the population at the best of times, but tonight this place seemed to be full of the Borrowers; as I shifted on my feet, my eyes instantly homed in on Freya and Hannah. Hannah seemed to be frantically rifling through the oversized bag she had been clutching like a lifeline all night, and Freya was shaking spilled booze from her bare arms.

I kept my feet planted on the floor, waiting to see what would happen now. I had hope that Freya would realise this was a lost cause and push to her feet. I hoped the sound of smashing glass would maybe snap her out of the crazy town she seemed to reside in lately, or that maybe I would see a glimpse of the woman I had once known.

None of those things were what happened next. Corduroy seemed to have taken it upon himself to become a one-man clean-up crew and was now swiping a bar napkin over the bare skin of Freya's chest without her even seeming to notice. The beast that usually lay dormant deep in my stomach was beginning to stir as I watched him pick up a dry napkin and repeat the same action, only this time his swipe ended at the exposed globe of her breast, the exact place his eyes had been fixed for the last hour. Seeing his fingers tighten and give it a rough squeeze that had her yelping and jerking back was enough to snap my last thread of control. I knew what those breasts looked like and I knew how they felt pressed against my chest. She wielded them like weapons against the opposite sex and they were a thing of fucking wonder. Pert, round, and high, begging to be cupped and squeezed—or in some of my wilder fantasies, bitten—but definitely not by some piece of shit in a dive bar, and most certainly not without her fucking consent.

My feet were moving before I even gave them permission, and I was across the bar faster than I had anticipated. I couldn't see the bottle-green colour of her eyes when she turned them up to me over his shoulder because, for one, the lighting was shit, and for two, she had put on so much mascara and eyeliner that seeing anything aside from that was fucking impossible. I scowled and I saw it register on her face, her nostrils flaring in defiance— the same defiance I had been forced to endure for the past eight weeks. Unlike all the other nights, tonight I had no patience for her shit. Freya Anson had finally gone too far, and as she stared up at my face and took in the muscle ticking wildly in my jaw, I couldn't help but feel as though she knew it.

Freya

I felt him before I even saw him, despite the throbbing in my tit from where that handsy bastard had just gotten a good squeeze. I'd fought the urge to smack him in the face and land him on his arse, and now I was glad I had because there was no way on God's green earth I wanted Knox Sutton to see just how badly the night had gone.

I could tell he wanted to burst into his usual lecture, the one I had heard so many times I could recite it almost word for word, but there was something else working behind his eyes. The skin on his face looked tighter than normal, and the pulse in his neck was hammering so hard I could see it from where I was sitting. I didn't much like the look on his face, and I'd be damned if he thought I was going to go running like a good little girl.

My nostrils flared as the reality of just how ballsed up this night had become settled around me. I had wanted to forget and lose myself. I had wanted to pretend the tight feeling in my stomach was not the loneliness Knox had told me it was three nights ago. I'd had every intention of just rolling up to this bar and drinking myself sleepy. I had never been able to get drunk the way other people did, and it was both a blessing and a curse. Lately I felt like getting drunk would be a good thing—at least people seemed to be happier when they were drunk. Lennon had been drunk just last weekend and it had been adorable and funny as hell. It was testament to how pathetic I was behaving these days that I was almost certain watching Lennon trip over Gabriel's boots while half out of her mind on tequila was the last time I had laughed. That was almost seven days ago, and even though I knew I had never been accused of being a happy-go-lucky kind of girl, I didn't remember ever being this much of a miserable bitch either.

Somehow my night of drinking alone in a bar I wasn't familiar with had been thwarted as soon as I'd stepped foot outside my door. Hannah had been standing on the other side, her finger poised over the buzzer for my flat and a funny look on her face that I couldn't quite read. I had asked if she was okay and she had returned it with a question as to whether I was on my way out. It would have been pretty bloody difficult to lie to her considering I was wearing next to nothing, had my favourite heeled boots on my feet and a face full of makeup, so I had opted for the truth. I'd stressed the fact that I was going to a loud bar that sold really cheap booze to put her off, but when that soft smile she wore had graced her lips, I'd known I was bringing a friend along. In hindsight, it would have been easier all around for me to just change my mind, take her back to the flat, and order takeaway, but I wasn't renowned for being the queen of good decisions. Instead I had hauled her over to the cab that was waiting for me and brought her here.

I had heard about this place at the bar I was at on Wednesday. I'd been talking to the fairly decent-looking bartender and he had mentioned working here at the weekends. That was right before Knox walked in and made a scene, the way he had every other time I'd gone out in the last two months. I still didn't have a clue how he found me because I made it my mission to go to a different bar every single time, yet he always showed up and he was always pissed off. Sometimes I was sober, others I was slurring a little, but every single time he appeared, I wasn't anywhere near happy or drunk enough not to notice the glimmer of disdain in his onyx-coloured eyes.

I was used to being judged by strangers and even by people who were semi-close to me. They all saw what I wanted them to see, and I never cared enough to correct their opinion. Just last week Hannah's boyfriend Ross had told her I was a bad influence. He had told her he wasn't certain I was the kind of friend she should be keeping, and every damn word had been heard out loud in my office because her phone had been on speaker and he hadn't let her speak long enough to tell him so. If I hadn't hated that dipshit before, I certainly did after. I'd wanted to march over to his pretentious flat and smash all the ugly prettiness he was blessed with into a mirror so hard it shattered beyond repair—not because I cared what he said about me, but because he had embarrassed Hannah so acutely. Having Ross Danes judge me, however, was nowhere near the same as having Knox Sutton do it. Knox had been a very different ball game from the first night we met, and even though I knew I couldn't afford to show my underbelly to anyone, least of all that brooding hulk of a man, it was hard to pretend it didn't hurt to see him look at me that way.

It shouldn't have surprised me that he would turn up now of all times because this night seemed determined to become a shit show. Honestly I wanted out, I just didn't want that self-righteous bastard to believe it was because of him.

"Come on baby," Cord—which I had named him because I hadn't seen anyone in trousers like his since the nineties—slurred into my ear as he leant his heavy weight against my side. "Don't you like it a little rough? You look like the kind of chick who would be up for the kind of games girls like your friend would turn their nose up at."

I fought the urge to roll my eyes, aware that Knox's were burning holes through my skin. I could feel Hannah's body trembling beside me even though we were barely touching, and I shifted my body away from his a little more. I needed to figure out a way to get us both back to the flat, but with the alcohol clouding my brain and his breath in my face, it wasn't easy to think straight.

"I think it's time to go," I said as gently as I could. I knew how volatile drunk men could get and I had no desire to poke the bear, especially with Hannah there. It was my fault she was being subjected to this bullshit, and I hated the thought of Knox spreading the word about my irresponsibility when it came to the gentle woman we had dragged into our circle.

"Yeah that's what I'm talking about, sexy girl." He seemed to be slurring harder now as he reached up to shift my hair away from my neck. "Time to go get to the good stuff." His hand trailed from my neck to my cleavage and I tried not to stiffen my muscles as I raised my own hand to grab his wandering one, but as soon as I came close enough to make contact, the weight of his body disappeared. I blinked as my brows furrowed, and then my eyes focused on the back of the worn-out band t-shirt Knox seemed to favour. It was stretched tight across all the prominent muscles of his back, and the seams in the shoulders didn't look as though they would be able to stay connected for much longer. I knew I shouldn't be admiring the way his back tightened and then released as he shoved my wannabe lover away from us, but I couldn't help myself. My brain didn't have to like him for my vagina to, no matter how irritating that small detail was.

"Is that Knox?" Hannah's voice sounded thready as she breathed in my ear, and her cold hand shook as she held out a tissue for me to take.

"Mmmhmm," I murmured as I took it from her and wiped the remainder of the sticky liquid from my arms.

Shouts filtered through the air behind us and I knew better than to turn around to try and get a better look at whatever was happening. Knox was a beast of a man and there was no way anyone was going to take kindly to him barrelling through a crowd and undoubtedly spilling several drinks.

"What is he doing here? Are you and—"

"No!" The word came out harsh and clipped as I stepped down from my stool and looked her in the eye. "None of this is what you think, all right? We should just get out of here." I reached out to grab hold of her, praying we could make it out before Knox surfaced from the ruckus behind us.

"Um…" She tilted her head forward slightly and I fought the urge to groan as his big, hard body pressed tight against my back. His rough hands cupped the bare skin of my shoulders and an involuntary shudder ran through me at the contact. It was the last thing I wanted to admit, but my body was even more in tune with him when we were skin to skin.

I wasn't sure what it was about him that my body yearned so hard for. I'd had my fair share of men over the years and I liked to think I kept my base urges sated well enough that they didn't need to hanker after things they could never have, but every time he came close to me, it all became a lie. Little coils of pleasure radiated through my stomach in a way that was impossible to ignore, and I didn't even want to think about the state of my underwear, especially right now with his thumbs pressing into my skin and liquid heat flooding between my thighs.

I had almost allowed this physical attraction to get out of hand twice before, but I'd be damned if I was going to let it happen tonight. It couldn't matter that I hadn't felt the release of an orgasm in more weeks than I liked to admit, or that my hormones were convinced he would bring me pleasure unlike anything I had ever felt before. The man was so in control and self-possessed that it was impossible to believe he would be anything but amazing in bed. I could not afford to go there with Knox Sutton, not when he was so entwined in my life, not when my best friend would find herself stuck in the middle when things undoubtedly went sour.

"You're not going anywhere without me." His voice was rough as he pressed his mouth against the shell of my ear and his hot breath fanned across my cheek.

I let out a harsh breath as Hannah's eyes widened even farther and I saw her bite down on her bottom lip. I shook my head at her, willing her to understand why I was about to pull away, but clearly giving away my intentions wasn't my smartest move because his heavy palm was sliding down my arm and he was turning me to face him before my brain had a chance to catch up. I was only at eye level with the base of his neck even in my heels and I knew that if I let him, he was going to continue to gain the upper hand with sheer presence alone. I had been caught with my armour down and there was no way I could let him take the first shot. I tipped my head back to look at him and felt my breath catch; there was a harshness to his jaw I hadn't seen before, and in the dim lights of the bar, I could see that his onyx-coloured eyes were blazing like hot coals. His wide chest was heaving with deep breaths and even though he was shielding my view of the bar behind him, I could tell from the noise that it wasn't good. Still, I couldn't seem to stop my mouth from running away with me.

"What the fuck do you want?" I yelled the words to be sure he could hear me over the heavy thump of the music.

"Now is not the time or the place for your bullshit Freya, and if you think I'm kidding around, think again. I can't even begin to tell you how fucking irresponsible you have been tonight, bringing yourself and Hannah here, and right now I don't have time to. You need to move." His voice was barely below a roar and I couldn't tell if the vein pulsing in the side of his head was because he was angry with me or because he was afraid of whatever was going on behind him.

"Knox—" I started to speak, but his grip on my arm tightened and he tossed one quick look over his shoulder before he surged forward, taking me and Hannah with him.

"What's happening?" she asked, her voice trembling.

"Just stick with me. Everything will be okay if you just stick with me." Knox's voice was as steady as I had ever heard it, which for some reason made my stomach clench even harder. He placed one of his hands on her shoulder and cupped the other around the back of my neck as he ushered us towards the front door.

"Knox—" I tried to speak once more, but again he cut me off as he shoved open the door we had walked through two hours ago.

"Promise me that no matter what happens next, you will let me explain, okay?"

Hannah's wide eyes swung to me and her nostrils flared as I sucked in a breath; the warning in that tone of voice was enough to make bile climb up my throat. His black eyes burned into me as the sound of glass smashing from inside the bar echoed into the chilly April air.

"Fuck!" He cursed as he shoved his hand in his pocket and pulled out a key fob. "Truck." He nodded towards the big silver beast of a car. "Get in and lock the doors." He pressed the key into my hand and when neither of us moved, he gave us a little shove. "I said go!"

I grabbed Hannah's hand and started to drag her towards the car before I realised I hadn't answered his original plea.

"I promise," I yelled, and the sound echoed around the empty car park just as the club doors were flung open again and several men spilled out into the night. It didn't take a genius to figure out who they were or what was going to happen, and it made me tighten my grip on Hannah's hand and pull her even faster.

"What's happening?" Hannah hissed in my ear as the nails of her other hand dug into my arm, her feet slowing down on the gravel beneath us.

"Knox told us to get in the car so come on." I tugged her the last few steps and pressed my finger down on the key fob. The car lights flashed and I wrenched the door open, shoving her inside before jumping in after her.

"Freya. Freya!"

"What?" I asked as I fumbled with the lock button.

"What if he gets hurt? There were a lot of them and only one of him. What if he gets hurt?" Her nails dug into my forearm again as she grabbed me. My blood felt as though it had chilled to freezing inside my veins as her words swirled in my head.

"I…I don't know," I admitted. The truth was, I didn't have the first idea how any of this was going to play out. I tugged open my bag, readying myself to grab my phone and call the police when Hannah's voice broke over the sound of my harsh breathing.

"Oh my god!"

"What?" I swung my head to look out the window into the black night, not knowing what I was going to see but not able to stop myself either.

My eyes were the ones to widen this time as I took in the scene we had only narrowly escaped being a part of. The guy who had been buying our drinks was off to the side, one hand clutching his face—which looked bloody and messy in the dim lighting—and the other was holding his stomach. There were two men crumpled on the ground and my eyes couldn't move fast enough to track down where Knox was straightaway.

"How did he do that?" she whispered. "How did he take them all on?"

"I've got no idea," I whispered back. "Where is he?"

"There." Hannah pointed a little way off to my left and I took in the sight of Knox's fist hurtling for the stomach of the only other man still standing. The guy toppled over like a toy soldier under his furiously swinging arms and his landing looked painful.

"Did he kill him?" Hannah sounded like she was going to be sick, and as Knox started to move towards us, I turned to look at her.

"I said we'd let him explain. You can't freak out Han." I grabbed her shoulders, forcing her to look at me instead of the straps of her bag, which were wound so tightly around her fingers, the tips were turning white. "This was all my fault! We need to let him explain." I pushed the unlock button and then turned back to her because she still hadn't agreed. I shook her a little bit and repeated myself. "Okay?"

"Yes." She breathed. "Okay." I let her go as the door to the truck flew open and he climbed inside.

"Keys." His voice was gruff as he thrust his bloodied hand over the back of the seat. My stomach twisted at the sight as I placed the keys in his palm, and within five seconds he had shoved them in the ignition and peeled out of the space, racing towards the exit.

I glanced over at Hannah, whose skin looked pale and clammy, and let my head fall back on the seat. I didn't like the speed at which he was driving, but I knew I couldn't say anything. I was going to need to suck this one up because without me, none of this would ever have happened. I looked down as Hannah threaded her slender fingers through mine and I squeezed her hand once, wondering how the hell I was going to make things any better.

chapter TWO

Knox

Blood was pumping hard and fast through my veins, thundering in my ears and drowning out every other noise, even the roar of my monster engine. I tried to breathe through it but it felt as though I had a rubber band strapped tightly around my chest. I felt exhilarated and disgusted at the same time, and I couldn't get my brain to slow down long enough for me to get a grip on either emotion. I knew it was the adrenaline and that when I came down from the rush it was going to be a long hard fall, but I couldn't control every response my body had, and this one was purely chemical.

I hadn't lost control to that extent in years. I had buried that part of myself in the same dark place I had buried almost every other part of my past, and that was where I had intended for it stay; the boy I had once been should have been nothing but a bad memory. I wanted to howl in pain because I had exposed that part of me to the two women in the back seat of my truck, and I had no idea how they were going to react. Their silence was starting to feel as though it was suffocating me, but I couldn't trust myself to talk yet.

I had known it was going to kick off as soon as I threw that arsehole off her. The look on his face had been one of a self-righteous piece of shit who thought he could buy anything he wanted, including women. I hadn't been able to stop myself from landing my fist on his cheekbone with enough force that he had crumpled to the floor like a pack of cards. I'd wanted him to understand that she was off limits, but what I hadn't taken into consideration was the fact that there was no way a sleazebag like him would be in a dive bar like that without his buddies. That arrogance alone proved I had been out of the game for a long time. Once upon a time, I would have known better than to go after my main target first. I would have taken my time, deconstructed his little gang one by one, and worked my way up to the main prize, but seeing him put his hands on Freya that way had stolen any sense of self-preservation I possessed and replaced it with red-hot, burning anger. I'd wanted him to pay for the way he had touched her and had allowed myself to just react.

I tightened my grip on the steering wheel, the broken skin of my knuckles screaming in protest at the action. I hadn't stopped to ask the girls if they were okay; the only thing I had wanted to do was get the hell out of there before any of the bodies littering the gravel really got a good look at me. The last thing I needed now was for the press to get wind of what I was really capable of. I had managed to keep the parasites out of my life all through my time in the band, and there was no way I wanted to hand them a front row ticket to it now. I was going to have enough explaining to do as it was.

I sucked in as deep a breath as I could manage before I got up the courage to look at the girls in the rear-view mirror. The sight was like a sucker punch to the gut. Hannah's eyes were wide in her face and she was staring at the back of my passenger seat headrest. Freya had her head tipped back and her eyes closed, her pouty mouth pursed in a thin line, and just the sight of it made my stomach twist. There was no denying that Hannah looked more terrified sitting in the backseat of my car than she had in the bar earlier, and I felt the self-hatred yawn in the pit of my gut. I'd never wanted anyone to look at me with fear in their eyes ever again, least of all two of the women who were so deeply engrained in my life now. I knew I needed to speak, to say something, explain myself, but none of the words wanted to come out. I clenched and unclenched my split and swollen hands around the wheel as I psyched myself up.

I swallowed hard against the ever-tightening strictures around my throat and pushed out the words that seemed the most important.

"Where do you need me to take you?" I held my breath, praying neither of them would request a trip to the nearest cop shop, and trained my eyes on the road in front of me. I heard whispering in the backseat but couldn't distinguish their words over the echoing thud of my own heart in my ears. I wasn't sure I even wanted to know what they were discussing, so I concentrated instead on keeping the car moving in a straight line.

I fought the desire to look in the rear-view mirror as Freya cleared her throat. I wanted to look at her, to make sure she was unharmed. I was almost certain she was as flawless as she had ever been, but I hadn't had the time to be gentle with her. I'd manhandled her in my haste to get the three of us out of there in one piece, and I was far from proud of it.

"Can you drive to Lennon's please?"

It was a soft request in a tone of voice I was certain I had never heard from her before. I couldn't blame either of them for wanting to get away from me as quickly as they could, but that didn't stop it from stinging. I had brought this into their world when I could have just followed them into the truck. My first thought had been to ensure they were both safe, and there had been enough time between them walking away and that first arsehole squaring up to me for me to have followed, but I hadn't. I had chosen to stand and fight. I had decided I was the one who needed to teach those bastards a lesson they would never forget. I had chosen to pummel my fists into flesh that wasn't mine and act like a caveman, a thug; now I had to pay the price that came with it.

"I can do that." I willed my voice to remain steady as I flicked my indicator on. The clicking sound filled the interior of the car in a way that made my teeth clench; it was too quiet and there were too many things running through my brain.

"I appreciate it." Freya's voice was cold and lifeless now, and it chilled me to the bone. I had fucked everything up before I'd even had a chance, and all because I had wanted to protect her.

By the time I pulled up in front of Gabe and Leni's front gate, I was wound tight. I wanted to speak to them before they went inside, wanted to say something meaningful because I wasn't completely certain I was going to get another chance. More than that, though, I wanted to ask them not to tell Gabe what had happened. I wanted to beg and plead with them to keep the whole debacle between the three of us, but I knew I couldn't ask them to lie for me.

I pushed off the steering wheel and forced myself out of the truck. Freya had already clambered down from the backseat and Hannah was following her onto the pavement, the straps of her bag twisted around her hands. I closed my door and leant against it, trying to keep my battered hands out of view.

"Look girls—" I started to speak, but my words were halted by the sound of Hannah's trembling voice.

"Knox." The sound of my name quivering from her lips felt like a dagger straight through the centre of me. I let my eyes slide shut as shame swamped me, so I didn't realize she had launched herself at me until her small body collided with the front of mine. I caught her in my arms as hers wrapped around my middle. "That was the scariest thing I have ever been involved in." She trembled a little bit and I wrapped my arms tighter around her. I wanted to protect her from the images that were no doubt playing on a loop inside her head even though I had been the one to put them there. I wanted to show her that I was still the person she had known all this time and not just some thug who was only good for his fists.

"I'm sorrier than you will ever know that you had to see that." I opened my eyes and looked over at Freya.

"That either of you had to see that." Freya's lips rolled between her teeth as she shifted on her heels, and Hannah sniffed against my chest before pushing back. I looked down quickly to make sure none of the blood splattered on me had rubbed off on her; when I was satisfied it hadn't, I found her eyes.

"It was scary to see you that way, but you saved us. If you hadn't been there, then who knows when things would have gone bad, and we would have been stuck. We would never have been able to get ourselves out of that mess, so thank you. Thank you for getting us home safely."

I blinked at her words because the last thing I had been expecting was gratitude. I leant forward and pressed as gentle a kiss as I could to her forehead as she squeezed my waist. The fight and the tension seemed to be leaving me, and as much as I knew I was going to need to explain myself to a lot of people come daybreak, I wasn't sure I had the energy left to deal with any more of it tonight. I wanted nothing more than to crawl into a dark room and stay there until my world tipped itself back on its axis.

"Thank you Hannah. You don't know what that means to me." I set her away from me and tried to smile as best as I could manage. "Get yourselves inside, all right?" She nodded at me as I stepped around her and yanked the handle of my door open before turning my head to look at Freya. "Take better care of yourself, okay?"

I didn't wait for her to respond, instead I continued tugging the door open the rest of the way and climbing inside. I rested my forearms and forehead against the steering wheel because the adrenaline was beginning to seep out of my body fast now, seemingly through my skin, which was covered in a fine sheen of sweat. My heart rate had slowed to a rattling thud and my muscles were burning. I was more aware now of the cuts on my hands and how badly I needed to ice them, but I had no idea where I was going to go because I really didn't want to have to explain the state I was in to the night doorman at our new apartment complex. I didn't relish the idea of being thrown out before I'd barely had the chance to live there, but I already knew what everyone would see when they took one look at me—there was no way to deny it when my clothes and hands were blood-stained and tattered.

I twisted the key in the ignition and was about to release the handbrake when the passenger door swung open and a rush of cold air flooded the inside of the car. The door clicked shut and the silence I had been using to calm myself suddenly became weighted and heavy. I knew she could feel it too because I saw her shift in her seat out of the corner of my eye, her long fingers tugging at the hem of her skirt and skating over the bare skin of her thighs. I could tell it was a nervous thing, but I wasn't sure I had ever seen Freya nervous before now, which could only mean it was me she was nervous about.

I closed my eyes again because I wasn't even sure how to begin to deal with that. I had wanted a chance. I had wanted to show her I could be someone she relied on, someone she could trust. I knew she wasn't the kind of woman to lean on someone easily and I had been determined to show her I was worth it, but now it was gone. It was all gone, and all it had taken was a couple of drunk arseholes and my temper coming off its leash.

I sighed and the sound echoed in the quiet. A few seconds later, the sound of her phone pierced the air and I watched her fumble for it. Her fingers tapped across the screen before she turned it to darkness and slid it back into her little handbag.

"My place." It was a statement, not a question, and it had my mind reeling. I had no idea why she wanted me to take her back to an empty flat when she could have just gone inside with Hannah.

"Freya—"

"Can you just drive, please Knox?"

Those were the only words she said before she turned her head to fix her eyes out of the passenger side window. I nodded even though she couldn't see me because it was clear there was nothing I could say that was going to make this any better. Freya was not the kind of girl to explain her behaviour to anyone, least of all the man she had just watched pummel four men into the ground, so I released the handbrake and drove the quickest route I knew back to the ramshackle block of flats she called home.

I parked the car at the foot of the path that led to the front door of the block and clasped my fingers tightly around the steering wheel, preventing myself from reaching out for her. I wasn't going to make this any harder for either of us; tonight had gone as badly as it could have, and even though I had been craving a resolution for all our drama, this was not the one I wanted. I had imagined finally getting her to stand still long enough for me to explain that the only reason I kept following her because I knew she deserved better than she was giving herself, and I wanted to be the one to give it to her. I had imagined finally getting the chance to put my hands on her the way I had been craving since the first night we met, but there was no chance of any of that happening now.

I needed her to get out of the car and go inside because there was no way I could press my game on her now. I had probably never had any right to dream of putting my hands on her or even to think of her the way I did, and now that I thought about it, maybe she had always known I was no good. The near misses were always interrupted on her end. The times we had danced too close to the flame, she had been the one to throw water on it and stamp it out. I had been foolish enough to believe our demons called to each other, but maybe in reality, mine had been shouting out every bad thing they had ever done so hers knew to run and hide.

Freya

I looked over at Knox as he pulled the handbrake up and sat back in his seat. His eyes were shut tight and he didn't seem to be making any move to get out. I had assumed he would understand why I had gotten back in the car and why I had asked him to come back here with me. I had presumed he would understand I was asking him to come upstairs so we could try to talk this out, but as I stared at his rigid form, it became pretty clear that I had given this man so many mixed signals, he wasn't even bothering to try to keep up with me anymore.

"Knox—"

I wasn't sure how to say the things I needed to, so I closed my mouth almost as quickly as I had opened it. I hoped he would at least speak now, say something to make this easier. I wasn't sure anyone really understood how hard it was for me to articulate the things that needed to be said. I was always the one ready with a quick remark or sarcasm. I was the one people looked to for a smart comeback, but that was all part of the armour I wore for the rest of the world to see. When it came down to saying the important things, I often found myself lacking.

"It's okay Freya, I understand. You can get out and go inside." He looked dejected, and it was not a look that suited him. Ever since the night we'd met, he'd had an air of confidence about him. It wasn't that he was arrogant or cocky; it was more a look of calm self-assurance the rest of us could only dream of having. He always seemed so effortless when he barked out commands or tossed out advice, and seeing him this way—shoulders slumped, face pained—made the sick, gnawing feeling in my stomach become more insistent. I was the reason he looked this way. I had brought this down on him, and now that I'd had the chance to really think about the events of the evening, I knew what it could cost him.

My mind had been whirring since we had sped out of that car park. My job was based on public relations. I dealt with publicity, both good and bad, on a daily basis, and I knew that if even one person had recognised him tonight, I was about to have rained a whole shit storm down upon him. It didn't matter that the band had stopped recording. It didn't matter that they had played their final concert over two months ago. None of that mattered because Acerbus was still Acerbus, and every member was still public property. Even if that weren't a problem, the fact that they were setting up their own record label would be. Who the hell was going to want to work with someone who had an assault charge against them? Would he even be able to do it if he got sent to prison?

I pressed my hand to my throat as those things settled even harder around me in the heavy silence of his truck. I hadn't just let Hannah down and hurt him tonight; I had potentially cost him everything he had worked so hard for. The helpless feeling I usually avoided at all costs settled heavily around my shoulders, and I knew I couldn't just sit here, waiting to see what would happen. I owed Knox Sutton. I owed the man I had been evading so much that I couldn't even see a way through it. If he went to prison, it would be my fault. If he lost his business, it would be my fault. If people looked at him differently, it would be my fault.

"Freya." His voice broke through all the possible outcomes that were spinning in my mind, and my eyes snapped to his face.

"I owe you and I swear I will do whatever it takes to put this mess right. I have money. I can pay them off. I can pay the tabloids off, or I can spin it if I need to. I can talk to people. I can…I can—" An unexpected sob tore its way through my throat before I could finish what I was saying. There was a pressure behind my ribcage I hadn't experienced in a long time, and a stinging sensation that I loathed rose in the back of my nose. The only person to blame was myself. I bit down hard on the inside of my cheek and willed myself not to lose it completely.

"Fire, you didn't do anything. This was me. It was all me."

My eyebrows pulled down over my nose so fast and hard that pain shot through my brain. I had never heard him call me that before; I could only be half certain he hadn't just said Freya and I was imagining hearing some sort of nickname slip from his lips.

"You didn't make me fight them. I chose to do that."

"You wouldn't have even been in a place like that if it weren't for me, Knox, so as much as I appreciate what you're saying—"

"I need you to listen to me." His voice was gentler now as he twisted his big body so that he was facing me a little more. "I'm not saying any of this to make you feel better. You should never have put yourself in the position that you did tonight, but at no point did you ask anything of me. You didn't ask me to lose control. I did that all by myself."

"I'm self-destructive, Knox. You already know this, and now, even though it's the last thing I want, I seem to be dragging everyone else into my spiral as well."

"Fire, please, will you look at me?" His hands were clasping the sides of my face, forcing me to turn my head in his direction, forcing me to meet his eyes as that name echoed between us once again. This time there was no way I was mistaken. The need to ask him why he was calling me that was on the tip of my tongue, but he spoke again before I could.

"You are not responsible for that. Sure, we wouldn't have been there if you hadn't decided to go, but as for the rest of it, that was bad judgment. No one stopped me from getting into the truck with you and Hannah. I could have picked you both up, bundled you into the car, and gotten us out of there without spilling even one drop of blood, but I didn't. I chose to stand and wait for them to come, to see what they could do. I can't explain why." His head dipped and his grip on my face weakened until his hands fell away and into his lap. His shoulders heaved under the weight of his breaths and the air he expelled fanned over my wet cheeks. I reached my hand up to press against the dampness and took in a breath; I hadn't cried in longer than I could remember. I had come to realise it was a pointless waste of time and energy to cry over things you couldn't change, but this night felt different.

When he didn't look up at me again, I immediately knew it was up to me how this went from here. We could either sit there and let it happen around us, or I could drag us both out of this car and try to do something to clean up the mess I had created.

"Come inside." I tried to keep my voice even, but the emotion I was so unfamiliar with was still clogging it. "Come in and get some ice, and I will try to figure out how to make this better."

"This isn't your fault," he murmured as he tilted his head to look at me.

"I disagree," I said as I pushed open the car door and jumped down onto the pavement. My ankles wobbled a little—one should never jump onto concrete in five-inch stiletto heels—but I made sure I stayed upright as I slammed the door behind me and stalked up the path. I needed a moment to myself because I hated to feel as out of control as I did right then, but I knew I couldn't have it until I'd put right what I had done wrong. I pulled the heavy security door open and then it was taken from my grip. The lift once again had its yellow *Out of Order* sign plastered to the front, so I headed straight for the stairs.

Knox was silent as we walked up the stairs, but I could feel his heat surrounding me. He was potent even now, and I felt my stomach coiling in response to his close proximity. My hand shook as I slipped my key from my bag and unlocked the door, letting us both inside. I had seen him in here only a handful of times, and most of those were when he was helping Lennon haul her things down to the removal truck Gabriel had hired. My heart tightened slightly as I made my way through the flat, flicking on lights as I went.

"It must be quiet here now." His voice echoed around us as he followed me into the kitchen. I had no idea how he had known what I was thinking at that moment, but it wasn't the time for pleasantries and small talk, especially not when I knew where the conversation was heading. I had heard the 'you're lonely' lecture countless times over the last two months, and I knew I wouldn't be able to stand up against it in my current emotional state.

I slammed the freezer door shut and dropped the ice cubes in my hand into the tea towel on the counter.

"Ice for your hands." I held it out to him and for the first time, got a really good look at the weapons he had been wielding against those men. His knuckles were swollen and ugly, and the skin was split. They looked raw and angry, much like his face had when he had been inflicting damage on those arseholes. I hissed out a breath through my teeth as he stepped around me and shoved his hands under the hot water tap.

"There has to be a better way of doing that." I winced at the sight of the blood as it coated the stainless steel of the sink and disappeared down the plug. "I think Lennon probably left—"

"This is good enough." His words were hard and conveyed finality, so I slammed my mouth shut and put the tea towel down on the counter. The best thing I could do at the moment would be to fix this mess so everything could return to the way it had been.

"I have to make some calls." I gestured in the direction of my bedroom and saw the shadows infiltrate his eyes.

"Yeah, me too actually." He nodded.

I dipped my head and made my way out of the living room. I closed my bedroom door tight behind me and pulled my phone from my bag. I found the number I wanted and it rang a few times before the call connected.

"Freya?"

"Jack." It was only as I had watched his blood wash down the drain that I'd realised I did know someone who could help.

"What's wrong sweetheart? Are you okay?" There were noises in the background that were nothing like the ones I would have heard had he been at home.

"Are you at work?"

"I am. You didn't answer my question." I let out the breath I had been holding because him being at work might make my request a whole lot easier to fulfil.

"I really fucked up tonight Jack." I pinched the bridge of my nose as I took a deep breath. "I dragged someone into it and now I'm terrified that it's going to cause him trouble. I didn't want to hurt anyone but I've managed it anyway."

"Okay darling, you're going to have to calm down and explain the situation to me properly. I'll help any way I can, you know this Freya." I thumped down on my bed and started to relay the events of the evening to the only person I knew for sure I could trust with them, the only person who might stand a chance of helping me right the wrongs.

chapter THREE

Knox

I couldn't see the door of her bedroom as I sat down on the sofa, but I heard it click shut. A part of me was glad she needed to make some calls because I did too, and after everything that had already happened tonight, I really didn't want her to hear what I needed to say.

I pulled my phone from my pocket and scrolled through my contacts. I knew it was probably out of order to call at this time, but I wasn't sure what else to do—I didn't want to be front-page news in the morning. I also didn't want Freya to be front-page news, and the only way I knew to prevent that was to throw money at it. It was Freya's words in the car that had highlighted it to me; her insistence that she had money to pay people off had lit a fuse inside my brain. I had money—lots of it—and if that was what it took to make tonight disappear, I was willing to throw every penny I had at it.

"Mathers." That familiar voice filled my ear and for a second I held my breath before releasing it.

"It's Knox."

"Bit late in the UK for a social call, isn't it boy?" His voice had relaxed somewhat and I hated to think that I was about to undo that.

"That's because it isn't really a social call." I cracked my neck as the tension crept up my spine. I heard the leather of his chair creak in the background and I knew that meant he had just sat forward. I had his full attention, and I hated every second of it.

"What happened?"

"I fought."

"Why?" I took another breath, this one so deep it had me seeing stars behind my closed eyelids.

"Freya went to a club; she's been going to shit holes like it for a few weeks now. I've been keeping an eye on her. I just had a feeling about tonight. I knew it was going to end badly, one way or another. I wanted to get her and Hannah out of there but...I got distracted. I had to pull some piece of shit off her—he was touching her without her consent." There was silence on the other end of the line so I continued. "I pulled him away, showed him up, there was a scuffle, and I knew I needed to get the girls out of there. The guys weren't far behind us. I made the girls get in the car and lock the doors. I didn't want either of them getting hurt."

"Why didn't you just get in the car Knox?" His voice was low and completely unreadable, exactly how I had expected it to be.

"I couldn't. It felt as though my feet were rooted to the floor. I stayed and I fought. I couldn't let him get away with touching her, mauling her like that. It made me feel fucking sick. It made me want things I haven't wanted in a long time, Cal." My chest ached once again as the memory of how I had felt, what I had seen crashed over me in waves. This was part of the reason I was glad she was out of the room; I didn't want to remind her of what she had seen in me earlier. For some crazy reason, she blamed herself. She had asked me up to her flat, and I didn't want her to remember why all of that was probably a bad idea.

"How many?" he asked, and as expected, I could hear the keys of his keyboard clicking.

"Four."

"You lay them all out?"

"Yes."

"Permanent damage? Breakages?" It sounded as though we were talking about an insurance claim, but I knew all Calvin wanted right then were the cold, hard facts.

"None. I was careful."

"Careful?" He barked out a laugh. "Careful would have been you sitting your arse in your truck and driving away."

"Are you saying you would have let someone get away with that?" The question was loaded in all the worst ways and I instantly wanted to apologise.

"Yeah, okay, you got me there."

"Look, I'm sorry Cal, for what I just said, and for calling." I scrubbed my hand over my face and acknowledged the fact that I felt as though I had aged about ten years in the last two hours.

"I'm glad you called me, kid. You know I will do all that I can."

"Money's no issue. I have money, so just send me the bill when this is over."

"Whatever kid."

"Calvin," I growled.

"You have more important things to worry about right now. Where's the girl?"

"In her room. She said she had to make a call. She's blaming herself and thinks it's on her to fix this."

"As much as we both know you wouldn't have been there without her, you gotta make her understand that that's bullshit. I know better than anyone that no one can make you do anything you don't want to do."

"I already tried to explain it to her."

"Then try harder Knox. You're going to need to take care of her tonight, you hear me? When that adrenaline wears off, she will crash."

"She's more than likely going to come to her senses and throw me out." I knew it was most likely the truth, but that didn't stop it from hurting. I liked being there in her space, and even though we had barely said anything to each other, I liked that we hadn't argued too much yet. I wanted nothing more than to stay and talk about what had happened, stay and make it right, but I knew that was most likely a pipe dream.

"Anyone ever reminded you that you don't know every little thing that goes on in other people's minds? Take it from an old man: if she blames herself, she ain't throwing you out, but it's your job to make her see that you have your own damn mind and you decided not to get in that car. Just take care of her tonight kid, and let me take care of everything else. I'll keep you up to speed."

The call ended and I pulled the phone away from ear, tossing it down on the coffee table and sitting back against the soft cushions of the sofa. Every part of me ached in ways that had once been familiar, ways I had once used to prove I was making up for everything that had happened before, but now the aches made me feel dirty. I needed to get my head on straight so that when Freya emerged—I couldn't even deal with considering that it might be an *if*—I would be ready to explain to her why the things she'd said in the car couldn't have been more wrong. Hearing her blame herself had shattered something inside me that I hadn't known existed. I never wanted to hear a woman blame herself for something I had done, least of all her. I had no idea how she had come to be the woman she presented to the world, but I knew for certain now that underneath it all was a woman who was running from things, and I could relate to that.

I let the soggy tea towel fall onto the coffee table as I sat forward. There was nothing I could do now about what had happened at the bar; it was in the hands of fate and Calvin and his team. The best I could do was try to get through to Freya.

I heard her bedroom door opening and sat up straight on the sofa. I moved in time to see her walking into the front room. Her shoes were gone and it amazed me how tiny she looked without them on. If I were to stand up, she would only come up to my chest. I watched her as she moved around the sofa and took a seat on the armchair.

"I've spoken to Jack, Maxine's husband." My brow furrowed slightly as she started to speak. "He's a cop." She swallowed hard and I felt it like a sucker punch. I had thought she wanted to keep the police out of it. I had been under the impression that she probably didn't want me to take a trip to the slammer.

I clenched my hands into fists as I realised I was being delusional. What possible reason would she have to want to save my arse? She had probably only gotten me up here so it would be easier for them to take me in.

"I've asked him to drive out there to see if they're still there, and to keep his ear on the hospitals and any calls of assault that might come into the station. It's a big ask, but he promised me he'd try."

I lifted my head to look at her; her jaw was flexing uncontrollably and there were bright red splotches on her neck and her still exposed cleavage. Her hair was no longer a waterfall, and instead, she looked windswept. Her bottom lip was raw and swollen from where she had clearly been biting down on it. She looked rumpled and far less than the perfect she always appeared to be, and I wasn't sure she had ever looked more beautiful.

"At least if he does that and he hears anything, then we will have a heads up and I can do whatever I need to do to stop it from becoming a problem." She nodded as though that action reaffirmed everything she had just said. "I know it's not much, not even close to being enough, Knox, but right now it's the only thing I trust. I don't want to call any of my contacts because you never know who's out to make quick money. I don't want to feed anyone a story in case they didn't recognise you." She clasped the back of her neck and shook her head. The look in her eyes squeezed my heart; she was hurting, and it was the first time she had ever allowed me to see an expression like that on her beautiful face. "I never wanted this. I didn't want anyone to get hurt."

I was moving from my seat before I even knew what was happening. I didn't have far to go and I dropped to my knees in front of her, her eyes widening momentarily as I clasped her around her waist and pulled her into me. Even kneeling, I was the same height as she was sitting, and it left us in the perfect position. I knew she wasn't a cuddler—Lennon had made reference to it on numerous occasions—but I couldn't help myself. She looked as though she needed someone to hold her together for a minute, and from the second I'd laid eyes on her all those months ago, I had wanted nothing more than to be the one who could provide that strength for her when her own was waning.

After a minute I pulled back, aware that her body was still stiff and her arms hadn't quite reciprocated the affection. I clasped her hands in my own, resting them on her thighs, and looked up at her.

"You have your man on it and I have mine; between them, they will help us fix this sorry mess. I have faith in my team and I can tell you have faith in Jack. I made mistakes tonight, big mistakes that I don't even know how to set about fixing, but I need you to hear me when I tell you that what happened isn't something I blame you for. It's like I said downstairs: I could have gotten in the car and driven away, but I chose to stay and fight. You didn't make me." I wanted her to really hear what I was saying, but I wasn't entirely convinced that I was succeeding until her fingers squeezed mine.

"Why did you want to fight?" She whispered the words and I shrugged, because the answer to that question was long, complicated, and not for a night like tonight.

"Because that's what I was taught to do Fire." I smoothed some of her hair away from her face as I answered and saw her brow furrow before she asked her next question.

"Why do you keep calling me that?"

"Fire?" She nodded. "When we first met, your hair looked like fire. I think I've probably called you that in my head ever since." I stroked my thumb over her cheekbone as I spoke because this was probably the closest I was ever going to get to touching her. I had gone way past any step we had taken before, and yet, she hadn't stopped me. I was pushing my luck and it was undoubtedly going to blow up in my face, but after what had happened, I needed the comfort of touching her. I needed her to ground me and to remind me of who I was now, that one slipup didn't mean it had all gone to waste. I could salvage myself from the mess of tonight; I just had to get my strength back.

Freya

Never in my life had anything felt as good as his thumb did skimming over my cheekbone. Nothing had ever made my chest warm or my stomach settle the way it did as his fingers brushed against strands of my hair. I had no idea what was happening, no idea what was suddenly making me feel this way, but it felt as though all the raw pieces of me that I had flayed open tonight—and even on nights before this one—were knitting back together.

I had denied my body's feelings for him. I had denied that I wanted him to kiss me the way he seemed to want to. I had denied that I felt anything for him at all. I had baited him. I had avoided him. I had treated him like he had the plague. I had dismissed him, and yet he had been there tonight. He had been in that bar and he had been watching out for me. He had saved me from myself and saved Hannah from my sheer idiocy, and there would never be enough words in my vocabulary to thank him for all of that. The power he possessed was what I had always been most afraid of, but tonight it had been my saving grace. A shudder ran through me as that thought settled on my shoulders.

"Are you cold?" His voice was gentle and it made me shiver again. "I'll get you something warmer." He pushed to his feet and as his body heat left me, I wasn't sure anything but him could ever make me warm again. I knew I was emotional. I knew it had been a long and exhausting night, but for once I didn't want to have to think too hard about the pros and cons of something. I wanted to feel. I wanted to feel something solid and real. I wanted to take the one thing I wanted more than anything else and hold on to it.

I pushed to my feet and snagged his wrist. He turned immediately, his eyes searching my face, looking for any sign of what had caused my sudden distress. I couldn't fight it anymore. Everything inside me was snapping and pulling back together in ways I didn't understand as his eyes swept over me and I pushed onto my tiptoes. I gripped the back of his thick neck in my hands and pulled his mouth down to mine. I obviously took him by surprise, because for a second he didn't move. I wasn't sure he was even

45

breathing, but I didn't pull away. I had pulled away from him enough, and now I had to follow through. I would probably regret it in the morning—fuck, he would probably regret it in the morning. I was sure this was a bad idea and every sensible part of me screamed to stop now before I made an even bigger mess than I already had, but I couldn't stop. I couldn't heed my own brain's warning because his hands were shifting into my hair, grabbing big fistfuls and tugging, sending tingles rushing across my scalp and my heart was pounding too loud for me to hear anything but the thump of desire that was crashing through me.

I pressed my fingertips tighter into his skin and felt the moan as it rumbled through his broad chest. One of his hands shifted from my hair and I felt the loss immediately, but then it landed hot and heavy across the base of my back. His hand almost spanned my entire waist, and I didn't consider myself to be a model-thin kind of girl. It made me feel small, dainty, and that was something no one had ever managed before. He was powerful and potent in all the best and most dangerous ways, and I couldn't seem to get close enough. I wanted to climb him. I wanted to scale him like an explorer on a mountain, and suddenly I couldn't remember why I had denied myself for so long.

I pulled my mouth away, reluctantly breaking our kiss, and forced my heavy eyelids to open so I could look at him. His mouth was parted and he was dragging in deep gulps of air as he stared back at me, his eyes glazed with lust, and it made the slickness between my thighs more obvious and important. His hands hadn't moved; he was still clasping me to him as though he was afraid I might disappear if he loosened his grip.

"Why were you there tonight Knox?" I whispered the question because I knew it was going to be one of the most dangerous things I had ever asked. His answer came instantly.

"For you."

The shudder ran through me again, but this time it had absolutely nothing to do with being cold. I was flushed. I was claustrophobic. I felt trapped and I wanted to be free. As if he understood the thoughts rioting inside my brain, he let his grip slacken a little and bent so he could trail his lips over the sensitive skin of my neck.

"I came for you. I came to make sure you were safe." I dug my nails into his skin harder than I meant to, but before I could pull away, he hissed out a noise that sounded like the purest pleasure. "Don't hold back. I need that. I need the pleasure tangled with pain so I don't know where either of them begin or end."

My stomach clenched at his words. I had never heard anything quite like it in my life, and I couldn't explain the effect it had on me. I dug my nails in again and raked them up his neck and over his shaved scalp as he bit down on the muscle between my neck and shoulder. My pussy clenched hard and I knew he felt it when my body jerked against his.

"I need you to be sure." His voice sounded pained, and I was certain that if I were to try to speak, mine would sound exactly the same. "I need you to be sure, because if we do this, there is no going back, no running, no hiding, no changing your mind." He brought his head up from where he had been dropping kisses across my shoulders, sending goose bumps racing up and down my arms. "I need you to be all in, because if I put my hands on you, I swear to God I won't be able to take them off." His eyes were imploring me to answer, but my tongue felt swollen, too big for my mouth. "Fire, please." He groaned, and I could see that it was taking every ounce of strength he possessed to hold on. I nodded shakily and he bit down hard on his lip. "Words. I need your words." His fingers clenched and unclenched reflexively on my hips as I shook the fog from my brain.

"Yes Knox."

That was all it took for all hell to break loose. He gathered me around the waist and carried me into my bedroom. The door slammed shut behind us, and I was about to ask him why he had worried about that when he pushed me up against it. My bare feet hit the floor and he dropped to his knees. His hands grabbed at my skirt, tugging it down my legs along with my knickers until they were both pooled around my feet.

"Knox." I gasped as he lifted my left ankle and tossed my leg over his shoulder. His tongue instantly made contact with my slick and swollen folds. I grabbed his head for leverage, to try to stop myself from toppling over as he swiped his tongue through my centre, stopping to pay special attention to my clit. I couldn't stop the scream that tore from my throat at the sensation. It was like nothing I had ever felt before, and I hadn't been expecting it. I never played with men who bothered with things like oral sex. I never went home with them; they never came home with me. We fucked where we met and that left little time for things like foreplay.

"God you taste even better than I dreamt you would." I jolted as his breath gusted over me and his free hand slid up the inside of my leg. "You taste even better than you smell. Fuck, you're like the purest alcohol, straight to my fucking head."

I didn't have time to respond, probably couldn't have even if I'd wanted to, because his questing hand had found its final destination. I felt two thick digits push inside me and curl in a come-hither motion as his lips wrapped around my clit and sucked hard. I detonated. I had no idea what happened next. The world seemed to dip and go black for a few moments, and when I opened my eyes, I was lying on top of my black satin duvet and he was beside me, leaning up on his elbow to look down at me with those heavily lidded eyes.

"That was…" I started, but I had to swallow hard. "That was… I mean, I've never…"

"You've never?" He raised a brow and I saw a light in his eyes dance.

"Never." I shook my head and he leaned down to press his mouth against mine. I could taste myself on him and it was the sexiest fucking thing I had ever been a part of.

I clawed at his t-shirt, dragging it up and over his head, and ran my nails over his back, scoring at the skin as he fumbled with his jeans. They eventually came free and he kicked them to the floor. As I pulled off my top and my bra instinctively, I heard his wallet thud on the floor and the tell-tale rip of a foil packet. I looked up at him as he grasped his cock in his left hand and a gasp escaped my mouth involuntarily as I tried to take in the sight of him kneeling before me.

"You okay?" he asked. He released his fully erect, fucking *massive* cock and moved towards me.

"I figured you'd be big, but fuck." I breathed the last word because my eyes were once again being drawn to the more than impressive package between his legs. I knew for a fact that if I reached out now, I wouldn't be able to wrap my hand the whole way around it.

"You want me?" He breathed the words, and I swallowed hard.

"Knox." I looked up at him as I lay back against the pillows. He didn't answer me, instead tightening his grip on his cock enough that his sore knuckles stood out in stark relief. It was far harder than I ever would have gripped a man, and it was only then that I realised why he was doing it.

"It's the way I like it, Fire." He breathed as he stroked himself hard and rough a few times. My pussy clenched once again as I watched him. My eyes were greedy because I had never watched a man pleasure himself before, least of all a man like Knox—not that I was convinced there were any other men like him. Even though it would probably all go up in flames in the morning, causing a world of pain and destruction, I couldn't imagine having anyone else in my bed.

"Jesus," I hissed out, and his chuckle echoed around the room.

"He's not going to help you now beautiful." His voice was deeper than I had ever heard it, and it sounded almost sinister as he snatched up the foil packet from the bed beside me. "You want me?"

"Yes," I whispered as he started to unfurl the latex down his thick length in a way that had me wanting to press my thighs together.

"Because I'm me or because I have a cock? Am I interchangeable?" My eyes widened as he looked up at me. "I need to know."

"What do you want from me? I've told you I want you. I've finally admitted it," I whispered as he moved up the bed, covering my body with his own. I curled my fingers around his neck as he dipped his head so that his mouth was pressed against my ear.

"The truth. From now on, I only want the truth. I need to know that it's me you want, so which one is it, the cock or the man?"

"The man." The words tumbled from my mouth as his hand skimmed down my side and across my stomach, my muscles fluttering in response to his feather-light touch, my body arching into his.

"So fucking responsive," he growled. "So fucking potent." His fingers trailed lower and once again, I felt them breach my entrance, plunging deep enough into me that I gasped out loud. "Need you ready for me beautiful." His fingers relentlessly plunged and retreated, stretching and testing me until I couldn't catch my breath. All that was left for me was the oblivion the black of his eyes promised. I pushed myself harder against the palm of his hand as he growled and murmured filthy things in my ear, and I finally let go in a gush of liquid pleasure that had me sinking into my bed sheets.

"It's too much," I groaned as he continued the push and pull of his fingers along sensitive flesh. My orgasm felt as though it was never going to end and I tried to wriggle away from it.

"It's not enough."

"Please."

"Please what beautiful?"

"Please just fuck me!" The words burst from my lips and his fingers stilled inside me. My eyes slid shut because I could hardly believe what I had just begged him for. Mortification was bubbling within me until his mouth came down hard on my own in a biting kiss that didn't last nearly long enough.

"One thing you need to know, Fire girl, is that even when you're so hot you feel like you're going to burn up, even if we get rough, I am never *fucking* you. I am never going to be the man who just ruts into you without a second thought. I am always"—his free hand clasped my chin until I was looking directly at him—"always going to be thinking about you. I am always going to be making it my mission to make it as good for you as it is for me. I am going to find your rhythm and I'm going to match it, and sometimes I'm going to smash it all to shit just because I can, because I know that this, with you, is going to feel better than it ever has with anyone else, and I'll be damned if I'm in it alone." His words had barely registered with me before he pushed against my entrance.

"Fuck," I hissed as he pumped his hips slowly against me.

After that speech, I had expected him to pound into me, to plunge in balls deep and punish me with his cock for all the times I had run away, for all the times I had hurt him, but he surprised me. I snaked my arms around his shoulders as best I could as he slid one hand in between us to work on my clit.

"God you feel so good, so tight, like fucking heaven."

"God…just…please." I couldn't get enough air into my lungs as I tried to beg him to go faster, to push into me harder.

"Tell me what you need." His voice was tight, and I knew it was because he was holding back. I unfurled my hands and let my nails drag over the soft skin of his back, and his body jerked against me.

"You, all of you."

Without another word he caught his weight on his elbow. His free hand grasped my leg, lifting it higher and wider to allow himself more access and leverage, and then he started to move. I lost my breath as he pushed and pulled against me. I could feel his fingers gripping my thigh, his other hand moving from my clit to tug at my hair as his mouth descended on my neck to suck and bite the tender flesh, and then I was flying, airborne. It felt as though I had left my body and landed somewhere nothing else existed but blinding, all-consuming pleasure. I was on fire and nothing had ever felt better.

chapter FOUR

Knox

I rolled onto my back and attempted to get my eyes to focus on the room around me. I had only caught a glimpse of it the night before in my haste to get inside her, but now I wanted to take a moment to observe. I knew a lot could be learnt about a person based on the things they deemed necessary in their personal space, and while I knew the flat as a whole had been decorated in neutral, soft tones and elegant touches, I also knew that those were mostly Lennon's doing.

I squinted slightly because the only light in the room was coming from the soft glow of the alarm clock on the bedside table closer to where she was sleeping and a small crack of light that was peeking in over the curtain rail. From what I could tell, the walls were all dark red except for the one directly behind her bed; that one was covered in a black damask-style wallpaper. I fought the urge to reach my hand through the wrought iron bedstead to touch it and see if it felt as much like crushed velvet as it looked, but I knew the movement would disturb her. The bed we were currently tangled in was larger than any bed I had ever slept in before, and the bedstead was the only defining feature I could find in the room. With its twisted metal vines, it had the part of my brain I tended to keep to myself running wild with all the ways I could put it to good use. Based on the satin I had originally laid her out on, I had expected her bed covers to be silky when we had finally slipped beneath them, but I had been pleasantly surprised to find a dark red flannelette sheet and a cotton duvet beneath the throw that had been tossed to the floor after round two because it really needed a wash. Freya's bedroom was exactly like her—raising more questions than it answered.

I turned slightly so I could bring her sleeping form into my line of vision and fought the urge to smooth away the tangled strands of hair that were stuck to her forehead. I knew if I touched her, she would wake and it would all be over, the bubble would burst, so instead I settled for watching her. The glow of her clock was more useful when I was concentrating on her, and I could make out the curve of her cheek and the small line of her nose. She looked younger lying beside me with her hands tucked beneath her cheek and her shoulder rising and falling with her deep breaths, but she still wasn't peaceful. There were small lines bracketing her mouth and her lips were downturned in a frown that made me want to change whatever had put it there. I had known from the first night I laid eyes on Freya Anson that there was a whole lot of pain bubbling away just under the surface, and I had wondered a lot—

especially recently—whether that was the reason she did the things she did. I could only guess it was the driving force behind how she treated herself so carelessly, and that thought alone made me want to beat down every demon she possessed.

I had always hated the way she seemed to short-change herself in every aspect of her life. I hated that she put herself in danger purely because she wanted to show everyone she was living life on her own terms, but now it felt different. The beast inside me was wide awake and fixated on doing all it could to ensure she never went back to that. I'd had her now, and I couldn't pretend otherwise, didn't want to pretend otherwise. Even though I knew it would mean I would probably have a fight on my hands, I wasn't prepared for us to go back to the way things had been before.

I watched as she shifted slightly in her sleep. One of her hands clenched and released gently before she fanned her fingers out against the bedsheet. I thought about reaching out and covering her hand with my own, if for no other reason than to get the inevitable fight out of the way, but before I could act on that impulse, her phone blared to life. The sound was obnoxious in the dark silence of her bedroom. She stirred beside me again and I considered reaching for the phone to shut the noise off, but she beat me to it. She went from lying still to sitting upright in less than a second, her hand shooting out to grab the phone and click the accept button without even looking at the caller ID.

"Jack." Her voice was huskier than normal and the sound went straight to my cock. I reached out for her and snagged her around the waist because I just couldn't help myself when all that naked flesh was on display right in front of me. Her eyes shot to mine and I could tell it wasn't confusion that flooded the bottle-green depths, but there was definitely something swimming in them that I couldn't put my finger on. I didn't let it deter me though. I tightened my hold on her and pulled her back so she was sitting against the pillows.

"Yeah I'm here. I was asleep. Okay." She murmured the last word and it had me sitting up straighter. "Oh god."

The whimper of sound that escaped her had every protective instinct I possessed firing to life. I tried to catch her eye but she didn't even seem to notice me as I hauled her body against mine. Her skin felt frozen as she collided with me but the grip she had on her phone didn't slacken.

"I don't even… I mean… Oh god." She breathed again. I was just about to snatch the phone from her hand and demand that Jack talk to me instead of her when her eyes finally swung up to mine. "He's here." She held the phone out to me and I took it from her wordlessly as my heart plummeted into my stomach. I couldn't imagine that this phone call would bring anything good for me, but I knew I had asked for it; I had courted trouble, and it had finally caught up with me.

I took the phone from her and as I pressed it to my ear, she slipped out of my hold and out of the bed.

"Fire," I growled as quietly as I could, and she turned back to look at me.

"Bathroom." Her head dipped and I blew out a breath of acceptance.

"Come back okay?" She nodded but didn't answer.

I watched her leave and pull the door closed behind her before turning my attention to the man on the other end of the phone. I had only met Jack Dalton once before at Lennon and Gabe's engagement dinner, and at the time he had seemed like a good guy. I wasn't sure my opinion of him was going to stay the same once I heard what he had to say.

"Hello?"

"I'm here. Sorry about that, Freya ran out." I tried to keep my voice as level as I could because I needed to hear what he had to say so I could plan accordingly.

"I thought she might, which is why I wanted to speak to you, Knox." He sounded weary and worried, and it caught my attention.

"Listen Jack, I know she asked a lot of you last night. Somehow, she got it into her head that everything that happened was her fault, and she wanted to make amends. It wasn't her fault, it was mine, so if you're giving me a heads up that you're heading down to haul my arse in, I completely understand."

"Not hauling your arse anywhere Knox." I heard a noise in the background that sounded like a mug being set down on a desk. "When Freya called me last night, I went out straight away. I took one of my men, decent guy, hates shit holes like that. We found two of them in the car park. They didn't look as though they were in any hurry to get moving. I told them we had received a call about a disturbance and had come down to look into it. The others were back inside."

"They were still there?" It seemed odd to me that they hadn't scarpered as soon as they had the opportunity, and I knew there was going to be a reason for that.

"They were. They didn't seem too pleased to have the cops showing up either. We questioned the two from the car park about why they hadn't reported anything and they said there was nothing to report. They said they had gotten into a fight with one another and it had just gotten out of hand."

"The fuck?" I breathed.

"Yeah. Considering I knew it was a downright lie, I pushed a little bit harder. We ran their names through the system to get some sort of idea of what we were dealing with."

I closed my eyes because now I felt like I knew where this was going.

"Freya gave me a pretty good description of the guy that started the trouble."

Suddenly the tone of his voice made a lot more sense to me—Jack cared about Freya, cared about both her and Hannah because they meant so much to his wife, and I knew that whatever he had found out terrified him.

"What's his deal?"

"Got out of lock up two months ago." He huffed out a breath again. "Rape." The word sliced through me and I pushed out of the bed.

"Did you tell her?"

"I did. I had to Knox. Is she okay?" I looked up at the open bedroom door and then back down at the sheets tangled on the bed.

"I don't think so."

"God." He sighed again, and this time I felt it. "You have no idea how glad I am you were there Knox. They didn't say a word about you. I'll keep my ears open, but I don't think they have any intention of making anything out of it." I expelled a breath as it felt like a weight had been lifted off my shoulders, but at the same time, a new one had been put in its place.

"I appreciate all you've done Jack. You'll have to excuse me though, I need to go make sure she's okay."

"No problem. Take care of her."

"Call me if you hear anything, okay?"

"Sure thing. How can I reach you?"

I rattled off my number and thanked him again before ending the call. I tossed her phone down on the bed and immediately stalked out of the room. I made my way across the hallway and pushed the handle on the bathroom door but it was locked, just as I had suspected it would be. I wanted to get my hands on her, wanted to hold her and promise her I would never let anyone hurt her ever again, but I couldn't do that if she kept me locked out. I let my forehead thump against the wood before I spoke.

"Fire, let me in."

There was no sound from the other side.

"Just unlock the door." I waited again, but there was still no sound. I rattled the handle. "Jack told me what he told you."

I pressed my ear to the wood, hoping to catch even the faintest sound.

"Okay, you have ten seconds to open this door or I kick it in, your choice. One…two…three…" If she thought I was messing around, she was sadly mistaken. I was getting my hands on her one way or another. "Four…five…six…seven…" I didn't relish the idea of the mess it was going to make to splinter the wood, but it seemed liked it was going to be a necessary evil.

"Don't make me do it. Just open the door beautiful." I expected her to cave. I wanted her to, but still nothing. I cursed under my breath before continuing my count.

"Eight…nine…"

Ten was on the tip of my tongue when the lock clicked. I shoved the handle down as quickly as I could and pushed the door open. She was scrambling back against the side of the bath, her knees pulled up to her chest and her arms wrapped tightly around them. She was wearing the tiny pair of knickers she had pulled on after round three and nothing else, and I could see the shivers rolling through her as she curled inwards on herself. The makeup I hadn't given her a chance to take off last night was now streaked down her pale cheeks, and it made my heart hurt to see her that way.

I turned around and made my way back into her bedroom. I grabbed the dressing gown that was on the back of the door and looked at it for a second. I had expected her to be the kind of woman who wore those useless silky things that only hit about mid-thigh, but instead in my hands was a soft fleece garment that probably fell down to her ankles. It had a hood and pockets and was covered in snowflakes of all shapes and sizes, just another piece of the jigsaw puzzle that was Freya Anson.

Freya

The words Jack had spoken were still ringing in my ears, even with the bathroom door wide open and the sound of Knox's bare feet padding across the wood flooring. Jack had warned me that he was going to say those words out loud to Knox, but what I didn't know was how he was going to react to them.

The sound of my phone ringing had broken through one of the deepest sleeps I'd had in a long time, and for a moment, I had forgotten all about the events of the night before. It was only a split second however, before every single detail came flooding back, and when Knox's arms had wrapped around my waist and hauled me back against him, I'd realised it hadn't all been a dream. I wasn't sure if I had expected him to have left in the middle of the night or not, but there he was lying beside me, half naked with every inch of corded and inked muscle on show and a look in his eyes that told me he saw too much. I hadn't had a chance to dwell on that, though, because Jack had said that awful word. After that, all I had been able to hear was the thumping of my own blood in my ears.

I looked up again as Knox reappeared in the doorway with my dressing gown in his hands. I had only just become vaguely aware that I was sitting there in just a flimsy pair of knickers, but it hadn't escaped him. He bent down and took my shaking hands in his, tugging me effortlessly to my feet before helping me slide my arms into the warm sleeves. He carefully pulled it around me, tying the sash around my waist and then ushering me to the closed toilet. I sat down with a heavy thump as he turned and opened the cupboard over the sink. I had no idea what he was up to, but I knew my voice wasn't strong enough to question him just yet. I stared down at my shaking fingers until he grasped my chin and tipped my head back.

"Close your eyes," he murmured softly, and I did as he asked.

I let my heavy, sore eyes slide shut and felt the cool glide of the wipe moving across them. I had never been without my makeup in front of a man before, but he wasn't quiet long enough for me to be able to think too hard about it.

"Jack told me. I know that piece of shit just got out of lock up, and I know what he did time for."

I heard him take a harsh breath, but the strength of his hands never faltered as he cleaned me up. I winced as my chest tightened, and I knew he had felt it. He didn't speak again right away, instead letting me soak in the feel of him for a minute. I had been taking care of myself for as long as I could remember, but sitting there, having him take care of me didn't feel as terrible as I'd always thought it would. My reprieve didn't last long.

"Fire, last night…me and you…"

There was a hint of trepidation in his voice, and suddenly I didn't want to hear him finish that sentence. I had known it was risky. I had known there was a chance it was going to blow up in my face in the cold light of day. We had both been emotional. We had both had a long and scary night, and I had sought comfort in his strength. I had always been aware that there would be consequences. Hell, I had expected to be the one screaming that it was a mistake this morning, so I could hardly blame him for feeling the same way. I hadn't anticipated the safe feeling or the deep sleep he had brought with him, and I should have known better than to enjoy either of them the way I had.

I pulled my head back and pushed to my feet. My knees felt like jelly and I could only pray that they would stay under me long enough to put some distance between us.

"Don't." I forced myself to look at him, even though it was the last thing I wanted to do. "Last night was last night; it was in the moment. I don't need to talk about it today." I stepped around him and turned to walk out of the bathroom, but his hand closed tightly around my wrist, preventing me from moving any farther.

"You might not want to talk about it, but I do. If you're dismissing me after what happened between us, the least you can do is explain it to me." I turned to look at him, confused by the words that were erupting from his mouth. "Twice before, we came close, and both times you ran off. Last night you didn't. Last night you made it really clear to me that you weren't running, so dammit, Freya, if you want to run today, the least you owe me is a fucking explanation."

My eyes were wide now as his words seeped beneath my skin. I had believed he was the one dismissing me. I had immediately attributed the apprehension I heard in his voice to him not wanting to have to untangle the mess we had created, but it hadn't been that at all. I swallowed hard.

"I know you just had a nasty shock. I just had a nasty shock too, but we need to talk about this. I need to know how you want me to take care of you." His broad chest was rising and falling rapidly as I tugged my wrist free from his grasp. I had expected him to tighten his grip, but instead he let me go, his shoulders slumping in that same defeated way they had the night before. I took a step closer and pressed my palms flat against his rock-hard abs, feeling the muscles jump beneath my touch.

"I thought you were the one dismissing me." I admitted the weakness out loud and waited for it to feel as though I was swallowing razorblades; when the sensation didn't come, I continued. "It sounded like you were going to apologise for what happened. I was afraid you were going to ask me whether or not there was anything clouding my mind. I'm the girl who runs, Knox, that's what that was."

I felt the air shift around us and saw his shoulders rise before he reached out to grasp my waist the way he seemed so fond of doing and tugged my body against his.

"I've wanted last night since the evening I laid eyes on you in Kenzo's, but you are right, you're the girl who runs. You're the woman who lives on her own terms, and I need you to forgive me for thinking I was possibly going to become a casualty of that. You were upset last night, and it could have been a heat of the moment thing. I need to know that you don't regret it today. I couldn't stand that, not after what we shared." His rough palm cupped my cheek and I leant into it.

"I've surprised the hell out of myself by how much I don't regret it, Knox, but it's messy. I expected to wake up this morning and wonder what the hell I had done, but I didn't. I don't." I bit down on my bottom lip as I stared at him. "I've never allowed it to wrap itself around me before, but you make me feel safe, and that in its own right is scary as hell for a girl like me."

"I understand that, but as long as there are no regrets, we can figure the rest of this out." His lips pressed gently against my forehead before he ushered me out of the bathroom and back into bed. I slid beneath the duvet and he pulled it up over me. "I'll be back in a minute."

I watched him leave the room before I let my head fall back against the pillows. I couldn't stop my mind from spinning now that heat was replacing the chill in my body. If Knox hadn't been there, there was a very real possibility that the previous night could have ended worse than I had ever imagined. The words he had shouted at me in that dark and dingy place were now echoing inside my mind. I had been more than just a little bit irresponsible; I had been downright fucking idiotic, and I had no idea how I would have ever gotten over it if that bastard had slipped something into my drink and gotten exactly what he had been suggesting all night. Even worse was how I would have dealt with it if he had turned his attention to Hannah instead.

I squeezed my eyes closed as memories assaulted me. He had told me he'd been watching us from his table. He had told me I was sexy as fuck and that no girl like me should be in a place like that. He had suggested that he wanted to get to know me with less clothing on. I pressed my hand against the phantom ache in my breast and bit down hard on my bottom lip. The night could have gone so wrong, all because I hadn't wanted to admit defeat. I had been stubborn and reckless and so fucking stupid.

"Hey." Knox's voice was sharp and brought me slamming back into the room.

"Sorry," I choked out.

"I brought you this, drink it." He held the mug out to me and I took it from him. The scent of coffee hit my nostrils and as I sipped it, I knew he had put something else in it, something stronger. "It'll help, Fire. Just drink it, okay?"

I sipped from the mug as I watched him move around the bed, and for the first time, I noticed that he had his own phone cradled in his hand, his eyes moving across the screen.

"Did they find anything?" I asked. Just because the guys he had fucked up hadn't squealed didn't mean we were home free yet. He looked up at me as he settled back against my pillows and held his phone out for me to take.

Calvin: I've had Melania, Cassie, and Nate on it since you called. There's nothing, not even a whisper. Obviously it's still early, but something as hot as that should have been in this morning's news run. I'm keeping the team on it, and they're going to rotate shifts so that we miss nothing. The big news stations and papers know that if they intend to mention an act tied to the company, they have to reach out and tell us or else we pull whatever support we offer them faster than they can say their own name. It looks like you're good son! I didn't get to tell you last night but I'm proud of you. I know that might seem like a fucked up thing to say considering what went down, but you protected those girls and for that, I am proud. I'll keep you posted, just keep your head down!!!

"Isn't Calvin that bitch's stepdad?" I asked as the name rattled around inside my head.

"Unfortunately for him."

67

"So he has newspapers and stations in his pocket and yet he couldn't find her?" I felt my brows knit together and even though I knew it was neither the time nor the place for that discussion, I couldn't seem to stop the words from escaping me.

"She turned up," he said gently, and I turned to look at him as I passed him back his phone. "A couple weeks ago. I'm not surprised Len didn't tell you, she didn't seem to want to hear it."

"Where the fuck is she?" The hatred I had for the woman who had ruined my best friend's life more than once was bubbling in my stomach, and if the man currently sharing my bed knew where she was, he needed to tell me.

"In a cemetery in New York City." I felt my eyes widen and the mug in my hand shook enough that he reached out and took it from me.

"What?"

"They found her body in a shallow grave in the middle of the Nevada desert. I say body, but it was more skeleton by the time they discovered it."

"She's dead," I said breathily.

"She is. You don't piss off the kind of people that she did and expect to get away with it, at least not if you have a shred of common sense. Turns out she had even less intelligence than we thought she did. Presuming you have men who allow weaker men to rack up hundreds of thousands in debt with no way to pay it off wrapped around your little finger is a foolish move." I ran my hands through my hair; it was barely even seven in the morning and I was beginning to feel like I hadn't slept in a week. There was too much information and far too much danger for me to be able to deal with rationally.

"So Calvin is taking care of it?"

"He is, and so is Jack. He'll be calling me from now on if he hears anything."

"Knox I—" I was about to protest that as it was my fault we were even in this mess, I should be the one to handle it, but I didn't get the chance because his mouth pressed hard against my own and his thick fingers twisted in my hair.

"I don't want to talk. There will soon come a time when we have to figure this out, but right now…" His eyes burned into mine, stealing the breath from my lungs with their intensity. "Right now I want to kiss and suck and lick every single inch of your skin that I can find. I want to trace these pretty tattoos with my tongue and pray that you let me hang around long enough to find out why you etched these particular things onto your skin. I want to feel the warmth of you engulf me. I want to see how far I can push your boundaries because I think that underneath it all, you and I are built so similar it's going to terrify both of us. Can you give me that Fire? Can we talk later?"

I nodded as heat flooded my body at his words and he nipped my bottom lip. I had no desire to talk in that moment either. I could dissect it all later, could have the what-ifs and maybes swamp me when I was alone, but right there and then, I just wanted to feel. I didn't want the fear that had settled in my stomach to be the overriding feeling anymore. I wanted the pleasure Knox could give me to take me over and make me settle again. I knew I was surrendering myself to someone. I knew I had sworn I never would, but I also knew that nothing had felt better than being with him and having him touch me and hold me in ways I had never experienced. As I looked into those dark eyes and caught a glimpse of the dimple in his left cheek that I had never noticed before, I knew the real world could wait just outside the door for a little bit longer.

chapter FIVE

Freya

As soon as the last suit walked out the door, I collapsed into the chair at the head of the room. I was exhausted, and after that meeting I felt as though I could crawl into bed and sleep for days—as long as sleep came for me and didn't evade me the way it had the past few nights.

I shoved my hands into my hair and sent up a silent request for a hairband to magically appear since I had left mine at home. I hated that I felt so off kilter and knew I couldn't go on denying that anything was wrong if I stuck around long enough for anyone to outright ask me. I had so far managed to avoid Lennon, and I could only hope I would be able to keep it up. I had no idea what to say to her when nothing about the weekend made any sense to me.

"How did it go?" I turned at the sound of Hannah's voice, wondering when she had snuck into the conference room.

"It went." I shrugged as she closed the door behind her and her heels clicked across the floor.

"I don't know if that's good or bad."

"Me either." I shrugged again, still not looking at her. I hadn't spoken to her since Friday night, and I didn't have the first idea where I was supposed to start now. As much as having meetings all day yesterday after a weekend of more ups and downs than my brain could seem to cope with had been painful, I had been grateful I hadn't had to face her and all the questions she was undoubtedly going to have.

"If you don't snap out of it, Lennon is going to swap me out for her. She interrogated me so badly on Friday night and she is dying to get her hands on you. I already had to buy her a chocolate muffin just to keep her in her office so I could be the one to come in and talk to you." My head snapped up from where it had been lolling against the back of the chair and I narrowed my eyes on her.

"Now I can't tell if you're winding me up or not."

"I'm not. Do you honestly believe Lennon is going to put up with not having spoken to you for four days? She's going pretty crazy right now."

"Fuck," I hissed as I covered my face with my hands. It was one thing to not really want to have this out with Hannah, but Lennon would be so much worse. I could just imagine the way her eyes would light up if she found out me and Knox had ended up spending the weekend together, and I didn't even want to hear the squeal that would come out of her if she found out we'd had sex

72

multiple times. I could hardly remember a time where that girl wasn't all up in everyone's sex lives because ever since Gabriel Delaney had popped her cherry, she had become a bloody fiend.

"Yeah exactly." Hannah's voice was quiet again and I looked up to where she was sitting with her hands clasped in her lap. "What happened after you left Freya? Where did you two go?" I raked my fingers through my hair and glanced down at Hannah's wrists.

"If I tell you, will you lend me your hairband?" I quirked an eyebrow at her and she shook her head with a soft smile as she disentangled it from her wrist and handed it over. Immediately I scooped my hair up off my neck and took a deep breath. "We went back to the flat. At first I didn't think he was going to come in—he was really messed up over what happened—but I managed to talk him into it. Then I realised that if anyone had recognised him, I would have just ruined his life."

She gasped as though the thought had only just occurred to her.

"Yeah, somewhere in the chaos I misplaced the fact that he is really well known. I called Jack and asked him to keep an ear out and Knox called his old manager for help. If it had gone badly, it would have been all my fault, Han." She reached across the table and rested her hand over mine.

"You didn't know Knox was going to be there, Freya. You didn't know he would come charging into the middle of that." I bit down on the inside of my lip as her eyes narrowed. "Okay, what aren't you telling me?"

"He's followed me before."

"When?" Her question came out louder than I think she intended it to and it made me sit back in my chair.

"The last few weeks. I don't even know how he knows where I am, but he always shows up."

"Have you been to a lot of places like that then?" I could hear the concern in her voice, and as much as I wanted to alleviate that fear, I knew I couldn't.

"Some of them were better. That place was the worst one." I tried to push the embarrassment out of my voice, but even I could hear it loud and clear. "Anyway, he normally shows up, we fight, I tell him to go fuck himself, and he glares at me. He usually just lets me walk out and get in a cab and we don't speak again until the next time. Friday night was different and I knew it. I really didn't think he would find us there, but I should have known better." I tugged my hand out from underneath hers and pressed it against my throat. I knew I needed to be honest with her about the guy who had been buying my drinks. I knew she had a right to know I had put us both in more danger than I ever could have realised.

"So after you spoke to Jack and he spoke to his manager, what happened?" I dropped my head into my hands and refused to meet her eye. "What happened?" she asked insistently as she sat forward in her chair.

"I might have thrown myself at him." I cringed because I still didn't like the way that memory played out behind my eyelids. I had never been that girl. I had never been the one to throw herself at anyone because I had learnt early on that if you wore the right clothes and walked around like you were in charge, you could very easily have men falling at your feet—granted, they were never men I really wanted, but I had always considered that for the best.

I wasn't the kind of girl who wanted to get caught up in feelings or emotions. I wanted to use men and sex as the release I so desperately needed from all the shit inside my brain, and if I didn't care for them, then it didn't matter.

I balled my fist as I realised that at some point on Friday night, or maybe even Saturday morning, Knox had shifted something inside me that I didn't know how to shift back. He was the perfect mix of dominant and gentle, the subtle line between submission and fight, and just thinking about it had me clenching my thighs together.

"What do you mean you threw yourself at him?"

"I mean one minute he was hugging me and telling me he was going to get something warmer for me to wear, and the next minute I threw my entire body at him and attacked his mouth with mine."

"And what did Knox do?" I swallowed hard because that was not the part I wanted to focus on.

"He kissed me back and took me to bed." I didn't dare look up at her because I didn't want to see the horror I assumed would be on her face. Hannah was not the type of girl to get drunk, cause a man to fight others, and then throw herself on his cock. Hannah was proper, a good girl, a gentle soul—the complete opposite of me.

"And how was it?"

"Sorry?" I gasped.

"What?" she asked with twinkling eyes. "I've read stories about guys who look and talk the way Knox does; I'm curious as to whether any of what is written is true."

"You are not supposed to be the one asking questions like that." I laughed.

"Ross hasn't wanted to sleep with me for months," she blurted out suddenly. "I've tried everything I can think of but he just tells me he's tired and can't be bothered." My bottom jaw dropped at the sound of those words from her mouth. "I'm not saying I'm living vicariously through you and Lennon but…well, I guess I kind of am."

"Why don't you just leave him Han?" The words were out before I could stop them and I wanted to kick myself. I had vowed I wouldn't get caught up in her business when I couldn't even sort out my own. She had seen me at my worst this weekend, and there was no way I should be dishing out any kind of life advice to her.

"It sounds easier than it is." She shrugged and brought her eyes back to mine. "So how was it?"

I cleared my throat because I knew she wouldn't give up until I told her, and honestly, I wanted to talk to someone about it even if I knew it was probably going to be a once-in-a-lifetime, never-to-be-repeated thing.

"The best I've ever had." The words felt bitter on the tip of my tongue. I had hoped I would wake up alone and think it was the worst sex I had ever had, because then I would have a reason to make sure it never happened again. Instead I had awoken to an ache between my thighs and the memory of his rough palms squeezing at my breasts; it left me with nothing but my own fears stopping me from going back, and I wasn't sure how I was going to make them stick. "I hate that it was the best I've ever had because it can't happen again."

"Why?"

"Because it's crazy."

"But why?" she asked again.

"Because I don't do relationships, Han, and he is so deeply engrained in our lives that I can hardly use him as a fuck buddy. Knox wouldn't go for that anyway. He's so intense and he made me make all these crazy fucking promises." I looked up to see she wasn't looking at me anymore but instead at her lilac-coloured nails. I screwed my face up and fought the urge to stick my tongue out like a child. "Okay so it was the heat of the moment."

"And if you hadn't been caught up in the moment or in him, then you would have had your brain working in typical Freya defence mode and you wouldn't have made the promises. As it was"—she finally looked up at me—"you were so caught up in wanting and needing him that if he'd asked you to marry him right there, you probably would have said yes." I blinked hard because as much as I wanted to refute those claims, I knew I couldn't. I probably would have said yes if he'd asked me to emigrate to another country with him in that moment. "What happened Saturday morning?" I rolled my lips between my teeth as I considered how to answer that question.

"Jack called to tell me that the guy who was buying my drinks, the one you hated—"

"The jerk with too much money?" she asked as she screwed her nose up.

"Yeah that one." I nodded. "Well apparently he just got out of jail for rape and I'm so fucking sorry that I took you to that place Han. I'm sorry I ever put either of us in that position." I winced as she gasped.

"He's a rapist."

"Yes." I nodded again.

"What did Knox say when he found out?" I was surprised she didn't have more to say about what a shitty friend I was, but I wasn't going to push it when she was letting me off so easily.

"He came and found me in the bathroom. We talked and then we had crazy sex again and then he ordered us lunch before spending two hours lecturing me about my behaviour." I scowled as I remembered the way he had refused to let me get out of bed until he was done informing me of all the ways I had been putting myself in danger.

"You had sex on Saturday?"

"Yes." I nodded yet again.

"Hmmm." She tapped her fingernails on the edge of the table before nodding. "Then what happened?"

"He left and I haven't seen him since."

"Has he called? Messaged?" I wanted to lie to her but I knew she would see right through it.

"Both," I admitted.

"And you ignored him." I didn't bother to answer her because it wasn't a question. "Freya, why? Why are you going to stop this from happening when it's so painfully clear that somewhere deep down you want it? Why would you do that to yourself?" I didn't know how to answer that so I kept my eyes trained on the glass desk between us. "Knox isn't like other men. He isn't like anyone I've ever met before, and he has his sights set on you. From what you've told me, I don't think you are just going to get rid of him by pretending the weekend didn't happen. You let him into your bed and he's going to want to stay there. He's not going to stand for you replacing him with another man every day of the week."

"I couldn't even if I wanted to," I mumbled.

"What did you say?"

I took a deep breath and looked up at her.

"I said I couldn't replace him with another man every night because I think he's broken me. He's inside my head like no one has ever been before and I can't stop thinking about how it felt to have him beside me when I woke up in the middle of the night. I can't stop thinking about the sex and how it was different with him than any other time I've done it. He's fucking broken me." I sighed as I ran my hand through my hair. "Have I turned into Len?" I pouted as I asked the question and was met by Hannah's gentle laugh.

"Maybe a little bit." She smiled. "But that's because you're fighting this the same way she was." Hannah pushed to her feet and squeezed my shoulder. "You're wasting your time because he will wear you down in the end, probably faster than Gabe wore Lennon down. What's the worst that could happen if you let him in Fray?"

"The worst?" I barked out a laugh as I closed my eyes. "I ruin everyone's lives when it all goes up in flames."

"Who says it will? Maybe it won't crash and burn. Maybe this is it. Maybe Knox is the man you've been waiting for. I saw the way he looked at you. I saw what he did to protect you, and that's not something you should take lightly. Think about it, Freya. Don't mess everything up before you give it a chance."

I sucked in a breath as her hand left my shoulder, and I heard the door click on her way out. I was terrified of the way he made me feel, but maybe Hannah was right—hiding from it didn't seem to be getting me anywhere either. I picked up my phone from the glass table and tapped out a message, hoping I hadn't already blown it.

I picked up our drinks from the bar top and smiled at the waitress; unlike the one I had encountered on the weekend, this one looked as though she actually enjoyed her job.

"If you need refills just give me a shout." She grinned wide and I smiled back before making my way across the room to where Asher was setting up the pool balls.

"Did you get her number?" he asked without looking up.

"Excuse me?"

"I asked if you got the barmaid's number." He straightened up and flashed me his trademark grin as he swiped the beer bottle from my hand and tipped an incredible quantity straight down his throat. "She was flirting so hard even I was getting uncomfortable, and I was all the way over here." He laughed and I shook my head at him as I swiped up one of the pool cues and lined up the white ball. "Sure, by all means K, go ahead and break."

"Don't mind if I do," I deadpanned as I hit the white ball with enough force that the other balls scattered far and wide across the green felt.

"Why are you being even more of a grump than usual, eh?" I didn't bother to look up at where he had perched his arse on the edge of the pool table. He knew it pissed me off when he did that, and I knew he was only doing it now to get a rise out of me.

"I'm not," I said as I lined up the white again and sent two of my balls flying into the same pocket. I shifted around the table, deliberately knocking into him, and bent low to pot my next one. His laugh was loud enough to draw attention our way and I scowled at the thought of being interrupted. "Do you have to be so loud?"

"Do you have to be such a brooding idiot?" he countered as I missed my shot and he swapped his bottle out for his cue. "Why don't you just tell me why you asked me to come down here with you? We already know you only ever voluntarily come to bars and play pool when something is on your mind, so it would be easier for both of us if you just spit it out."

I stared down at the man I considered more a brother than a friend and let that thought settle in. I hadn't realised how predictable I was, but now that he pointed it out, I could see where he was coming from. It didn't make me any more ready to talk, though, so I changed the subject instead.

"Have you spoken to Ari lately?" I knew the topic was a sore spot for him, but it was something that needed to be spoken about. In spite of their age difference, Arielle and Asher were the two closest siblings I had ever met, but ever since she had accepted a marriage proposal from her piece-of-shit boyfriend, the brother-sister harmony had descended into chaos and discord.

"Nope." He popped the P on the end of the word and I sighed.

"Has she called?"

"Once." He shrugged as he stood up and glared at me. "But if you won't talk about whatever's going on up there"—he poked his finger into the side of my head—"then don't expect me to, big man."

I sighed because I should have known it wouldn't be that easy. To most people, Asher was happy-go-lucky and not all that perceptive—he was usually off in his own world—but to me he had always been the opposite. I scratched the back of my neck as I surveyed the pool table, looking for my best shot.

"I slept with Freya." The sound of smashing glass had me rolling my neck forward on my shoulders and bending over to take my shot. There was no way my admission had warranted him dropping his beer bottle on the floor, but he was ever the drama queen.

I made my way around the table, potting the rest of my balls while he helped the barmaid with the big smile clear up the mess he had made. By the time he was done, so was the game. I reached into my pocket to pull out more change, but he shook his head at me.

"Don't even think about distracting me from what you just said with another game. Sit your arse down. We need to talk."

"We do not need to talk."

"Yes, we do. Sit." He pointed at the table closest to us and I reluctantly did as he asked. "You slept with Freya…our Freya…Lennon's Freya."

"Yes Ash, how many other women with that name do you know?" I knew the sarcasm wasn't lost on him as he narrowed his eyes.

"When?"

"Friday night." I watched as the wheels started to turn in his brain. I could see that he was trying to think back to what had happened Friday night, so I decided to make it easier on both of us and give him the whole story in one. I leant forward on my elbows and twisted my water bottle in my hands. "I followed her to a dive bar. She's been going to them a lot since Len and Gabe got engaged. She's lonely and she won't admit it, so instead she finds the shittiest places where no one knows her and sets about getting herself blind drunk. I overheard her on the phone to Len the first night asking her to go along, but she and Gabe were going to Darragh's so she declined. She mentioned a place called Habits so I went there. I'd been trying to get her on her own anyway, and it seemed like the perfect opportunity, only it went to shit pretty quick. By the time I got there, she was well on her way to being drunk and was fondling this bloke through his jeans."

"Sounds like Freya." He sighed and I raised my head to glare at him. I didn't like that he thought that was typical behaviour for her, and I didn't like the way he acted as though it didn't matter, because it damn well did. He raised his hands and met my stare with his own. "Hate it all you want, man, but that does sound like Freya. Carry on."

"I walked over and broke it up, sent him packing, and she stormed out of the club the way I had expected her to. I followed the cab she took home and walked upstairs with her much to her irritation. I was on my way out when Edie, Nell's grandma, came out of her flat. She asked me inside and I wasn't about to tell her no. I thought maybe she needed a hand fixing something, but she didn't. As soon as I crossed the threshold, she started telling me about how Freya needed someone to help her, to look out for her, and that I was clearly that person. I didn't argue with her because that was exactly what I wanted to do. Edie texts me every time Freya turns on her get-ready playlist and I drop everything and head over there." I winced as I said the words out loud for the first time.

"So let me get this right," Asher said slowly as he sat forward. "You are in cahoots with Grandma Edie, and she helps you stalk Freya."

"It's not stalking," I protested.

"It is, brother, not that I disagree with your motives, but it's still stalking. I can't believe Edie came up with that. She's a sly one." Asher laughed and I shook my head.

"She really cares about Freya," I said as I rolled my water bottle between my hands. "And after the shit show Friday night became, I'm glad."

"Tell me what happened then."

"It was different. Before we even set foot in the shit hole she had chosen, I knew it was going to blow up somehow. It was like all the places Eli used to frequent and it made my skin crawl."

"Shit man." He sighed again and I knew he understood.

"It was dark and seedy, and she had Hannah with her."

"Excuse me." His beer bottle slammed on the table, hard enough to send vibrations up my arms.

"Don't get all twisted up. Hannah was coming into the flats as Freya was coming out. Freya tried to send her home, but Hannah was adamant that she didn't want to be alone and insisted on going with Freya. She was out of place in there though—they both were. Anyway, the jackass who was buying the drinks started pawing at her—"

"Hannah?" His voice sounded unnaturally high pitched and I sat back in my seat.

"No, Freya. Hannah was pressed against the bar trying to disappear."

"Okay." He nodded.

"I pulled him off her but I was running on anger and didn't stop to think about the consequences. I tried to get the girls out but it kicked off quickly. I managed to get them in the truck and I had time to follow them, but I didn't. I stuck around."

"Shit man." Asher moaned.

"I know, all right. Believe me, I know, but fuck I needed to. I needed to feel flesh colliding with my fists. I needed that piece of shit and his friends to understand that they couldn't put their hands on a woman that way, and I'm fucking glad I did because the next day I found out he was a fucking rapist. If I hadn't been there and pulled them out, at least one if not both of those girls would have been his next victim." I clenched my hand around the water bottle tight enough that the plastic protested.

"Fucking hell!" He sighed long and loud as he drank more beer.

"I took Hannah to Leni and Gabe's—"

"I know, I was there, and she didn't say a damn word to any of us about this."

"Don't be mad at her Ash. I was messed up and Freya was with me, and I'm not surprised Hannah didn't have the first clue what to do—it isn't exactly run of the mill for her is it?"

"I just wish I'd fucking known. Where did you and Freya go?"

"Her place. I spoke to Calvin and he spoke to Maxine's husband, the cop, and between them they managed to ensure that my arse never found its way into the fire." I rubbed my hand across my forehead, aware of the pain I had been fighting off that was building behind my eyes. "Freya was frightened, vulnerable, and I was trying to take care of her. I've wanted to get behind her walls for so long, and suddenly I was there. When she launched her body at me, I didn't stop her. I couldn't, because every single fucking part of me that I buried so long ago was suddenly wide awake. I could feel and I reacted, because apparently when I'm around her, that's all I'm capable of. I took her to bed and I lost myself in her. I forced her out of her own mind and then she fell asleep in my arms. Fuck!" I cursed as I scooped up my water bottle and took long gulps.

"You didn't take advantage of her man." I blinked at the sound of those words coming from Asher's mouth. "I know that's what you're afraid of. I know you're fucking terrified of turning into your brother, but I can tell you right now, you didn't take advantage of her."

"She was upset. Jesus, she had just watched me beat the shit out of four men."

"K, look at me." His voice was hard and I snapped my eyes to him instantly. "You did not take advantage of her. If you'd frightened her or made her feel anything other than safe, she would not have let you into her bed. Are you listening?" His hand slapped against my wrist where I had propped my head on my fist and I jerked with it. "Has she gone to bed with you before now?"

"No."

"Exactly, jackass. You didn't take advantage, so just get that out of your damn head."

"Then why is she ignoring me? I spent the day there on Saturday and we talked about the danger she had put herself and Hannah in. I thought she heard me, thought she understood that I wanted to be there for her, so when she asked me to leave so she could work, I did. I thought she needed some time to get her head together and I was happy to give her that. Fuck, I've known this was my end game since the first time I laid eyes on her. I thought she just needed to catch up, but she's ignored me ever since I walked out the door. I've called her and texted her and nothing, absolutely fucking nothing." I tugged my phone from my jeans and slammed it down on the table between us. "What the fuck am I supposed to do with that?"

"Calm down maybe?"

"She will use any excuse she can to get rid of me Ash. She's already done it twice."

"Twice?" His eyebrows rose and the light glinted off the metal he had shoved beneath his skin.

"The first night after I took her and Len home, I almost kissed her. Then the night you met Hannah, I followed her outside after watching her play up to Fiore. I went out there to warn her away from a man like him and I almost ended up kissing her again. I wanted to, fuck I wanted to, and I was so close, but then her phone rang and she took off into the night. I know what she can do when she puts her mind to it, and I don't want it to happen again. I want her. I want us to see what this thing is between us because it melts everything in its path, but how the hell do I get a girl like her to take a chance on a guy like me? She won't even answer me." I gestured at the phone again as the screen lit up.

"I presume she is *Fire* so it looks like she's answering now." Asher stacked his hands behind his head and let a shit-eating grin take over his face. I lunged for the phone, almost dropping it in my haste to open the waiting message.

Fire: Good weather today eh?

I barked out a laugh at the message and rolled my eyes before passing it across the table to Asher, whose brow furrowed before he shook his head.

"Well she's really good at playing it cool." He smirked as he handed the phone back to me. "Show her how it's done, big man—for everyone's sake." He pushed out of his chair and looked down at me.

"I don't fucking know how it's done. I've been celibate for the last five fucking years and the extent of my knowledge before that was how to make a girl come solely with my mouth."

"And that, my friend, is a fucking stellar skill to have mastered." He laughed. "I'm going for a slash. Tell the damn girl you're taking her on a date, and don't let her wriggle out of it." I looked back down at my phone and typed a reply.

Me: Weather's decent actually! When can I take you on a date?

Fire: A date?

Me: Yes, a date. I know we have done this a little back to front, but I'd like to rectify that. When are you free?

The phone started to ring in my hand not five seconds after I hit the send button, and I was surprised when I saw her name flashing back at me. I hit answer before she could stop the call and pressed the phone to my ear.

"Why do you want to take me on a date?" She sounded breathy, and I was certain it was more to do with panic than excitement.

"Because that's what you deserve and it's what I should have asked for months ago."

"I thought this was just sex." I pinched the bridge of my nose because I had seen this coming, and I steeled myself for what I was about to say.

"I like having sex with you a whole fucking lot, but I don't want that to be all there is. I want your mind and your intelligence and your sense of humour. Hell, I even want your sarcasm. I want to take you on a date, so can you tell me if that's okay?" She was quiet for what felt like forever, and I glanced up at the bar to see that Asher was getting in another round.

"Okay," she whispered finally. "But I don't know what the hell to do on a date with you Knox," she warned, and I couldn't help but laugh.

"Me either, but I think we can probably just wing it until we figure it out. Let me set something up and then I'll give you the details."

"Okay, I'll talk to you then."

"No," I said quickly, and I heard her intake of breath. "No, I don't want to wait until then to speak to you again. When I call, can you just answer if you're not busy? No pressure, nothing heavy, I just want us to be able to talk." Again the silence on the other end of the phone had my fingers clenching around the piece of plastic against my ear.

"This whole thing terrifies me but I'll try, all right? It's the best I can do."

"That's all I'm asking for Fire." She ended the call without saying another word and I pulled the phone away from my ear as Asher took his seat.

"Well?"

"I'm taking her on a date." I couldn't fight the smile stretching across my face, and even though I knew I probably looked like a total tool, Asher smiled back at me.

"Yeah you fucking are." He laughed before his face turned serious. "You need to get it out of your head that you're like him though, K, because you couldn't be any more different if you tried. Find something fucking awesome to do with that girl and make her see that she needs to give you a chance, okay?"

"Thanks man." I held my fist out across the table and he pounded it. It was easy to promise him those things, but it was going to be something else altogether to make myself believe it.

"Now can we shoot some proper pool? A game where you let me at least touch a ball would be fucking awesome."

"No one likes a cry baby Sterling," I said as I stood up and pocketed my phone.

"And no one likes a game hogger. Get us set up and I'll get some music on," he said as he tossed some coins at me and sauntered off in the direction of the jukebox. I groaned inwardly because with the mood he was in, I had no idea what we were going to end up listening to.

chapter SIX

Freya

I pressed the off button on my speakers and smoothed by hands over the red fabric of my dress. I hadn't been lying when I told him I would try, and he hadn't been lying about expecting me to answer the phone when he called. We had spoken every day since he asked me on a date, but Knox had been insistent that we wait until tonight before we saw each other again. I had never gone the traditional route with a man in my life before, and the anticipation it had built felt like butterflies swarming in my stomach as I wondered what the night would be like.

Hannah's pep talk had gone a long way towards making me see I didn't need to be so reticent, but Knox's patience and understanding had cemented it. I didn't have any idea what that meant for me, but as he had reminded me so often over the past few days, I didn't need to have all the answers, I just needed to give us a chance. It was a foreign concept to me to let things just happen, but I was trying. More often than not, my fingers and brain still itched to take control, but I was trying to trust him the way he had implored me to.

I ran my brush through my hair for the five hundredth time and turned to look at the clock on my bedside table. He had told me he would be here at seven thirty and it was already seven thirty-two.

I grabbed my clutch and my leather jacket and tried not to let the voice inside my head—the one that wanted me to believe he had changed his mind—get too loud. He had assured me he would be here. He had assured me he had our entire evening planned. There was no reason for him not to show up aside from the fact that people rarely ever did what I needed or wanted them to.

I stepped into the living room just as the door buzzer let out its shrill sound. I wheeled around and snatched it up.

"Hello."

"Hi beautiful. I'm downstairs."

"Okay."

I slammed the receiver back into its holder and headed for the front door. I locked up and shoved my keys back into my bag.

"Going somewhere nice?" I spun around at the sound of Edie's voice and couldn't fight the smile that was begging for a place on my face as she stood up from where she had been watering the potted plants she had on either side of her front door. It never failed to amaze me that they always stayed in bloom despite the fact that we lived in a block of flats.

"I have date." I blurted the words out and then bit down on my bottom lip.

"I'm glad to hear it." She smiled that soft smile of hers as she made her way across the landing towards me. "I hope it's with a gentleman who's going to treat you like Gabriel does your Lennon." She raised one pale eyebrow and I found myself nodding at her.

"He's definitely a gentleman."

"In that case, don't let me keep you. We don't want your carriage turning into a pumpkin." She winked at me before heading back to her plants.

"Thanks Edie, have a good night." I walked over to the stairs, feeling much calmer than I had when I had first walked out of the flat, and made my way down them.

I pushed on the security door and stepped out into the cool spring evening. I let my eyes roam over the immediate area until I saw his beast of a silver truck gleaming at me from the parking bay opposite.

I let the door swing shut behind me and headed in that direction. As I got closer, the driver's side door swung open and he emerged, knocking the air from my lungs as his feet hit the concrete.

Knox Sutton was dressed to impress, and I had never seen anything that made me want to orgasm on the spot more than the sight of this man wrapped up in a suit to end all suits. My eyes were greedy as I did my best to take it all in before we were toe to toe, because in all the time I had known Knox Sutton, I had never seen him in anything more than a t-shirt and jeans. The black shirt he was wearing now looked as though it had been lovingly molded to wrap around his torso and pull tight across the muscles of his shoulders and chest. I couldn't see well enough in the dim light, but I was almost certain that if I got close, I would be able to trace every corded ridge of muscle currently indented in the cotton. The grey waistcoat hugged him in a way that made him look undeniably powerful, and as my eyes roamed farther down his body, I found that his thick legs were wrapped in a charcoal grey material that matched the waistcoat. The muscles in his thighs were pushing against the fabric in all the best ways, and I knew that if he got even a little bit excited tonight, the evidence would be on full display for anyone who got the chance to look at him. I couldn't help the grin that tickled the corner of my lips as that thought swirled in my mind. He took a step closer as I came to a stop in front of him and he grabbed my hand in his, twirling me once.

"You look absolutely stunning," he murmured when I was facing him again.

"Me?" My voice came out slightly squeaky so I coughed to try to clear it and then looked back at him. "I think you might have that the wrong way around."

"Did Freya Anson really just use her words to pay me a compliment?" I knew he was teasing, and as much as the insecure part of me wanted to bite down on my lip and wonder if I had done it wrong, the sarcastic part of me chose that moment to rear its ugly head. I dropped his hand like he'd burnt me.

"Well I didn't know you owned an actual shirt since I've only ever seen you in those ratty old t-shirts you always—" I squealed as he swept me off my feet and the rest of my sentence got lost as he pressed his nose against mine. My feet were dangling several inches off the floor and I kicked my legs to get him to put me down, but it only made his grip tighten.

"I liked it when it was a compliment." I blinked as his eyes burned into my own and dipped my head in acknowledgement of what he had said. My feet made contact with the pavement again as his hands roamed from my back to the curve of my arse. "I feel like I should warn you now that I am not averse to spanking this sweet arse when you sass me. In fact, I'm not sure many things would give me greater pleasure." An involuntary shudder ran through me as his mouth suckled on the tender flesh of my neck.

"You know you're a cliché right?" I whispered as my fingers clutched at the fabric of his clothes, trying to get some traction.

"You know I don't fucking care, right?" His hands squeezed the globes of my arse and I rocked my pelvis hard against his, earning myself one of his signature growls.

"Yeah I was getting that." I breathed as I started to lose myself in the sensations he was bestowing on me. My pleasure lasted only a moment before he was straightening back up and smiling down at me.

"I like that pretty pout on your lips." He smiled as he tapped my bottom lip with his index finger. "But we have somewhere we need to be, and I want to get us both there while we still look presentable to the outside world. Come on." He tipped his head in the direction of his car and I fought the urge to tell him to sod the date and just come back up to the flat. "We're not just going to have sex tonight, Fire girl. You said I could take you on a date, so that is what we're doing."

"I feel like we could have more fun upstairs," I grumbled as I climbed into the passenger seat and fastened my belt. When I looked back up, his face was only inches away from my mouth and his black eyes were glittering.

"I'll show you all about my type of fun when you let me bring you home later." He winked as he straightened back up. The car door slammed as he stepped back and I watched his big frame move around the front of his car. I had never paid too much attention to it before now, but he moved like he was stalking prey all the time. There was no denying that the man was all predator, and everything about it made my mouth water. For someone who spent years professing to be perfectly fine being in complete control of herself and her life, I sure was making myself look like a liar.

"What is your type of fun then?" I asked before he even had a chance to put his seatbelt on. The sound of his chuckle filled the warm interior of the car, caressing every inch of my exposed skin.

"I thought I gave you a good idea last weekend," he answered as he shifted the car into gear and pulled out of the space. I tightened my grip on the door handle just a little bit as his foot pressed down on the accelerator.

"Oh."

"Are you disappointed?" His eyes moved from the road to me when he asked the question, and I felt my heart kick against my ribs.

"Could you maybe look at the road?" I had wanted to ask the question calmly, preferably without fear colouring my voice, but I knew I had failed miserably.

"I am in complete control of this car, I promise you."

"You think you are," I countered, even though I was begging my lips to stop moving. I didn't want to start a conversation about this because I knew how much Knox could push when he got his teeth into something.

"I know I am Freya. I've been driving for a long time."

"Do you honestly think that matters?" I curled my hands into fists and pressed my nails into the centres of my palms as the sound of his indicator filled the interior of the car. I knew we couldn't possibly have arrived at the destination of our date yet because we had only been driving for a few minutes, which meant he was only stopping because I was behaving like a total idiot. "What are you doing Knox?"

"Waiting for you to tell me what that was all about," he said as he pulled up the handbrake and shifted his body in his seat until he could look at me face on. "One minute we're talking about the games I like to play and my mind is running wild with all the things I'd like to try with you, and the next you're acting like I'm about to drive us off a cliff." I winced involuntarily as those words fell from his mouth. "What did I say?" he asked instantly.

"Nothing." I shook my head and turned away from him, my grip on the door handle tightening even more.

"Fire, tell me what the hell is going on." His voice was full of demand and I felt something inside me snap at the sound of that barked command. I'd been an idiot to think this would be a good idea—to do something like this, you had to be willing to share yourself with another person, and there was no way on this earth I had the first idea how to share all the parts of me with somebody else, especially not somebody like Knox.

I pushed the release button on my seatbelt and shoved the car door open, grabbing my bag from the foot well as I climbed out.

"I'm sorry I've wasted your time Knox. I don't think this is a good idea anymore." I slammed the door shut behind me and moved a few steps back in the direction we had driven. I hadn't gotten far when I heard his door slam, and a moment later his hand was clamping around my wrist and turning me to face him.

"No way are you saying that and walking away." He shook his head at me and his jaw was set, so I knew he wasn't messing around.

"It would be best for all of us if you just let me go."

"It would be best for you because then you can go back to telling yourself I'm not what you want, you mean?"

"You don't know what you're talking about." I shook my head as I tugged my wrist from his grip and took another step forward. This time it was his front that collided with my back, and his arms snaked around my middle. I didn't bother to struggle against him as he leant down far enough that his breath ghosted over my neck.

"I don't know what the hell just happened, but somehow we went from sexual promise to fight town in less than five seconds. If you just get back into the car with me, I promise you I will keep my eyes on the road." I let out a heavy breath as he tugged my body tighter against his. "I apologise for whatever I said, you just bring out a side of me that doesn't think too hard before he opens his mouth. I promise I will work on that if we can please just go back to where we were when I picked you up."

"Knox…" I shook my head gently.

"Just get back in the car and come to dinner with me." He spun me in his arms until our chests were pressed together and tilted my chin to look up at him. "Forgive me?"

"There's nothing to forgive Knox—" I started to speak but he interrupted me before I could finish.

"That's settled then. Come on." He tugged me back to the car and helped me back into the seat before walking around to his own. "I can be a hot-headed jackass sometimes, so you might need to get used to that," he said as he turned the key in the ignition. "But I can promise you one thing Fire: when you are with me, you are always going to be safe." The words wrapped around me like a warm hug, and as much as I knew he couldn't really make promises like that, for a moment I found myself believing his words.

"I don't know what you're doing to me Knox, but everything feels as though it's upside down." I whispered the words because I wasn't even sure I was supposed to be saying them out loud. "Everything I thought I knew seems muddled up. Everything I told myself I wanted seems to have been scribbled out. I don't know which way to turn anymore, only that whichever way I choose, I always seem to bump into you. I don't know how to handle that and I don't know how to explain any of it because I haven't had to explain myself to anyone in so long."

"It's okay." His voice was gentle as he stroked his fingers over the bare skin of my arm. "It's okay for this to be scary as hell because it's no different for me. I don't think either of us ever expected to find something like this in our lives, but we have. We've found it and I'm ready to accept that because I've known you were it for me since the first night I laid eyes on you. You've never been on the same page as me, but I'm hoping you'll catch up."

I turned my head to look out the window as he pulled the car away, the declaration and promise in his words hanging heavy in the air between us.

"I'm trying Knox. For the first time, I'm really trying."

Knox

I had no idea what it was about the woman sitting beside me, but I kept finding myself making her promises I knew I shouldn't. There are no guarantees in this world and I knew that better than anyone, but every time she showed me even a hint of vulnerability, I couldn't seem to stop my mouth from running away from me. I wanted to make things better for her. I wanted to bring something to her life that she clearly hadn't had before, and if that meant making her endless promises, that was what I was going to do.

Those whispered words that dropped from her pretty red lips as I moved the car forward to our destination were enough for me to know that as long as she was trying, I was staying—and if I was honest, I would probably stay long after that.

"Where are we going?" The car had been silent for far too long before she uttered those words and I had to brace myself before I answered. The place I had chosen to take her was a risk and I had known that as soon as the google search had thrown up the top ten places to take a woman on an unforgettable date, but I hadn't been able to get it out of my mind. Sure, I could have opted for something simpler. I could have told Asher to find himself somewhere else to be for the night and cooked for her, but I wanted it to be a new experience for both of us, and this was definitely going to be that.

"A restaurant I found."

"A restaurant?" I couldn't quite read her tone but I had already learnt better than to take my eyes off the road when she was in the passenger seat, so I forged on.

"Yeah a restaurant."

"Why would you take us to a restaurant?" she asked, and this time the sharpness in her tone wasn't lost on me.

"Where did you think I was going to take you?"

"I don't know, to your flat maybe, or the studio, or somewhere without a ton of people who are going to be climbing all over you. I'm not Lennon, and I think we need to be really clear on that right now."

I hit the indicator as the turn off for the car park came into view, and I waited until we were parked with the engine off before I answered her.

"One, I am fully aware you are not Lennon. Two, why the hell would I take you to my studio on our first date? And three, why would I take you to my flat when we both know Asher would be climbing all over us?"

"He could have gone out."

I stared at her for a long minute before shaking my head.

"If you really don't want to do this tonight, you should just say so Freya." I let my head fall back against the headrest and called myself every kind of idiot for thinking this would be as easy as us both getting dressed up and heading out for a meal.

"Jesus I'm fucking this up." She sighed and I couldn't help but laugh.

"Ya think?"

"I'm no good at this Knox, and I warned you I wasn't."

"And I told you we could do this together, but you seem insistent on ruining it before we even get started."

"I just thought we'd have more privacy while we figured it out. I don't like the thought of being on show when I'm floundering."

"Fire, you're not floundering." I turned towards her and caught her hands in my own, tugging her close enough that I could put my lips on hers. "We're learning, and we won't be on show."

"It's a restaurant where there will undoubtedly be fans."

"Even if there are, we won't see them."

"Did you book a private room?" she asked, her eyebrows pulling down over her nose slightly.

"Not quite." I shrugged as I reached across her and popped the glovebox open. "Here." I placed the red velvet case in her lap and cocked my head to the side to take in her bewildered expression.

"What is it?"

"Open it and you'll find out." I saw the tremble in her hands as she lifted the lid slowly, but what I wanted to see more than anything was the look on her face when she saw what was inside. Her eyes widened as her fingers stroked over the black silk dotted with little black gems.

"A masquerade mask." She breathed the words before turning her face up to mine. "Why?"

"I wanted you to feel comfortable. You can choose whether or not you want to wear it." I was leaving that entirely open for her because honestly I didn't mind either way. Her fingers lingered over the mask for a second before she plucked it from the box and held it out to me.

"Can you tie me up?" I caught the gleam in her eye before she turned her back to me, and as I leant forward to place the mask over her face, I let my tongue trace the shell of her ear.

"Any time you want, any way you want."

"Is that a promise?"

"What do you think, beautiful?" The words rumbled from my chest as I tied the black satin in a bow at the back of her head. When it was in place, she turned to face me.

"How do I look?"

"Better than I imagined. Wait there." I climbed down from the truck and made my way around to her side, opening the door and taking her hand to help her down to the uneven gravel of the car park. Her head tipped back as she took in the black and chrome exterior of the building.

"What is this place?"

"Nothing you've ever done before." I squeezed her hip as we made our way towards it.

"This isn't a secret sex club is it?"

"One thing you need to know is that I don't share." I turned our bodies until we were facing and caught her beneath her chin. "What we do alone is between us and nobody else. There are no sex clubs in our future, do you hear me?"

"I don't want to go to one," she said, her nose crinkling beneath the mask.

"Good, then we're on the same page." I pressed a kiss to the top of her head and pulled open the door to the restaurant. Stepping inside, I noticed the lobby was empty save for two couples who were both sitting in booths with eyes only for each other.

"Mr Sutton, so glad you could make it."

"Good to see you again Warren." I smiled as he turned his attention to Freya.

"And you must be Mr Sutton's lovely lady. It's a pleasure to meet you."

"Likewise. This is a lovely place you have."

"Thank you very much madam. Now if you'd both like to follow me, I'll show you where the lockers are."

"Lockers?" She squeaked and I tightened my grip on her waist.

"Yes miss, for your coats, bags, and watches. Each party has their own locker so there will be plenty of room for all your belongings."

"Why do we need a locker?" she hissed as her elbow jabbed me in the gut.

"Because it's part of the experience." I pulled my watch from my wrist and moved to place it inside the open locker before turning back to her. "Just play along okay? If you relax, then you might have fun, and if you don't like it, we can leave, agreed?"

"Fine." She huffed as she pulled off her coat and stuffed it inside the locker along with her bag. She turned away from me as soon as she had done it and looked at Warren. "Ready." She said it with a smile, but her voice was that sugary sweet one she used when she didn't mean a damn word that was coming out of her mouth. There was no point in me arguing about it with her because we needed to get inside.

I placed my hand on the small of her back as we both followed Warren into what I knew was the large dining room, although neither of us could see a damn thing considering it was pitch black inside. Freya's feet stopped moving almost instantly and I felt her hands groping for me in the darkness.

"Fire?" I murmured.

"Why is it dark?" she demanded as her hands finally made contact with my waist and her nails dug into me.

"It's part of the experience."

"Stop saying that. Why is it dark Knox?"

"Mr Sutton." Warren's voice floated over from the left and I steered her unwilling feet in that direction.

"Just trust me."

"You keep saying that too, and you already know shit like that isn't easy for me. Knox—"

"Sit and you'll understand." I interrupted her words because now Warren was in hearing distance and I really didn't want anyone else privy to our conversations. She finally did as she was told and as soon as she was situated on the bench, I was satisfied that I could sit down as well. Instead of sitting opposite her as I would in a normal restaurant, I took the seat beside her.

"I'll be back with the others shortly and I'll explain everything once everyone is situated." I heard the shuffle of Warren's shoes as he moved away and Freya's arm instantly smacked into mine as she turned around.

"Ow," I complained, even though it hadn't hurt at all.

"You're sitting stupidly close to me," she growled. "Where are we Knox? What the heck is this place? And why did you have me wear this mask if no one can see me anyway?"

"It's called Tenebris, which is Latin for dark, and I had you wear the mask because you look hot as all hell right now, and also because I knew you would be more comfortable. I told you that in the car and—"

"Okay but why are there no fucking lights in here? There aren't even any candles."

"Like I said to you twice before, it's part of the experience. Basically you sit in the dark and you have to use your other senses to enjoy your meal."

"How can I read the menu if it's dark?"

I took another deep breath because if she was already annoyed, this was probably going to make it much worse.

"There are no menus." I heard her groan but forged on. "But there are some options. You can choose between a meat or vegetarian meal, and you let Warren know if you have any allergies or anything you really don't like to eat and then they bring you food accordingly."

"Are you seriously telling me I don't even get to pick what I put in my mouth tonight?"

"I am." I nodded even though she couldn't see me.

"Are you crazy?"

"No."

"Then why would you do something like this? You know I like control. Everyone knows I like control. It's probably the world's worst-kept secret, so you had to know this was a really bad idea."

"Actually…" I sighed as I shifted even closer to her. I could feel the heat of her thigh pressed against my own and

I reached out so I could touch the soft skin of the inside of her wrist. "I think it's one of my better ideas." I traced small circles as I spoke and felt her muscles contract and release beneath my fingers. "I think the need to be in control runs you hard sometimes, beautiful. I think it hounds you and plagues you even when you sleep, and it's about time someone helped to lighten that load."

"Knox—" she interrupted, but I leant down to press my mouth against hers. It was lucky for both of us I had spent a lot of my childhood in the dark because I was remarkably good at finding my target even when I couldn't see. I pulled back slightly but stayed bent close to her.

"You need someone to lighten that load. Something like this isn't something you need to control. It isn't something you need to hold on to so tightly. You can just let go, let someone else worry. I want you to enjoy yourself tonight, and you won't if you don't relax." I pressed my mouth to hers again. "Someone else is going to worry about what you eat. Someone else is going to worry about preparing it, and you just have to sit back and revel in the flavours they provide you with."

"I don't do out of control," she whispered back.

"Then use that pretty mask to pretend you're someone else. Just trust me that nothing but good things will happen to you tonight."

"God you make it really hard to stay angry," she hissed as she moved away slightly. I let the chuckle bubbling in my throat come loose as I leaned closer again.

"This is the first date I have ever been on, and you can't blame a man for wanting it to be really memorable." She pulled back and I felt it. I wasn't sure how she was going to take what I had just said to her, but it needed to be said. I needed her to understand that I was just as much of a blank page as she was.

"How is that even possible?"

"How many dates have you ever been on?" I countered. I already had a feeling I knew our answers were going to match considering what she had told me previously, but I needed to hear her say it.

"None," she whispered. "Until now that is."

Satisfaction slithered through my chest at the sound of that.

"Then thank you for being my first."

"What if I ruin this?" she asked, and I was almost certain she had only said it out loud because we were sitting in darkness and I couldn't see her face. There was something about the dark that often gave people loose lips. It was what I had been banking on.

"How will you ruin it?"

"Because I've already freaked out, had a meltdown, given you attitude, and made myself look like a bitch in front of the waiter."

I laughed low and soft as I tugged her towards me.

"You haven't ruined anything. I know you, Fire, as much as you would like to believe otherwise. I know how you get and I knew exactly what would happen when I brought you here. It would have been foolish of me to believe you would come quietly, and that's why I needed to do this. I want to share new things with you, new experiences, and this is only the beginning. You and I, we've been living a certain way for a really long time, and I think we are about due for a break. We don't need to live in the dark anymore. We can have more. We can have the kind of light Lennon and Gabe have, we just have to loosen the chains of the past enough to reach out and grab it. I'm right here and I'm waiting for you to grab on to me the way I've been trying to grab on to you since day one." I heard her breath quicken as I spoke. It was amazing just how quickly your other senses stepped up to the plate when you cut the main one out. "And you could always consider this foreplay."

"Foreplay?" she said hesitantly. I leant down and traced the shell of her ear with my tongue again, but this time I bit down on the lobe. Her body jerked and I knew that if I were to slide my hand up her bare thigh, I'd find her hot and ready.

"Mmmhmm. Sensory deprivation is highly erotic, and with me sitting beside you whispering dirty things in your ear while you eat your dinner, there's no way this couldn't be considered foreplay." I shifted my hand so I could press lightly against her throat with enough pressure that she knew I was holding her there. "There is a whole world of things I want to show you and share with you, beautiful, and I plan to tick them off one by one." I closed my lips around her earlobe again but instead of biting down, this time I sucked, and her body shuddered.

"Jesus you're good at that." Her voice was hoarse and low as she spoke.

"At what?"

"All of it." I chuckled again as the door to the room opened and I shifted back slightly in my seat.

"You ain't seen nothing yet, darling."

chapter SEVEN

Knox

I pushed open the door to the restaurant and stepped out into the car park. We were the first ones to leave and again, I was glad I had money. They didn't care if you played by your own rules when you left a really hefty tip on top of the already weighty bill.

I turned my face into the breeze, willing my blood to cool down. It had been burning hot and thick in my veins ever since I had made the stupid mistake of pointing out the foreplay side of things to Freya. I couldn't get enough air or get comfortable after that, especially as I had to live up to my promises and spend two hours whispering every filthy thing I could think of into her ear while she fidgeted and shuddered beside me.

I had told her things I had only ever dreamt of being able to say out loud to a woman. I had told her how much I wanted to see my fingerprints on her creamy thighs for days after we had sex. I had told her I was dying to see how her dainty little wrists would look bound to that wrought iron headboard of hers. I had run my tongue over the fragrant skin of her neck as I told her I wanted to delve into her bedside drawer, pull out her little box of toys, and use them all with her and on her, one after the other, until she passed out from pleasure.

I gripped my rock-hard cock as hard as I could through my trousers and willed myself to calm down. I couldn't recall a time I had ever been this turned on and as I squeezed my eyes shut, I wasn't braced for her to collide with me. I straightened, trying to keep my balance as she locked her arms around my neck, gripping the back of my head tightly between her hands and yanking me down until our mouths collided.

I had kissed this woman a few different ways so far. I had kissed her soft. I had kissed her sweet. I had kissed her with passion, but I hadn't yet kissed her with starving hunger, and I knew that was exactly what this kiss was going to be.

My hands gripped her arse of their own volition, kneading and squeezing the tight globes and using the leverage to pull her tighter against my body. There was no possible way she couldn't feel my erection through the trousers, which seemed to have no fucking give in them. She herself had commented on my size, and I had never felt as hard or swollen as I did right then. Her mouth hungry against mine as her tongue slipped in and pushed against my own, tangling and twisting as though she couldn't get close enough or far enough inside me.

I shifted one hand up to tangle in the hair she had made look so fucking pretty for our first date and felt a tinge of regret as I twisted the silky locks around my fist, but it passed as quickly as it had come when she moaned into my mouth. I had kept this part of me under lock and key for so long and now that it was finally getting the chance to come out and play, my brain was exploding with what it wanted to try with her next.

"Knox...Jesus." She moaned against my damp mouth, her breath coming in harsh bursts as she trembled against me.

"I know," I answered as I combed my fingers through the tangles I had made in her hair.

"Can we just go home now?" She was panting and half deluded with lust—I could see that much through the slits in the mask she was still wearing. Her glassy eyes were staring up at me and I couldn't stop the warmth spreading through my chest at what she had asked. Freya Anson had just asked to go home with me. She had made us a pair without even thinking about it, and I wasn't sure anything would ever feel sweeter than that.

"We can go home." My voice sounded rougher than usual even to my own ears, but I knew it could be easily explained away as being lust filled. In reality, though, nothing could have made my voice sound that way aside from pure emotion.

I gripped her hand and towed her as carefully as I could to the truck. I opened the door, helped her inside, and sent a prayer out into the universe that I could make it back to the flat without busting a nut. I took a deep breath before I pulled open my own door and climbed in. Sitting down on the plush leather seats of my almost brand-new truck had never been so fucking uncomfortable.

Freya's breathing was still uneven, and I couldn't ignore the way she was shuffling against her seat. I turned away and pulled out of the car park. I couldn't even think about what was waiting for me when I got her naked and splayed out.

I turned the car onto the main road and tried to force myself to relax, but every muscle in my body felt as though it was coiled too tight and was going to snap at any minute. I clenched my fingers hard on the steering wheel and tried to run through the set list for our last concert in an effort to gain even a little control of myself.

"Knox." Her voice sounded strained and I knew she was struggling as much—if not more—than I was.

"It won't take us long to get back," I said without taking my eyes off the road

"Knox." She bit my name out and I waited until I rolled to a stop at a shitty red light before I turned to face her. The sight in front of me had me almost swallowing my tongue. Her tight red dress was hiked up around the top of her thighs, her cheeks and chest flushed with arousal as her fingers pressed tight circles against the place I wanted to be buried.

"Fuck!" I didn't know what else to say. I didn't know what the hell she was up to or why on earth she had decided to do it. I didn't want her to stop, but at the same time I didn't want her in full view of any arsehole on the road.

"I just… It's too fucking hard to wait." She hissed the words through gritted teeth as her tiny hand worked in tighter, harder circles. My cock jumped and pressed even harder against my zipper in a way that was far more pain than pleasure. "Fuck…" She moaned again and I made my choice.

I hit the indicator and turned down the nearest side road, looking around to see how busy it was, and my eyes snagged on what looked like an industrial estate. I hit the accelerator—she was already too far gone to notice the speed of the car—and pulled into the car park. I parked in the darkest, farthest corner and ripped off my seatbelt before releasing hers in a rush of activity. Her lithe body was slumped in the seat, her skin glistening with a fine sheen of sweat, and I wanted in. I wanted in more than anything I had ever wanted in my life.

Every part of me that had spent so long buried in the dark was roaring to life and demanding that I feed it. I could feel it surging through me and there was no way to control it. There was no reason to fight it even though I knew my demons would burst into fucking flames when they met hers, because there would never be anyone else I would rather go up in fire and smoke with.

A growl radiated through me and turned into something more like a roar that caught her attention as I snagged the silk ties at the back of her head and the mask fell from her face. Those bottle-green eyes that I loved to look at so much turned to me, and I knew she saw something on my face she had never seen before. I expected fear to pass through her eyes but it didn't come; instead something seemed to settle in those dark depths and I knew, I just knew she had realised the same thing I had.

"Knox." She was breathy and her voice rattled through the interior of the car.

I watched her small hand move out of the way and I dove. I had my hand in her knickers quicker than she could blink and she screamed as my hard, calloused fingers replaced the soft brush of silk against her swollen clit. I went to work instantly because there would be no mistaking who was getting her off if I had my way. I leant across the gearstick and pressed my mouth to her ear as I rubbed her in tight, hard, unrelenting circles.

"We're gonna burn, Fire. We're gonna burn so fucking hot and so fucking bright." I grunted as I slipped my hand lower and pushed two fingers deep inside her greedy channel. She clutched me as her body convulsed and I dragged my fingers out over swollen and sensitive tissues before shoving them in harder. "I wanna hear you scream. I want you to scream so fucking loud my ears ring for days. I want you to scream while we burn." I bit down hard on her earlobe and she rewarded me with the sound I was looking for.

I knew she was close; I could feel it in the way her body tensed so hard around my fingers that I could barely move them in and out of her. I could feel it in the way her skin was burning and her fingers were clutching at anything and everything to try to get some tether to the universe. Her hips were bucking wildly with no rhythm and the only sounds emanating from her were moans and whimpers.

"I said I want you to scream. I need to hear you scream." I growled in her ear. "Scream while you come for me." I curled my fingers in the way that made her detonate around me and I was rewarded with a sound that was like balm to the raging beasts inside of me. It was long. It was loud. It was broken and strangled, and as her body tried to calm, I couldn't seem to stop my fingers from plunging and withdrawing from her depths. I wanted it to go on and on. I wanted it to last forever. I never wanted to forget the way she looked right then for as long as I lived.

When the scream dissolved into gasps, I knew it was over. I withdrew my fingers and covered her back up, skimming my fingers over her exposed cleavage. I had broken her apart and now I needed to soothe her, calm her, hold her. I shifted so I could tug her a little bit closer; it was a shitty thing to try to manoeuvre around the accessories of the car, but I was determined to do my best. What I didn't account for was her eyes opening and staring straight at me. For the first time since I had met her, they were clear, sharp, and focused so intently on me that I felt my skin tighten. It was like a break in the clouds on a summer day—strong, piercing clarity.

"Fire—" I started, but my voice got lost somewhere between my throat and my mouth and I could only watch as she twisted in her seat. I braced myself for the yelling, the screaming, and maybe even the hitting I was sure was about to come. Most women would have been pliant and sated after an orgasm like that had torn through them, but I should have known better than to believe Freya would be that way. She looked ready for battle and I didn't know what I was supposed to do. "Look, I…"

I couldn't help but want to explain myself. I had thought burning together was a good thing. Fuck it had felt good to have her at my mercy, to push her to heights she had never experienced, but now I was crashing. I was coming down from the high as she stared at me, and there couldn't possibly be a safe place for me to land.

"Fire—" This time it wasn't me tripping over my own words that brought me up short; it was her lunging for me.

Her slender fingers hit the button on my trousers and yanked down the zipper with such force that the vibrations ricocheted through my cock and a groan of pleasure and pain vibrated through my chest. For most men it would have been too much, but not me. I craved it. I ached for it. I had told her that and here she was handing it to me without so much as a raised eyebrow.

I sucked in a harsh breath that almost had my chest exploding as those talented hands of hers wrapped tightly around my erection, so tightly that my balls pulled up hard with the first stroke. I fought the feeling of it snapping up my spine because there was no way on earth I was going this early. There was no way I wasn't going to soak up every single second of pleasurable torture she was bestowing on me. Those clever hands of hers were twisting, pulling, and changing direction and pace so quickly now that I couldn't keep up. My brain was scrambled. My pieces were scattering and I felt the demons within me scream and squeal in pleasure. The sound of their excited cackles echoed inside my head as it rolled backwards against the seat.

"I burnt for you, now you burn for me." Her hot breath ghosted against my ear as she spoke my own words back to me. "I want to hear you scream now. I need to know they scream as loud inside of you as they do inside of me." Her voice caught and I turned my head slightly to catch her eye. "Don't fucking hold out on me Knox. Don't leave me out here alone."

I didn't get to say anything. I didn't get to press my mouth against hers. I didn't get to stroke her face and soothe her the way I had intended to because she was gone and her hot mouth was closing around the head of my cock and pulling it deep into that sweet cavern. I felt the muscles of her throat contract around the too-sensitive head and I lost the ability to do anything but feel.

I grunted and groaned as she worked her mouth over me in tandem with her hands. There was push and pull, soft and hard, pain and pleasure. They were rioting and pushing against me until I couldn't fight them. I couldn't stop the grip they had on me. I couldn't do anything but listen to the roaring sound of blood in my ears.

My hand was tangled in her hair but I wasn't pushing or pulling—I wouldn't have had the strength even if I'd wanted to—I just needed to know she was real, that this was really happening. I groaned long and loud as she cupped my balls and squeezed, and then her teeth scraped over that little rim of sensitive flesh beneath the head of my cock. It might not have been the scream she was asking for that tore from my throat as I lost it into her hot, sweet mouth, but it wasn't silence. It was a roar, an animalistic lion's roar that didn't seem to have an end. I clutched at the steering wheel, clutched at her soft hair, and I let it roll through me from my toes to my head. Even as she rose from my lap and her eyes found mine, I couldn't stay quiet. My chest was heaving and the moans that were left behind were something I couldn't even name.

"We burnt," she said the words loud like a declaration, and as I watched her, a satisfied smile passed across her lips.

"Not yet." I shook my head against the headrest. Despite the fact that my chest was still tight and I couldn't quite regulate my breathing, I knew we weren't done yet. We needed one more match to be lit before we really went up in flames, and as though she could read my mind, I saw her eyelids drop. It was a heavy-lidded look that I had once been convinced was mythological because I had sure as fuck never seen a woman wear it before, but this woman wore it well.

I grabbed her waist, pulling her over me as I reached down and pushed the chair back as far as it would go. My other hand found its home between her thighs, sliding the damp silk out of my way. I had expected to need to get her hot again, but as my fingers made contact with her soft flesh, I found her soaking wet.

I leant forward in my chair and grabbed a fistful of her hair, tugging her head back with it so I could skim my nose up the length of her throat and chase it with the tip of my tongue.

"You're fucking soaking. Did sucking my cock get you this wet?"

"Yes." She whispered the words and it wasn't good enough. I tugged her hair a little harder and heard her moan her pleasure.

"If it made you this wet, be fucking proud of it. Don't whisper it, shout it. Tell me," I demanded as I released her hair so she could look at me. "Tell me sucking my cock made you horny. Tell me it made you fucking drenched." Her eyes met mine and her nostrils flared at the challenge. She leant forward so her nose was pressed against mine, her quick tongue darted out to swipe across my lips, and her words ghosted across the damp trail she had made.

"Sucking your cock made me fucking drenched. Sucking your thick, hard cock made me so horny I—"

I cut off her sentence as I thrust up into her and swatted her arse with my open palm at exactly the same time. The words got lost and were replaced by a sound that made the windows rattle. I gripped her hips hard and pulled her up and then down again to meet my hard thrusts. I had no idea how I was still hard after coming in her mouth the way I had, but I would be damned if I was going to squander it. Her hands went to my chest, clawing and ripping at the buttons of my waistcoat and shirt to expose my flesh, and as soon as it was bared to her, her nails sunk into me. I growled, and she moaned.

"I want to mark you." I groaned as I bottomed out inside her again. "I want to leave my marks on you. Fingerprints. Bite marks. Rope marks on your wrists. I want you to see me every time you take a shower, every time you change your clothes. I want you to know you're mine. I don't want you to forget that you're mine." Her nails scored down my chest as I felt her insides clamp down around my cock. She was gone. She was flying and I followed her—I just couldn't help myself.

As her body relaxed, she fell against me, her chest pressed against my own, our bodies rising and falling with our uneven breaths. I let my eyes slide closed and as they did, I heard her whisper against my bare skin, "I am yours."

Freya

I stared out of the windscreen, my eyes unfocused on the dark velvet of the night sky that reminded me of the eyes of the man sitting beside me. The car was almost silent now, nothing like the frenzied moaning and growling that had filled it only minutes ago. I had no idea how to break the quiet, no idea what the hell I was supposed to say considering it felt as though I had been turned inside out and none of the pieces of me seemed to fit back in the same holes anymore. I was scrambled, off balance, and I had absolutely no idea how to deal with any of it.

Dinner had been a success, no matter how much of a bad start I had gotten us off to. I hadn't been able to stop myself from running my mouth and accusing him of having no idea what he was doing. I hadn't been able to prevent the attitude I used to protect myself from running away from me. Luckily he had used it as fuel to strengthen his own resolve, and for once I was glad Knox Sutton didn't take my shit; if he had, I would have missed out on one of the best experiences of my existence.

I would never have dreamt that a place like that would be something I would enjoy. The control freak in me would never allow it, but he seemed to have taken her, spanked her arse, and shoved her in the corner for the night. The guy who had shown us in had returned while my earlobe was still stinging from the sensations that had been thrust upon it by Knox's wicked mouth, and it had taken every ounce of self-control I had to dial myself back down to a more acceptable place. I had turned my body slightly away from his in order to concentrate on what the guy was telling us about wine and letting our table waiters know our choice of menu, but Knox hadn't been okay with that. I had felt his big hands circle my waist and pull me closer to him. I had felt the thick, hot outline of his erection through material of his trousers, and I'd almost lost my ever-loving mind. He had kept me distracted, only letting me go long enough to tell the waiter we both ate meat. Knox had stayed true to his word and spoke dirty, filthy things in my ear as I tried to swallow the food that was placed in front of me. I'd had no idea why the man had chosen for us to have the full five-course experience, but he had assured me the wait would be worth it, and fuck had he been right.

I turned my head just slightly from where it was lolling against the passenger seat headrest and saw that his eyes were closed. His wide chest was rising and falling and he still looked pretty out of breath, which made my brows furrow. I knew he was fit and spent a lot of time in the gym, so I couldn't understand why he wasn't able to get control of his breathing. I had managed to and I was about as allergic to exercise as any one person could get in life. I turned my head back to the windscreen and let my mind get lost again.

I hadn't really thought about jumping him as soon as we got outside. Of course I had wanted to—hell, I'd wanted him to shove my main course off the table and fuck me across it at one point—but I had respected the fact that I was certain he would make me wait. For all that Knox was, I hadn't expected him to be the kind of man who was happy to fuck in his car, but as soon as we were closed inside of it, I hadn't been able to stop myself from pressing my hand against the throbbing, painful heat between my thighs. It had been steady all through dinner, but as soon as his big hands had curled around the steering wheel, it had exploded. For the first time in so long, there had been no thoughts inside my head, no words on the tip of my tongue, no push and pull within me. For the first time, I had looked into someone's eyes and felt as though they understood all the darkness that coiled and swirled inside of me, felt that maybe they knew how it felt to fight a battle every day that you were never sure you could win. As his words had ghosted over my ear about burning together, I hadn't been able to stop the detonation. I hadn't wanted to. I had felt the battle leech out of my body as his fingers moved into me in that perfect way. It was a moment of sheer clarity, the first moment in so long where I felt as though I could breathe. Now that the frenzy, the crazy, the breath-stealing minutes were over, I wasn't sure what to do with myself. I had never had anything like this before, and I didn't know how to deal with it. I didn't know how to take care of it the way other people did.

"Stop." Knox's voice was hard but quiet, and I turned to look at him. "Stop, Fire." His hands reached out and wrapped around my wrists, tugging my arms away from where they were twisting around my middle as I emerged from my post-orgasmic haze.

"I'm not doing anything," I whispered, even though I knew it was only partly true. I was doing something, but I didn't want to be doing it. He tugged on my wrists until my arms were completely free from my body and then wound his fingers through mine. I sucked in a breath and belatedly realised that the car reeked of sex.

"I don't want to lose you after what we just shared. Actually, no, fuck that—I *can't* lose you after what we just shared, so you are going to have to get used to me being here. You"—he tugged on my chin and turned my head to face him—"are going to have to get used to talking to someone and telling them what is on your mind. I want to be in this with you more than I have ever wanted anything in my life, and I'm not going to have you checking out on me if things get a little rough."

"What happens now?" I put voice to the question that had begun to circle in my mind. "I mean, we just did that, and now I don't know what happens. Do you go home? Do you drop me off? Do I text you tomorrow? Do you call me?" I squeezed my eyes closed because clearly this was going to be the night I started to show my hand.

"What happens now, beautiful, is that you are going to pick your pretty mask up from the floor and I will take us back to your flat. You will let us inside and I will take care of you. I know no one takes care of you and I know you have been looking after yourself for a really long time, but so have I, so I know sometimes it would be nice for someone to take care of you. Fuck, I'd love someone to take care of me for a minute. Fighting so hard and fast for so long is exhausting beautiful. Let me take the load for tonight, and then you can have it back." His hand squeezed mine and he didn't wait for me to respond before turning the key in the ignition and pulling out of the industrial estate.

I didn't speak anymore. I simply did as he said and picked up my mask, settling it back into its box as he drove us back to my place. I let my eyes slide closed after a minute or two and allowed myself to just feel. I felt the car moving steady beneath me; he hadn't pressed too hard on the accelerator since my freak out. I felt the way his rough hand rubbed against my smooth one. I felt the wind blowing across my face from where he had cracked the window, and I felt the vibrations of his humming as he moved us forward. I had no idea what he meant by taking care of me, but I did know that for once, I was determined not to get in my own way. I was going to zip my mouth shut, shove down the barricades I kept between me and the world, and allow this clearly wonderful man to do exactly as he pleased, because so far he hadn't failed me.

I jumped as the car rolled to a stop and his fingers released mine.

"You dozed off." He smiled over at me before hopping down from the truck.

I shook my head, trying to push the fog of sleep from my brain as I released my belt and reached down to pick up my bag. The door opened and he caught me around the waist, lifting me down from the truck but not letting me go.

"What do you dream of?" The words were spoken so softly I wasn't even sure I had heard him right.

"Sorry?"

"What do you dream of? I've watched you sleep more than once now. I know you don't even get any peace when you are meant to be at your most relaxed." I felt my body stiffen and I knew he felt it too when he sighed. "Something else you don't talk about?"

"No." I shook my head. "I didn't know I dreamt of anything." I watched his dark brows pull low over his eyes as he considered my words.

"No one's ever told you?"

I took a deep breath in through my nose as I realised the only way forward was to be honest. If he was putting up with me, I needed to make an effort too. I squeezed his wrists as I rested my hands over them and opened my mouth.

"I know I used to dream as a kid. I used to talk in my sleep as well. Apparently I would sit up and have a whole conversation sometimes." My lips quirked slightly as I allowed the memory a few seconds of my time before I shut it back down. "I haven't shared a room or slept with anyone who didn't have their own nightmares since I was sixteen." I bit down on my lip hard enough to draw blood and he tugged it free with his thumb, allowing me to continue. "So, I didn't know I still dreamt. I never remember it." I shook my head and let my shoulders lift and fall to emphasize my point. Instead of tugging me into him to pity me the way I had expected him to, he turned and slammed the door of the truck shut and tugged me towards the flat.

I walked up the stairs with his hands on my hips and his body pressed tight against my back. I unlocked the door and no sooner had I stepped over the threshold than I heard it slam shut behind me. I expected him to pounce. I expected him to strip me naked and haul me against him, but it didn't happen. I turned on my heel to see what he was doing and found him with his back pressed against the wall and his chin pressed against his chest. Panic shot through me unbidden as I dropped my bag to the floor and hurried towards him. I got my fingers beneath his chin and tipped it up so I could see his eyes.

"What's wrong?"

"You slept with me." His words were low and gruff and I had to get really close to be able to hear them.

"I know." I nodded.

"Why me, Fire?"

"Excuse me?"

"Why me? Why did you let me stay? And don't say it's because I wouldn't leave, because we both know that had you meant it, I would have gone when you asked me to." His hands shifted from his pockets and shoved into my hair, bracketing the sides of my face. "Why did you let me stay? Why let me in?"

"I don't know." I answered honestly because I had made myself a promise to do so. "I have no idea why I let you stay. All I know is that it didn't feel wrong. I didn't want to run and I didn't want to hide. I just wanted to be."

"Is it because you were vulnerable?" His tone was pleading, but I had no idea what he was pleading for. I shook my head sharply.

"No. I went to bed with you because I'd wanted to for longer than I'd liked to admit. Those near misses…I thought they were for the best. I convinced myself a long time ago that there was no place in my life for another person—ask Lennon, she'll tell you. It's really hard to undo years of telling yourself one thing, and you were so strong and dominating. You terrified me, Knox, because I could see myself coming undone with you. I fought too hard and too long to just hand myself over, but that night, after seeing what you did for me, after watching you put yourself in the firing line for me, I couldn't deny it anymore. I couldn't fight the pull. I didn't even think about letting you stay. I just fell asleep." I grabbed his face more firmly in my hands as I looked him in the eye. I needed him to understand that what I was about to say wasn't something to be taken lightly. "I never fall asleep. I have sex where I meet men. I have had sex in club toilets, against brick walls, in cars. I've had sex in a ton of different places with more men than I'm proud of, but I've never been with a man the way I have been with you." The hands he had in my hair tangled deeper and pulled a little tighter.

"I never want you to be with another man again." The words sounded as though they had been torn from him. "I never want to see another man put his hands on you, because none of them deserve you. Fuck, I don't deserve you, but I'm just smart enough to know that if you are telling me these things, it's because this means to you what it does to me. I won't let you down."

"Knox," I whispered as his mouth came down on mine. It wasn't hard or frantic this time; it was slow and it was soft. I'd never been kissed with reverence, but I had seen other people do it. I had watched Lennon kiss Gabriel the way Knox was kissing me right now, and I felt something coil, tighten, and snap inside my chest as I wound my arms around him and let my body fall into his. I trusted him not to let me fall without a fight. I trusted the words he was telling me and I trusted the way I felt around him. I didn't want to fight anymore. I didn't want to make myself miserable. For once I wanted more. For once I felt as though I deserved more.

chapter EIGHT

Knox

"Viva!" I yelled as I pushed the already open front door the rest of the way with the toe of my boot. "Viva where are you?" I called again as I stepped into the empty hallway.

"I'm here." Her soft voice floated towards me from the back of the house and I scowled. I slammed the door shut and walked towards the sound.

"Do you want to explain to me why the hell the front door wasn't locked? I know this isn't a totally shit neighbourhood, but nowhere is safe and you know better than to—"

The sound of her mixing spoon clattering into the bowl of god knows what she had been stirring echoed through the room as she spun around to face me. She was a tiny little thing—all of five feet—but when she looked at me this way, with fire in her eyes and a scowl on her face, I knew I was in trouble.

"Do you want to try walking into my house again? With better manners this time would be appreciated." I stared at her for a second as I tried to figure out whether she was serious, and when her hard posture didn't give, I knew she was.

"Veev—" I started, but her hand shot up to stop me.

"I said, try walking into my house again, and this time do it without yelling and hollering at the top of your lungs. Go!"

I fought the urge to roll my eyes as I turned on my heel and walked back in the direction I had just come. I needed to rein in the panic that had flooded me when I saw the door open that way. I knew she wasn't stupid, and I knew Viva didn't take her safety—or anyone else's—for granted, but old habits seemed to be rearing their heads all over the place lately and I was having difficulty coming to terms with that. I made my way to the front door as I tried to get a hold of myself before turning around and heading back towards the kitchen.

"Veev," I said gently as I crossed the threshold. She hadn't gone back to her mixing the way I had assumed she would, instead I found her standing with her arms crossed on top of her pregnant belly and glaring at me.

"What was that?"

"The door was open."

"The door was unlatched."

"It's the same thing."

"No it isn't." She shook her head and I saw her brow furrow slightly. "What's going on with you?" She asked the question straight out and I sunk into one of her kitchen chairs as the weight of the last few weeks suddenly felt heavy on my shoulders.

"How are you?" I asked, avoiding the subject in the only way I knew how. "How are you feeling?"

"I'm fine, the same way I was when you called and asked if you could come round." I sighed and reached out to place my hand on the protruding baby bump that seemed to fit her.

"How's she cooking?" I asked, looking up at her as her small hand covered my own.

"She's good." I could hear the smile in her voice as she looked down at our hands. "Not much longer until I can get all the men in my life off my back." She turned away from me and picked her mixing spoon back up.

"What did we do now?"

"Well you, Matt, and my father seem to think I have suddenly become an invalid. I'm pregnant, not ill, and this isn't my first rodeo." I felt a smile teasing the corners of my mouth. Viva had always understood me, had always known what I needed, and no time or distance had ever changed that. I tilted my chair slightly to look around.

"Where's Kale?"

"School, K. It's Thursday lunchtime."

"Oh shit, yeah," I said as I glanced down at my watch.

"Okay that's enough." The bowl in her hands thudded against the table as she plopped down in the chair opposite me. "Can you just spit it out? You know you can't lie to me. You know I can see straight through it, so please just get on with it so I can fix it."

"Who says you need to fix something?" I peeked up at her and she pursed her lips.

"The look on your face tells me. You called me, K. You asked to come over. You wanted to talk, so talk, because I'm listening." I sighed as I scrubbed my hands over my face, my head, and finally clutched at the back of my neck.

"I met someone." It seemed like the easiest place to start seeing as I had never been brave enough to tell Viva anything about Freya before now.

"You met someone," she repeated, but unlike the strain that had been in my voice, there was undeniable joy in hers. I stared at her as she clapped her hands like a schoolgirl and beamed at me. "Who is she? What's her name? What does she do?" Her questions shot at me like tiny bullets and I knew my confusion was showing on my face when she took a deep breath and shook her head, causing strands of her raven hair to come loose from her trademark braid. "What's her name?"

"Freya."

"Okay." I could tell she was fighting the urge to bounce in her seat as she asked her next question. "How old is she?" I shifted my eyes away from hers as I tried to remember if she had ever told me how old she was. I knew we hadn't done a whole lot of talking and some of that had been my doing, but sitting there and not knowing, I felt like an idiot. How could I claim to feel the things I did about this woman when I didn't even know her damn birthday? It was just one more thing to add to the pile of not-so-awesome I had been building up behind her back.

"I'm not sure." I winced. "I think she's about twenty-three."

"You think she's twenty-three?" Viva's dark eyebrows rose, and I didn't like the look of censure on her face.

"She doesn't like to talk about herself much." It sounded pathetic, but it really was the truth. Freya didn't like to get into deep conversations, and I had been avoiding them like the plague. I knew we sounded like a terrible pair, and I saw Viva's excitement drain from her face.

"Is that what you need to talk about?"

"No." I shook my head, because I had called on a whim. I knew I needed to tell Freya the truth about who I was, but I wasn't sure how to do it without causing her to run screaming. The last thing I wanted to do was lose her, but I couldn't demand honesty from her until I gave it myself. "Freya is Lennon's best friend." Her eyes widened, but I didn't give her the chance to interrupt me. "I don't know all the basics about her because the only thing that matters when we are together is the raging inferno that sparks between us. I know how she looks when she cares. I know how she trembles when she's afraid of something. I know what she sounds like when she can't see anything but me and that's all that's mattered to get us to this point, but I want more. I want everything from her, and I know I can't demand any of it until I'm honest with her about who I really am."

"Oh." The sound was soft and more like a breath of air than anything else as she sat back in her chair.

"That is why I called Veev. I've never told a woman about any of it, least of all a woman who already holds my whole world in the palm of her hand. I don't want to lose her." I looked up at her and saw the fine white lines of tension that were now bracketing her mouth. "Shit!" I cursed as I grabbed her hand, holding on to it as tightly as I could. "I don't want to rake up the past for you Veev. I don't want to hurt you, but you're the only one who understands. You were there and you made it out the other side. I just want your advice. Fuck this was a bad idea!"

There was silence between us for a long minute, but when she didn't pull her hand away from mine, I took it as a good sign. Finally she let out a breath and her free hand rubbed her stomach.

"You're not hurting me K. I've been waiting for this day for longer than you know."

"You have?"

"Of course I have." Her hand moved from her stomach to cup my cheek and her smile was watery. "I knew you'd find the woman who turned you inside out one day. I've hoped for so long that you would come ask me how to tell her, and that I wouldn't have to beat you with my rolling pin to get you to tell her everything. There shouldn't be any secrets between you two, not with the way you look when you talk about her. She's really it for you, huh?"

"She's the only person I've ever met who fits me. She can see the darkness, recognises it. She has the same inside of her, and when we come together, those monsters that torment us…they go quiet for a minute. It's great, and I know the only way forward is to be honest. I need her to see all of it and still want me, but how the hell do I make that happen?"

"Have you told her anything about yourself Knox? Anything at all? That you're an uncle, maybe?"

"Not yet." I wasn't able to meet her gaze so I kept my eyes trained on the grain of the table. I had wanted to talk to Freya about Kaleb and Viva a hundred times, but every time I came close, she would want to know all the ugly parts that went along with that story, and until now, I hadn't had the strength to face them. "I couldn't tell her about everything else so I couldn't tell her about the two of you."

I was ashamed to hear those words from my own mouth and my head dropped forward on my neck and my eyes trained on my boots. Viva's stomach came into my line of vision as her arms wrapped around my neck and she cradled my head to her shoulder. At only three years older than me, we shouldn't have had the kind of relationship we did. People on the outside would have called it a brother-sister relationship, but I knew it was far closer to mother and child. Viva had been the only person in my life to take care of me for the longest time. She had been the one hounding my arse to go to my exams, the one to put food on the table when I got up in the morning and when I came home at night, and the only one to recognise my desire for more. I hadn't wanted to live the life I had been stuck in for so long, and she had held out her hand to me and dragged me out of it without fear of the consequences.

"What do you think she's going to do K? Do you think she's going to blame you for the things that were done to you when you were a kid? Do you think she is going to judge you for the stains on your conscience that someone else put there? If that is what you think you need to get the hell out now, because she is not the woman for you." My eyes snapped open as the words flowed from her mouth, her voice harsher than it normally was and giving me pause.

"I don't think that." I shook my head as she released her hold on me slightly. "She's ballsy and she's strong in her own way. I don't think she'd blame me, but I'm fucking terrified knowing what I am truly capable of is going to change the way she looks at me." I sighed as I thought back to the look on her face when I had been washing the blood from my hands in her kitchen sink. "She's seen me fight, but she's only seen the tip of the iceberg, Veev. As much as she was glad I protected her and her girl, there was still fear in her eyes." I didn't miss the way Viva's nostrils flared at the confirmation that I had been fighting, but I was grateful she didn't dwell on it.

"Back then, you were nothing but a scared little kid, and nothing you did or saw can ever be blamed on you. You can't go back and change it. Believe me, I've wished a thousand times that we could. I wish I could have met him earlier, got you out sooner, changed him forever, but the fact is, it's an impossible dream. I was blindsided by him; it was the effect he had on people. Jesus, it was what made him so damn good at the life he chose because he could manipulate and get people to do the things he wanted without you even noticing." She sucked in a shaky breath and it hit me that this was the first time we had spoken about any of this; it was no wonder I had so much trouble voicing it to anyone else. "I wish things had been different for all of us, K, but they weren't. You live with the things you did because you loved him and so do I. That's our lives, and it's what's made us who we are right now."

"You make it sound so much better than it was when you say it like that." I sighed.

"That is how it was. You were a baby." Her hand clasped the side of my face and turned it back so I was looking at her. "You've been so wrong for a long time, and now I know how badly we should have had this conversation before now. Our stories are so similar, but what you need to know is that Eli never loved himself. The only way he could measure his worth was by testing how much he could make others do for him to prove their love. He played you, K. He played both of us because it was all he knew. I'm not making excuses, but he was fundamentally broken and the rest of us didn't stand a chance in the face of that."

I rubbed at the pain behind my eyes as her words settled into my reality. I had been so consumed blaming myself for all the wretched things I had done, I had never considered the motives behind it all. I had told myself for so long that I had done it because that was what was inside me, but maybe that was what I had needed to tell myself at fifteen years old just so I could step foot outside the door and carry out the orders the man I had looked up to had given me.

"And if Freya deserves you, she will see that. If she doesn't, then as much as it will hurt, she isn't the woman for you." I hated the way that sounded, but I knew she was right. "I was terrified when I told Matt, but when he took my hand and told me we all had scars and he could live with mine as long as I could live with his, I knew he was it for me. You'll know once and for all if Freya is it once your truth is out there." Her thumb skimmed over the back of my hand before she continued. "You're a good man. You're one of the best I have ever met. You deserve a woman who sees that too, and maybe if she's damaged then you'll iron out each other's kinks and cobble yourselves together." I let out a long breath and leant forward to press a kiss to her forehead.

"When she's ready, can I bring her to dinner?"

"There's the boy I know." She smiled. "We would love to have you both when you're ready. Don't drag this out, K. Tell her soon, promise?" She reached out her pinky and I hooked mine around it.

"Promise."

Freya

"Lunch?" I turned my head at the sound of Lennon's voice. I was surprised it had taken her this long to corner me because I had no doubt she knew there was something going on that she wasn't privy to.

"Lunch sounds good."

I spun my seat back to face my computer so I could close the presentation I was meant to have been working on for the last hour and a half. It hadn't changed since I'd opened it, and I knew that was because my mind kept wandering to Knox. I wanted to know where he was and what he was up to because he had seemed distracted when I'd left him half naked in bed. I'd written and deleted no less than ten text messages since I had walked into the office, and between that and my daydreaming about my now suddenly exotic sex life, I was running on empty.

Instinctively I glanced down at my wrists and tugged the sleeves of my black shirt down over the raised red marks that marred the skin. I liked looking at them just the way he told me I would when he'd fastened my arms to the iron bars of my headboard and proceeded to tease and tantalise me into three mind-bending orgasms before he had even pulled his cock out of his boxers. I shuddered at the errant thought and turned to see Lennon now perched on the chair on the opposite side of my desk.

"I thought we were going to lunch."

"I brought lunch to you. I assumed you were going to claim to be too busy to go with me seeing as you're always busy lately." She didn't even try to hide the smirk on her pretty face, which meant fighting mine was nearly impossible. "I knew it!" she exclaimed as she emptied all the cardboard containers out of the white carrier bag in her hand. I recognised the logo on the side instantly and could have kissed her for bringing me Chinese food. "I knew there was something going on."

"You brought me Chinese food as a bribe?" I gasped in mock horror even though we both knew it was her go-to thing. My two long-held vices were Chinese and Indian food, and seeing as she was allergic to anything even remotely spicy, she always held Chinese food as her golden ticket into my mind.

"Yes and no." She shrugged as she opened her container and forked a heap of noodles into her mouth, slurping loudly on the ends. "I miss you." She said the words so matter-of-factly that I almost missed them, but when her blue eyes turned up to mine, I could see the fine sheen of tears in them.

"What's wrong?" I asked, instantly dropping my own fork back into my beef and broccoli.

"God I'm so ridiculous." She sighed as she pressed the back of her hand against the tear that had leaked from her eye.

"Oh shit." I sighed as I shoved my food to her side of the table and made my way around to sit in the second client chair. I snatched up some tissues from the box on my desk and held them out for her. "Talk to me Len. I can't help if you don't."

"That's just it." She laughed and my brows furrowed. "There's nothing to help. Life is good Fray, really good, and even though I'm probably going to bash Gabe over the head with a paint tin any day now, I'm happy."

"Then why are you crying?"

"I just miss you and I've been trying to give you space because I know something is going on with you and Gabe said I shouldn't climb all over your arse about it."

"He said that?" I asked, picking my food back up now that I knew she wasn't going to descend into a full meltdown.

"Something similar." She tossed her growing hair over her shoulder and sat back in her chair. "So I've been trying to wait for you to come to me but you haven't."

"So you've been working yourself up," I finished for her.

"I guess." She peeked up at me from beneath one blonde eyebrow, and for the first time since starting this thing with Knox, I wanted to talk about it. The words felt as though they were crowding the tip of my tongue, and even though I'd spoken briefly to Hannah, it wasn't the same as confessing everything to the woman who had been by my side for so long.

"I wouldn't have told you," I admitted, and I winced at the hurt that flashed across her face at my badly thought-out words. "Not because I don't love you or trust you, but because I wouldn't have known how to. You know me Len, you know I'm no good at the talking and feeling stuff."

"Does that mean you want to talk about it now?" I could see that she was physically restraining herself from asking a million questions, and I knew I needed to put her out of her misery.

"I think so." I nodded before quickly shovelling food into my mouth to give me a chance to get my heart rate back under control.

"Okay, I can work with that." She nodded as her foot tapped against the wood of my office floor in an anxious rhythm that was at complete odds with the look on her face. "It's about a guy right?"

"It's about a guy," I confirmed.

"Okay. How long have you known him?"

"A long time," I said carefully.

"And how long has it been more than just friends?" I raised my eyes towards the ceiling as I counted back to that night at the bar.

"Almost four weeks." As I said the words out loud, I realised it felt as though it had been much longer than that. It was amazing to me how I had changed so much in such a short space of time. The thought of sharing a bed with him didn't freak me out, and if anything, I missed him when he wasn't there. The flat was too empty, my bed was too big without his hulking frame, and those dark eyes of his took up every inch of my space and my mind. "It feels like longer."

"Really?" I looked up at the sudden escalation in pitch of Lennon's voice and she winced slightly. "Sorry, I'm so excited, but I'm trying really bloody hard to keep a lid on it. You have no idea how difficult it is."

"Thank you for trying, I appreciate it. I'm starting to sweat by the way." I motioned at my suddenly damp palms and she sat back in her chair.

"Do I know him?"

"You do," I confirmed.

"Can I guess?"

"If you want to." I laughed as I swapped out my container for the one I knew was going to be the home to some spring rolls—there was no way Lennon would bring Chinese food as a bribe without investing in spring rolls.

"Is it Paul?" She squealed his name and instantly slammed her hands over her lips, her eyes darting around to look out my window almost comically. I'd stupidly just taken a bite of a spring roll and my throat seized as a too-big bite slid down without permission. "Shit, sorry!" she exclaimed as she reached over and banged my back in the most unhelpful way. I managed to swallow the rest of the deep fried goodness and snagged my water bottle, taking a couple of big gulps to ease the stinging the food had left in my throat. "I didn't know you were going to choke," she said with her hands held up in surrender.

"Neither did I." I rubbed at my throat as I settled back down and shook my head at her. "But no, it isn't Paul."

"Oh." She sighed.

"Did you want it to be Paul?"

"Well, he's cute and kind and stuff, so yeah, I thought he could make you happy." She twisted her mouth to the side as though she was deep in thought, and I knew it was time to put her out of her misery.

"Knox makes me happier." The words seemed to echo in the space around us as I waited for her reaction. I had no idea if she was going to go nuts or be happy for me.

Paul was close enough to be familiar but not too close to cause any problems, but Knox was a very different story. He was completely embedded in her life and by default, in mine, and Lennon knew me better than anyone. I crossed my fingers as I watched her face; there was a lot going on behind her eyes but nothing coming out of her mouth. "Jesus Len, please say something. Yell at me if you need to." I tipped my head back on my chair and looked up at the ceiling; as much as I had given her permission to yell, I really didn't want to have to look at her while she did it.

"Fuck yeah!" She whooped as she leapt out of her seat and did a little shimmy dance. I raised an eyebrow at her as I pulled my head up, and she grabbed my face between her hands. "You just earned me five hundred quid. I fucking love you Freya Anson." She pressed a smacking kiss to my forehead before resuming her crazy dance while I gawped at her like a total idiot.

"Do you want to tell me what the hell you're doing?" I asked incredulously after what felt like an eternity of her butt shaking far too close to my face. She pirouetted on the spot and then flopped back down on her chair, beaming widely at me.

"Gabe and I had a bet."

"You had a bet?" I asked slowly.

"Mmmhmm. I bet him five hundred quid you two would finally give into it before the year was out and he bet you wouldn't. I think he was banking on it happening during the party we're planning for New Year."

"You're planning a party for New Year?"

"Oh yeah, it's going to be amazing. Fireworks, champagne, cocktails, Twister—all the best things."

"That's nearly eight months away."

"I know, but you have to start planning early." She beamed as I rubbed my fingertips against my forehead.

"We've gone off course," I muttered as I shook my head. "Why were you betting on us?"

"Because it's been obvious from the beginning to anyone with eyes that you two were into each other."

"It has?"

"Fuck yeah. You two melt everything around you even when you're bickering like an old married couple, so we thought we'd make it interesting." She shrugged as if it was no big deal. "The only rule was that we weren't allowed to meddle and we didn't, so yay." She tossed her arms in the air before laughing at me. "You look scandalised."

"I feel it," I admitted. "I can't believe you two were making bets on us. Don't you have anything better to do?"

"Oh we do." She winked. "But you know all about that already, and I want to hear about you." She pointed her finger in my direction and for the first time since I had started having sex, I realised I didn't really want to talk about the things I was getting up to in the bedroom. It wasn't that I was ashamed or that I thought my once virginal and pure best friend would be freaked out; it was because it was suddenly a lot more personal than it had ever been before. "You don't want to talk about it do you?" I had expected her face to fall a little bit, but instead her lips turned up in a softer smile than I had seen on her face so far.

"I'm not ashamed," I said quickly.

"I know you're not, you just want to keep it private, between the two of you."

"Yeah." I nibbled on my bottom lip as she nodded at me.

"Do you have any idea how long I have waited for this Fray?" I shook my head and she continued. "I've waited forever for you to find someone who makes you feel like this because it's what you've deserved all along. You deserve to cherish the thing between the two of you and keep it close to your chest because that is how you know it means something. I love him for you, and I only wish things had happened sooner for the both of you."

"I don't." I shook my head because I knew I could say this with complete confidence. "I wasn't ready for Knox before. He was too much for me then—sometimes he's too much for me *now*, but I'm learning to talk it through rather than run, and he's patient with me." Her fingertips smoothed over my cheek as she bit down on the inside of her mouth to halt the tremble in her bottom lip.

"I trust him with you, Fray, and I know that you do too, because you wouldn't give him your time otherwise. Let him take care of you, and when the time comes, you take care of him right back. I'm not saying it will always be easy—you are both fiery—but ride it out and hold on tight because the end is so much sweeter that way."

"You're going to make me cry, Walsh, and I don't cry." I sniffed as I pulled back slightly, she laughed the way I had hoped she would, and then she pushed to her feet.

"This deserves a celebration. Up you get, Anson. We are going to the salon."

"It's the middle of a work day," I reminded her even as I pushed to my feet and walked around my desk to retrieve my bag.

"I know, but there's no way on earth I'm concentrating now. Gabe is taking me out tonight so I want to look pretty, and maybe you can ask your man around and show him a buffed and shinier version than he's seen so far." She winked as she picked up her bag.

"He's seen me with no makeup on." Those simple words felt so powerful when I said them out loud, and when her chin dipped and her eyes glossed over, I knew she understood.

"And when you're ready, you can show him you without the armour." I nodded as I got to my feet and pulled by handbag out of my desk drawer.

"What about Hannah and Max?" I asked as I made my way around my desk to where she was standing.

"They went out for lunch together, said they'd be back later."

"They've gotten close," I commented as I pulled my phone from bag and finally started to type the message I would actually send.

Me: What time will you be home? I'll order a takeaway.

"Yeah I think it's good for Han. I'm hoping maybe she will let Max in further than she's let us."

"I hope so," I agreed as we stepped into the lift and the phone buzzed in my hand.

Knox: Forget the takeaway... I'll be home at seven and I'm cooking, all you need is your appetite Fire girl xxx

I took a deep breath and inclined my head towards Lennon. I might not have been able to tell him with words what he meant to me, but I knew there was a way I could show him.

"Do you think Ramone is working today?"

"Why, are you dying your hair again?"

"I think it's time." I nodded.

chapter NINE

Knox

I pulled up the handbrake and looked up at the shitty block of flats my girl called home. I hadn't heard any more from her after that one message, but that didn't surprise me. I was coming to realise that Freya was so much more than I had believed because every time I peeled back a layer, there was another waiting just beneath.

I had managed to rein myself back in from the meltdown I almost had at Viva's kitchen table when she texted, and for the first time in my life, I felt as though I could believe in things like fate. In that moment, I had needed nothing more than to hear from her, to know she was invested in this. I was used to her being on radio silence during the day—she wasn't the kind of girl who wanted to come across as needy or even one to make small talk—so I knew when she messaged me it was because she had something she felt needed saying. In some ways it was probably better for us that she was that way because I knew she would never give me anything simply to placate me the way people so often did.

I pushed open the car door and made my way around to the boot. Viva had given me a crash course in all of her best recipes and the bulging sight of my shopping bags was testament to that fact. I could only hope I had memorised them properly.

I closed the boot and made my way towards the front door. I pressed my finger down on the buzzer for her flat and waited for her to answer. When there was no response, I pressed a little harder, and again I was met with silence. I was just about to put down my haul and drag my phone from my pocket when the door swung open from the inside. I looked up into the beaming face of Nell, Freya's teenage neighbour who I had met a few times. I knew she had once been a big Acerbus fan, but she never got starry-eyed when she saw any of us and I appreciated that more than anyone knew.

"Going in?" she asked with a wide smile. From what I recalled Lennon telling us once, she hadn't had the easiest of lives; her mother had given birth to her at a young age and left her to be raised by her grandmother. I couldn't recall ever having seen the woman who spawned the pretty teenager, but Grandma Edie was the one I had to thank for the way my life was now; just looking at Nell, it was easy to tell she had learnt her ways from her.

"Sure am." I nodded as I scooped my bags up. "Heading out?"

"Yup," she replied as she let me step inside. She spun around and pointed at the logo on the back of her t-shirt.

"Heading to work." She looked so damn proud of herself that I couldn't help but return the smile.

"New job?"

"Yeah." She practically vibrated with excitement as she bounced from foot to foot. "I got this awesome job at a tattoo place not far from here. It's called Porcelain. It's still fairly new, but I went in there with Lucy last week and they set me up with a job on the desk. It beats flipping burgers hands down, and the owners are really cool. Callum, the one who manages it, even said he'd teach me the ropes so I can get into the art side of things." Her joy was palpable and I couldn't stop myself feeling happy for her. I knew how hard it could be to drag yourself out of a less-than-stellar life, and just the fact that she was trying her hardest and doing it with an infectious smile on her face made me want to cheer her on.

"That sounds like you got yourself a sweet deal Nell. Congratulations."

"Thanks Knox, that means a lot."

"It's nothing." I shrugged before continuing. "Make sure you let us know when they start letting you wield the good stuff and I'll get you to book me in."

Her dark eyes went wide in her face and her jaw dropped. "You'd let me tattoo you?"

"Once they train you up, I'd have no problem with that. I've got some blank space left." I chuckled as she squealed and bounced on the balls of her feet.

"Oh wow, thanks!" I expected her to kiss my cheek or something when she lunged forward suddenly, but instead her fist hit me solidly in the shoulder and she smiled before checking her watch. "I've gotta run, but Freya came in about an hour ago. I'll let you know when I can book you in. Have a nice night!"

I let the door slam shut behind me and headed for the cement stairs that would lead me to my girl. I was glad I could put a smile on Nell's face over something so simple, even if it had landed me a hearty punch. That girl could certainly wield her fists as weapons, and I knew I shouldn't have been so surprised because there was no doubt Edie was still as scrappy as that even at her age. I smiled to myself as my eyes drifted over to Edie's closed front door and then I turned my attention back to the one I wanted to be behind. I lifted my hand and knocked hard enough to have the letterbox rattling. There was no answer and I frowned because Nell had clearly seen her come home, and Freya had asked me to come around so should have been expecting me.

A slither of dread spread through my chest at the thought of something being wrong with her. Bad things could happen to people when they were alone: she could have slipped and cracked her head, had a heart attack or seizure. Panic flooded my veins and I lifted my hand again, smacking it hard against the piece of plywood that separated me from her. Suddenly the door wasn't beneath my palm anymore and I blinked back in shock that I could have actually busted it down without using my boots or my shoulder, but my shock was short-lived as the sight of Freya standing just inside the door in nothing but a small white towel met my eyes. I swallowed hard as I stared at her. Water droplets still rested on her skin and her face was completely bare. Long tendrils of fiery orange were escaping from the rough messy bun she had pulled her hair up into and I blinked as her luscious mouth curved into a stunning smile. It wasn't a smile I could ever recall having seen on her face before, and it was damn beautiful.

"Hey." Her voice sounded huskier than normal and it slid over my skin, snapping me from the lust-induced haze.

"Why are you answering the door naked?" I growled, and those mossy eyes of hers rolled exaggeratedly in her head.

"I'm not naked, see." She laughed as she tugged on her top of the towel, which was only just covering her beautiful breasts.

"You're naked," I repeated as I stepped inside and slammed the door shut with my foot. My bags fell to the floor as I reached for her, and her laughter faded into a whisper of sound as I tugged her against me.

I skimmed my thumb over the high ridge of her cheekbone. It wasn't often that she let me see her fresh-faced like this. Sure, I had seen her without makeup, but rarely with the flush of a warm shower in her cheeks. Her skin was baby soft beneath my touch, and the message was sent directly to my cock because I already knew of the intimate places where she was always soft and silky like that.

"You're definitely naked," I whispered again as I felt the water from her skin start to seep into my clothes.

"I'm not naked." She bit down on her bottom lip and peered up at me through her lashes. The woman was a seductress without even trying, and I knew I would never be able to let her go. "Anyway, I knew it was you—no one else has ever pounded on my door the way you do." Her hand slid up the centre of my chest and it took every ounce of self-control I possessed not to whip that towel away from her and go to town on all the sweet naked flesh it would reveal.

I wanted nothing more than to trace the fine lines and intricate designs of the markings on her body. I wanted to trace every dove etched into her left arm with my tongue. I wanted to run my nose over every pretty red rose that blossomed between the serene birds. I wanted to smooth my fingertips over the melting clock and the broken hourglass that covered her right arm. I wanted to kiss away the pain that had forced her to etch the thorns around the timepieces. I wanted to turn her around and get a good look at the fallen angel that sat with its head on its knees, weeping at the base of her back. My cock pushed against the zipper of my jeans and my abdomen contracted hard enough to make me suck in a breath as I clenched my hand tighter on her hip—where the dreamcatcher was etched— and let my forehead fall against hers while her fingers danced along my beard.

"It's getting longer," she whispered, and I couldn't stop the grin from tickling at the corner of my mouth.

"Just means you'll feel it even more." A laugh escaped her, but it sounded more sultry and needy than amused as my eyes met hers. "Hey, by the way—"

"Are you done being a caveman now?"

"I still don't like you opening the door naked, but I've needed to see you all day." Her brows furrowed as she stepped back to look at me with concern. My heart thudded more insistently as that look took its place on her features. I wanted her to care as much as I did, and if she was worried about me, that meant I was finally cracking through the steel that surrounded her.

"What happened?" she asked as she got herself out of my grip. The towel had slipped slightly when I had pulled her against me and I caught a flash of a perfect, pale pink nipple before she could hide it. My mouth flooded with moisture and I knew she caught the gleam in my eye before I could mask it. She pulled the towel tighter and fixed her gaze on me a little harder. "Knox, why did you want to see me?"

"Just did." I shrugged. "I missed you."

There was no way I was going to bare my soul right now. I needed a little more time to show her that she wanted me. I needed to prove that I was someone she should keep around before I set about tearing down everything she thought she knew about me and replacing it with the ugly truth.

"You dyed your hair." It was stating the obvious, but in my haste to get my hands on her, I had forgotten to mention it. I reached out a hand now and fingered a bright orange tendril.

"I did." Her eyes dipped away from mine and landed somewhere on my boots. For someone who always oozed confidence, she suddenly looked nervous. I straightened as I looked at her.

"Why won't you look at me beautiful?" I kept my words gentle because I had no idea where her head was at. Trying to keep up with Freya was sometimes like trying to keep up with the weather in the middle of a storm.

"I'm looking at you." Her words were soft as her eyes rose to mine and she pushed her shoulders back. I watched as her chest heaved with a deep breath and she licked her lips. I wasn't going to interrupt because it looked as though she had something she needed to say and I wanted her to say it. "Lennon knows about us. They took bets on how long it would be before we gave into each other, and she won five hundred pounds. I know I didn't speak to you about it first, but I couldn't lie to her anymore. I needed to talk to her. Are you pissed at me?" Her bottom lip twisted between her teeth and I closed the distance between us once again and pulled her against my chest.

"Nearly everyone knows already. I think it's only Gabe and Cam who are still in the dark." I laughed as she traced the muscles in my shoulders with her fingertips.

"Well they'll know now." She choked out a laugh and I matched it with one of my own.

"So who owes her five hundred?" I asked; it didn't surprise me in the slightest that our friends had started taking bets.

"Gabriel, so we went to the salon to celebrate on him." I barked out a laugh that had her fingers curling into my chest, because of course that was what they decided to do. "You called me Fire girl in your text right as I got in the lift so…" She shrugged and shook her head a little as her sentence trailed off. The meaning behind her words hit me square in the chest and all laughter fled my body.

"Are you telling me you dyed your hair because of what I call you?" She shook her head and I could see apprehension swirling in the bottle green, but there was something else there as well. As her chin tipped up slightly and her jaw set, I recognised it as determination.

"No, I'm telling you I dyed my hair for you. I dyed it orange because you told me you liked it. I dyed it because I want to show you the things I can't say with words. I'm not like Lennon or Hannah and I never will be, so showing you things will always be easier than telling you." She squeezed her eyes shut as the declaration wrapped itself around my heart and squeezed tight. This woman, this vivacious, independent, infuriating woman, had dyed her hair because she knew it meant something to me. No words she could ever have said would have made me feel the way this did because I knew her appearance meant everything to her.

I licked my suddenly dry lips before I pressed them gently against hers. Her mouth flowered open instantly and I dipped my tongue inside briefly before pulling back.

"Do you like your hair this colour?" I needed to know she was okay with it before we went any further.

"Yes." She nodded and relief washed over me.

"No one has ever done anything like this for me before and damn, a few weeks ago I never thought I stood a chance with you, but this…" I reached up to tug the hair tie from her hair, allowing it to cascade past her shoulders in a fiery river. I tangled my hand in it and smiled. "This is everything. You're everything."

Freya

I couldn't escape the way his eyes burned as he made that declaration. I had no idea what I had been expecting his reaction to be, but I hadn't anticipated the glassy sheen that seemed to be reflecting my face back at me, and I hadn't expected to feel the way I did as I told him. For once, I wanted to be better. For the first time in a really long time, I wanted to be more for someone. I had kept Knox out of my life for so long and had denied us both all the things that made the world feel right. I knew Lennon had a point and we more than likely did have a long and bumpy road ahead of us, but I wanted to walk that road with him.

I took a deep breath as I let all of my thoughts and feelings swirl for a second before they settled down in a new way. I wanted this more than I had wanted anything in so long, and I wanted it with the man standing in front me.

"You okay?" His voice was still low and I felt the vibration from the deep timbre where his cheek was pressed against mine. I reached up and wound my arms around his neck, not caring anymore if my towel hit the floor. I wanted him and I knew he wanted me.

"Intense moment," I murmured, and his strong arms tightened around me.

"Best moment," he murmured back before pulling away.

I frowned because I had no idea where he was going. I was more than halfway naked and after what he had just said, I needed to feel his body against mine to ground me. I wanted to feel his hands on my naked skin and his bulk looming over me because I had never felt safer in my life than I did when our bodies were joined in the most intimate of places and his hands cradled my head. Sure I liked it rough with him; I liked it when he pounded into me and I liked it when he pulled my hair. I loved it when his fingers gripped my skin hard enough that it felt as though he was trying to meld us together, and it made my brain explode when he spanked my bare arse or tied me up, but those quiet moments when his orgasm was crashing over him and mine was waning were my real favourites. I loved lying beneath him and watching the pleasure contort his face. As much as I had grown addicted to the sweet bite of pain he had told me countless times he needed, I liked that in those last few moments, he didn't need them at all. There was no room in his brain or his body for anything but the pleasure mine offered him, and it made me feel like a goddess.

"Don't pull that face." He smiled as he smoothed the frown lines from my forehead with the tip of his finger. "Go get dressed and I'll get dinner started." My eyebrows shot up as I let my jaw drop.

"You want to cook right now?" I clarified because I could hardly believe what I was hearing. "I'm nearly naked and I want you inside of me, and you want to cook." I raised my hand to his forehead, pretending to check his temperature, and he laughed before tugging my wrist away.

"Yes I want to cook for you. I promised you I would and I told you to stay hungry,"

"Oh I'm hungry all right." I pouted as my eyes dropped meaningfully to the very hard bulge confined in his jeans. His palm covered up my view and his other hand came up to cup my chin.

"I'm hungry too, Fire, but I want to feed you. I can't explain it any better than that. Just play along and I promise I'll make it worth your while." One onyx-coloured eye slid closed slowly in a wink and I pursed my lips. As much as it was going to suck to wait, I couldn't say no to him. I nodded slowly before glancing down at the discarded shopping bags on the floor.

"You actually went to a supermarket?" I asked.

"I did." He bent down and scooped the handles into his big fists, heaving them off the floor effortlessly. I wasn't sure I would ever get enough of how strong he was or the way the muscles in his biceps bunched so deliciously.

"Well then I guess I can't say no, can I?"

"No you can't, and if I had any hands left, I'd swat your arse for the sass. Get dressed." He tipped his head towards my bedroom before walking away. "Meet me in the kitchen when you're done."

I shook my head at his bossy words and then did exactly as he'd asked. I pushed my bedroom door closed behind me and looked at the clothes I had laid out to wear before I had gotten in the shower. I wrinkled my nose at them and turned my attention to my armoire. I wrenched open the second drawer and let the light shimmer off the silk and satin it was home to. There were times—more often than not—that I needed to feel sexy. I had never allowed myself to admit it before, but I wanted to be desired. I wanted to be caressed and adored, and wearing silk nighties and satin pyjamas had been the only way I could achieve it. The men I had been wasting my time on were simply a means to an end, and sometimes for a few moments, I felt cheap and dirty. Those were the nights I dressed up and took myself to bed, but tonight I wanted to wear these pretty things for a whole new reason.

I selected a raspberry-coloured calf-length nightdress that had lace working its way from the hem up to my thigh on the left side and a slit up the right side. I dropped the towel and pulled the silk over my head. It slithered down my body, kissing every inch of overly sensitive skin as it did. I turned to look in the mirror and for the first time in forever, I really smiled at my reflection. I reached for my hairbrush and tugged it through the waves of my hair. Knox had only seen my hair natural when I woke up in the morning, but that was nothing close to what happened when I got out of the shower. He thought he had seen it wild and untamed the first night we met, but he hadn't seen anything yet. The strands sprung back into curls and soft waves, and I watched it happen with fascination. For the longest time I had been using straightening irons on my locks to keep them tame, but tonight I didn't want that. I couldn't tell him about my past yet, but I didn't want to hide anything else from him anymore. I felt as though we had turned a corner today, and I wasn't sure if it was because Lennon knew now or because this was just the natural progression, but it felt good.

I considered putting on a little makeup, but then a snapshot of his face as he stroked his thumb over my cheek flashed through my mind and I snatched my hand away from extensive stash of lotions and potions. I had no idea what his reaction was going to be, but I was hoping for all the best things.

The floorboards creaked beneath my feet as I made my way down the passage, so I pushed onto my tiptoes to go the rest of the way. I didn't even think about it as I pushed into that familiar stance and my feet tingled. I hadn't stood on my toes since I was a little girl, and I had no clue what had possessed me to do it in this moment. I pushed the errant thoughts from my mind and concentrated on my task. I wanted a minute to look at him before he realised I was there, and I wasn't disappointed by the sight I was met with. Knox was standing at my counter, bare from the waist up, the t-shirt he had been wearing was now shoved into the back pocket of his jeans, which had dropped low enough that I had a healthy view of the black boxer briefs he seemed to prefer.

I shifted my weight a little to get a good look at the way his back muscles pulled taut and rippled as he cut up whatever was on the chopping board I hadn't even realised I owned. There were jars and vegetables scattered all over the place, but I couldn't begin to figure out what on earth he was mixing up.

"You can come help instead of standing there ogling me if you want to." His voice was full of humour but he didn't turn around. I dropped onto the soles of my feet and padded across the floor into the kitchen.

"You should know now that I don't cook." It seemed like a sensible thing to put out there as I hoisted myself up onto an empty space on the opposite side of the cooker.

"Good thing I do then isn't it?" He smirked up at me.

"What is that?" I nodded to the green thing in his hand and wrinkled my nose.

"It's an avocado." He lifted it up so I could get a look at it and I frowned again.

"That's in guacamole right?"

"You really don't cook do you?" He laughed. I kicked out at him and he dodged me as he scooped the inside of the avocado into a bowl. "I'm making guacamole. The salsa is already there." He nodded at the bowl I hadn't noticed was sitting on the other side of me. "Tortilla chips are behind you, and by the way, you look fucking stunning." I smiled because I couldn't help myself and I saw him lock his jaw.

"Why are you scowling?"

"Because you knew what seeing you in that was going to do to me, and I can't do anything about it."

"Oh I don't know." I smirked as I scooped some salsa onto one of the tortilla chips and brought it close to my mouth. "I think you could do plenty about it, but you don't want to." I popped the chip into my mouth and the flavours exploded on my tongue. It was better than any I had ever tasted before and I knew my enjoyment showed on my face because he broke out that wide grin of his that would have made my knickers damp if I was wearing any.

"I'm glad you approve of my skills."

"You have to make me more of that, like tubs of the stuff so I can just pull it out of the fridge," I demanded. He laughed as he mixed the contents of the bowl he hadn't stopped adding things to and then washed his hands. I cased his every move as he picked the bowl back up and walked over to me, held it out between us, and slipped his other hand inside the slit in my nightdress.

"Try this one."

"I'm not a big guacamole fan," I admitted as his fingertips caressed my skin, sending little zings of promise to the place I craved him the most.

"Just try it."

I reached out for another chip and scooped some of the dip onto it before popping it into my mouth. I pulled my hand away as the flavour exploded the way the salsa had and my eyes widened. My hand didn't get very far though because he caught it in mid-air with both of his and tugged it towards him. I watched and tried to swallow as he sucked the tip of each digit into the hot cavern of his mouth and liquid warmth flooded the space between my thighs. There was something undeniably, unexplainably fucking hot about watching him suck my fingers through those plump. When he was finished with his task he leant closer, circling his hands around my hips and palming my arse through the silk.

"Knox…"

I had no idea what else to say. I wanted to ask him to touch me. I wanted to beg him to kiss me again. I wanted him to do every single damn thing I knew he was capable of. I gripped his broad, bare shoulders and tried to get myself under control as he pressed his open mouth to my neck. Everything inside me pulled taut in anticipation and I knew he felt it.

"I want to have dinner with you beautiful. I want to sit down together and talk. I want to know everything Len said when she found out. I want to know when your birthday is and your favourite colour, but you make it so fucking hard when you come out here looking like a goddess." His voice sounded strained and a flash of satisfaction shot through my blood, mingling with the desire that was threatening to overflow.

"I'm a strong man, Fire, and when you find out more about me, you'll understand that I mean that in every sense of the word. As much as I want to strip you out of this hot-as-all-hell silk, as much as I want to run my hands and my tongue over every single inch of your naked skin, as much as I want to pull you to the edge of this countertop, shove this pretty nightie up to your waist, and lose myself in your tight, wet heat, I'm not going to." His hands released me and I had to curl mine around the edge of the counter to stop myself from falling into him. My eyes could barely focus on him, glazed with lust as they were, but I tried my damnedest. "I'm not going to do that because I want more from you than just your body. I want all of you to be in this with me, and not just my cock. I don't want to cloud your judgment with sex because when we come together, it's powerful and potent and you'll only end up hating me if I wield that against you like a weapon. I want you to walk into this with me with your eyes open. Don't ever think this is easy for me, beautiful, especially not when you're looking at me the way you are right now, but know that I am always trying to do what is best for us." He stepped forward once more and pressed a gentle kiss to my forehead. "Now take your chips and your dips and have a seat. I'll be in once the rest of this is done."

I could barely hear him over the roar of blood in my ears. The words he had spoken felt both suffocating and freeing at the same time, and I couldn't stop the hole that ripped wide open in my armour as I ran them through my mind again. Knox wasn't going to wield the connection between us against me. Most men would have with a girl like me—heck, a few had even tried over the last few years, but there I was, having dinner cooked for me by a man who recognised that he could manipulate me in that way but was choosing not to.

I let him help me down and pressed my hands against his chest.

"I know you wouldn't do that to me, Knox. Just promise me you won't withhold this"—I dragged my hand down his chest and cupped the prominent bulge in my hand, grinding my palm against it just a little bit—"all night." He hissed out a breath between his teeth and caught my shoulders in his grip. In a flash his mouth was pressed hard against my own and his tongue was delving inside to tangle with mine. I let him play for a minute before the need to fight him back engulfed me. My hands went to his neck and I pushed my entire body flush against him, trying and failing to get closer to him. His hands flexed where they were now gripping my waist and he pulled us apart.

"I couldn't even if I wanted to Fire girl." A rush of air left me as I turned to scoop up my presents from him. He watched me the whole time I walked from the kitchen to the sofa and when I sat down, I tipped my head in his direction.

"Just in case it gets tough for you to keep your promise, I'm not wearing any knickers." I winked before dipping another chip in the heaven sauce he had made and let my head fall back against the sofa. I really was turning into someone I didn't recognise, but I'd be damned if all of a sudden it didn't feel like the best thing to happen in forever.

chapter TEN

Freya

"Where are we going again?" Hannah asked as I pulled the security door open and stepped outside. I turned to look at her and frowned. Hannah was the one who normally had the details memorised, and the fact that she was asking me again made me pause.

"It's a place called Derail, some bar Len found," I said gently as we made our way down the path to where the sleek black BMW was parked. Knox had taken it upon himself to organise our transport for the evening, and Alberto had been waiting by the curb for the best part of an hour. As we approached, the driver's door opened and the smiling face of the older man greeted us as he made his way around to the pavement.

"Oh yeah, I remember now," she said quietly as he swept open one of the back doors for us.

"Good evening ladies."

I cringed slightly at his politeness because I hated that he had been waiting this long. I made a mental note to chew Knox out for sending him round so early before turning and smiling at him.

"Sorry you had to wait so long. We didn't know you were coming until you were already here."

"It's not a problem at all Miss Anson. Mr Sutton advised that he wasn't sure when you would be ready and I'm used to it anyway, part of the job."

The way he spoke you would have expected him to have a little chauffeur's hat that he could tip at me while I climbed inside, and I had to admit, I was a little disappointed he didn't.

Hannah slid in beside me and I focused my attention back on her. I had noticed that over the last few weeks she had been quieter and more distant than usual, and it didn't sit well with me. Her hands were clasped over the bag she was holding against her stomach and her eyes drifted out the window.

"Are you okay Han?"

"I'm fine." Her voice was as gentle as ever, but there was a hint of something colouring her tone that sounded a lot like sadness.

"You know you can talk to me right, or Lennon if you need to."

"I know." She nodded as she turned slightly to look at me.

"And I also know that the last thing you want right now is for me to start babbling on, but I've noticed, Han, and I can't pretend I haven't." Her chest rose on a deep inhale but I forged on anyway. "I know I've been a pretty shit friend lately, especially since that night at the bar because my head has been so full of me and Knox, but I'm worried about you."

"You don't need to worry about me." She shook her head even as her chin trembled slightly. "I'm trying to grow up and I'm trying to figure things out, it's just not as easy as I hoped it would be."

I reached out for her hand, finding it icy cold as I wrapped my fingers around it.

"It's not a bad thing to ask for help sometimes. I know that probably sounds really hypocritical coming from a girl like me, but I'm learning. I'm changing, we all are, and Han, if that's what you need, we can help you with it. Please don't isolate yourself."

"I'm trying not to, but it isn't as easy as it sounds. I love you all, you know that but lately it feels like I'm trapped in this vortex and there is so much push and pull on all sides that I don't have the first idea how I'm going to make it out without someone getting hurt."

I took a deep breath because I didn't like the sound of that at all. I might not have been Ross' biggest fan, but I also knew that our very verbal dislike of the man wasn't helping. I didn't want him around any more than he wanted to be around us, but if it came down to it, I didn't want to lose Hannah because of him either.

"Hey listen, why don't you and Ross come for dinner one night, with Knox and me? The big man is an insanely good cook and it's only fair that I share that every now and then." I forced my smile to be as genuine as possible, already knowing Knox was man enough to go along with what I was offering without me having to ask him first.

"I'd really like that," she said softly before her eyes dipped away from mine and looked down at our joint hands. "But I'd have to ask Ross first. He's really busy with work and stuff right now."

I knew she was lying and I knew she knew I did, but it was not the time to call her out on it.

"Just let me know what he says and we can set something up yeah? Otherwise, if he's busy, maybe me, you, and Len could have a sleepover or something, buy loads of takeaway and some cheap wine, watch chick flicks and eat popcorn, just the three of us."

"Yeah I'd like that a lot." Silence fell between us for a beat before she broke it again. "I appreciate you trying so hard. I know you don't like him and I know he's never had anything nice to say about any of you. I'm really sorry for that, just so you know."

"Whatever Ross thinks of us is on him, not you. You don't need to apologise, and honestly I'm not blind enough not to see why someone's boyfriend wouldn't want someone like me around them, but like I said, I'm changing. I'd like to build some bridges, make your life easier, because the last thing any of us wants to do is lose you."

"Did Len say what this place was like then?" she asked, changing the subject quicker than I had expected her to.

"Not really, but she said it wasn't far from home and that it was nice. God knows what the urgency for girls night was though—did she say anything to you?"

"Just that I should be here at seven and to make sure I had a good meal before I came."

"That sounds ominous." I laughed as the car pulled up to the curb and the line that stretched from the front door right around the side of the building came into view. "And that looks painful."

"We're never going to get in." Hannah sighed as I pushed the car door open and stepped onto the pavement.

"Thanks for the drive Alberto," I said before I closed my door and fumbled inside my handbag for my phone. "I'll call her and see where she is. Maybe we can find some place close by."

I was bummed because from what I could see of the bar, it looked nice with its partially frosted windows and classy exterior. This place was far too classy for the girl I had been the last six years, and it made sense now why I had never heard of it before. It was the kind of place I would have sneered at because I had no doubt the drinks were going to be expensive, and there would probably be actual chairs to sit on. Tonight though, it looked perfect. For the first time, I wanted to sit with my girls and finally feel like I had something useful to contribute to the conversations they had about the men in their lives. Tonight I wouldn't have to rely on sarcasm or heavily loaded sexual innuendo. I was finally one of them.

"Where are you?" Lennon's voice was muffled by the sounds of people talking and music when she finally picked up.

"Outside Derail, where are you?"

"Inside!" she yelled. "Hang on a minute,"

"She said she's already inside," I said to Hannah as Lennon's muffled voice moved away from the phone speaker. "She's talking to someone."

"Okay just come up to the front door," Lennon said. "Someone will meet you there." With that, the line went dead.

"She said go to the front door and someone will meet us there."

"She wants us to walk right up to the door when all these people are waiting?" Hannah asked with wide eyes as she gestured at the queue.

"Apparently Gabriel's celebrity tendencies have rubbed off on her." I sighed as I linked my arm through Hannah's and straightened my back. "Better own it." I laughed as I dragged her up to the doorman and pasted on my best smile. "Hi there I'm Freya Anson, my friend is—"

"Inside." I looked up at the smiling face of the man who had just stepped out of the bar and finished my sentence. He looked like he had stepped out of a Viking movie. The wave of appreciation rippled out over the women behind me, and I felt like I now understood why the line was so long.

"Ladies, if you'd like to follow me." He motioned for us to step inside the bar in front of him so we did. "I'm Heath Carson, part owner of this fine establishment, and you must be Freya and Hannah."

"Lennon sent you to do her bidding for her did she?" I asked with a smile.

"We like to treat our customers well here at Derail." He smiled back.

"Is that code for Delaney asked you to keep an eye on his wife-to-be while she was in your care?"

"I like you." He laughed as we came to a stop at a secluded wraparound booth. "I bring your friends safely to your table, Miss Walsh."

"Thanks so much Heath. Hey it's so crazy out there right?" She laughed as she motioned out the window behind us and got up to kiss my cheek. Hannah had already slid into the booth beside Maxine.

"Yeah I think we got death-glared a shit ton, especially when you sent the Norse God to come collect us."

"Well I guess he's pretty nice to look at." She smirked as she nudged me with her elbow, and I couldn't help but laugh as I slid in next to her and got a good look at the two ice buckets holding champagne bottles that were already on the table in front of us.

"Are we celebrating?" I asked as Lennon leant across the table to give Hannah a kiss on the cheek and Maxine's eyes met mine.

"Well it's not every day I get all three of my girls in the same place unless we're stuck behind our desks." She smiled.

"And that calls for champagne?" I asked, turning my attention to Lennon, who was now chewing on her bottom lip.

"Well not exactly," she hedged.

"What's going on?" Hannah asked as she sat forward in her chair slightly.

"Gabe and I have set a date for the wedding and booked a venue." The words tumbled out of her mouth in a rush and I twisted to face her sharply.

"You didn't say you were looking at venues!"

"It was an accident. We were driving past this really beautiful hotel on the way home the other day and I sort of fell in love with it. We stopped to ask them if they provided weddings and they said they did and they had a cancellation."

"A cancellation?" Hannah asked.

"Yep, in October." Lennon paused for a minute with her teeth stuck into her bottom lip before breaking into the biggest smile I had ever seen on her face. She was practically radiant with excitement and it broke through the fog of surprise that had settled over us. "Gabe never wanted to wait, and well, I don't want to wait any longer either. We are getting married on October fifteenth and I need as much help as I can get." Her eyes flitted across all of us as if she didn't think we would help in any way we could, and I shook my head at her.

"I'd have been more disappointed if you hadn't needed help, kid." She threw her arms around me and squeezed me tight as a champagne cork popped beside me.

"I have to ask you something too," she said quietly as Maxine and Hannah got busy pouring champagne into glasses.

"You do?"

"Yeah, I need to know if you will be my maid of honour."

My eyes widened and my jaw went lax as her words hit me. I had never expected her to ask me that. I had presumed I would get tasked with invitations or something because I was fairly decent on design software. I could see she was holding her breath and her nails were digging into my arm as my silence seemed to stretch.

"Cam's going to be Gabe's best man so you'll walk down the aisle with him, or maybe you could walk with Knox if you wanted to, I don't really mind. Knox and Ash are going to stand up with Gabe too and—" I pulled her body into mine and squeezed her as hard as I could without breaking any of her bones, and her mouth snapped shut.

"I'd be honoured." She squeezed me back before extricating herself from my grip and reaching for two champagne flutes. She passed one to me and took one for herself before Maxine pushed to her feet and raised her glass high in the air.

"To Lennon and Gabe, may your wedding be stunning, may your married life be blissful, and may your children be beautiful."

I raised my glass and toasted to Lennon and Gabriel before taking a sip of the bubbly liquid. The minute the bubbles hit my tongue, my nose screwed up in distaste. It was a pretty vehement reaction even for me because while I was more accustomed to the oaky taste of whiskey, I wasn't a stranger to more feminine drinks. Lennon had already turned to Maxine to discuss wedding favours so Hannah was the only one to notice as I put my drink down on the table and pushed it away from me.

"Are you okay?" she asked, her brow scrunched in concern.

"I'm fine," I nodded. "Champagne isn't really my kind of drink."

"Okay," she said with more of a smile on her face than I had seen in weeks as she turned back to join in their conversation.

Two and a half hours later I found myself standing in front of the mirror in the bathroom. The décor matched the opulence of the bar area and I found myself musing over the fact that it was probably one of the better public bathrooms I had ever been in. It was unusual for me to be sober enough to notice something like the interior design of a bathroom, but I had given up on the idea of alcohol after my mishap with the too-bubbly champagne and had been firmly on soft drinks since then. The same could not be said for the three women with me.

Times had definitely changed, and looking at the glassy eyes of the woman who had just fallen through the bathroom door, I couldn't say I missed the old me very much. I knew what it was like to lean because you couldn't stand up, and I knew what it was like when you overstepped your limits and the churning feeling in your stomach was the only thing you could concentrate on. Hannah had those looks in spades as she came up beside me and leant her head against my shoulder.

"You okay?" I asked quietly as I found her eyes in the mirror.

"Why you so sober?" she slurred.

"Because I haven't been drinking champagne like it's going out of fashion."

"Fash-nun." She snorted as she twisted the tap on the sink and cold water splashed over both of us. "That's a funny word."

"Is it?" I asked as I reached out and turned the tap off.

"I'm hot," she whined as she twisted it back on again and shoved her hands underneath it. I shifted slightly and she wobbled. I steadied her automatically.

"You're wasted." I shook my head on a laugh and she squinted up at me.

"I am." She nodded. "First time ever."

"This is the first time you've been wasted?"

"Mmmhmm." She nodded so hard I was afraid she was going to topple over before she leant her weight on the sink and squinted at me in the mirror. "It's not ladylike to drink." The words came out slurred but the meaning wasn't lost on me. "Ross lets me have *one*." She snorted as though the words were amusing but her eyes were cold. "One wine with dinner, then water. *You were taught better, Anna. You were raised better, Anna. Be a lady, Anna.* Do you know something?" she yelled suddenly as she whirled around to face me. "Do you know something?" she asked again as her caramel-coloured eyes met mine.

"What Han?"

"I fucking hate that name. I hate when he calls me Anna because it isn't even my name." She barked out another dry laugh before turning back to the mirror. "I hate it and it's all he calls me."

I didn't want to state the obvious by asking her if she had told him she hated it, so I kept my mouth shut and my hand on the base of her back to keep her steady instead.

"He's supposed to love me. He said he'd take me away, to the Lake District, but then he forgot. Did I tell you that?"

"You didn't." I shook my head, my heart feeling heavier with every word that passed her lips.

"I need to make it work. I need to make us work because it's what they all want. They've always wanted it. It's perfect, the perfect match. I have to make it work Fray, but every time I see you and Knox and Len and Gabe I just…" Her sentence trailed off as she ran her hands through her hair. "Ash calls me Punz." Her eyes were glassy now as she tapped her fingers against her lips. "I have to make Ross and me work. They expect me to."

"What about what you want Han? What about what you deserve? Surely they want you to be happy." She twisted to face me, her fingers reaching out to play with a strand of my hair.

175

"I don't even know who I am." Her words were a whisper. "I don't have a clue."

"Then maybe you need to find out. Take a step back and find out who you are and what you need." She nodded up at me as she took a step back.

"I need to pee." She shook her head as she darted away from me and disappeared into one of the toilet stalls. The door slammed shut and locked behind her.

"Everything okay?" Maxine's voice was soft as she stepped inside the toilet and her eyes fell on the closed door.

"I have a really bad feeling that someone's gonna get hurt," I whispered as I walked by her. She caught my wrist and held me steady.

"It's going to happen, Fray. Best we can do is cushion the blow." I nodded just once before exiting the bathroom, my hand immediately going for my phone.

Knox

"You done good in here man," I acknowledged as Gabe handed me another bottle of water. I took it and twisted the cap as I studied my surroundings properly. Gabe's man cave had definitely exceeded my expectations, and his insistence that we eat upstairs now made a lot more sense. I had assumed he was exaggerating when he described it to us a few nights ago at the studio, but I was dead wrong. The walls were slate and blue, there was a U-shaped sofa of black leather in the centre of the room that was big enough to comfortably seat at least ten people, and a cinema-sized screen hung directly opposite. I had caught a glimpse of several video game consoles beneath it but I hadn't had the chance to see what they were yet. We were currently sitting in the kitchen area, which was kitted out with a fridge, a sink, and a microwave oven, and on the opposite side of the room, there was a pool table and several sweet-looking vintage guitars along with Gabe's first ever acoustic. I was in awe of his space and I couldn't deny it.

"I wish I could take the credit for it," he mused as he popped the cap off the bottle of beer in his hand and sucked down half the contents in one swallow.

"Are you saying my baby cousin is responsible for all this?" Cameron motioned around the interior of the room and Gabriel nodded.

"She's become queen of homemaking." He beamed with pride and I couldn't help but feel happy for him. It had been a long and painful road, so I was glad they had fully come out the other side of the tunnel. "I wasn't expecting a man cave. I was assuming we would just use the basement as storage or something, but she decided we should split it in half and do whatever we wanted with it."

"Well I guess that leaves upstairs free to be family only," Asher said with a smirk as he came up beside me and propped himself on one of the stools.

"Are you and Len…?" Cameron asked, his eyes unnaturally large for his face.

"Not yet." Gabe laughed as he reached out to shake Cameron. "But I plan on having babies with the woman I love in the not-too-distant future, so you might need to get ready for that, man."

"I don't think I'll ever be ready to watch you procreate with my little cousin," he grumbled as he took another long pull from his beer.

"I never thought I'd hear myself say this, but domesticity suits you Delaney," I said as I gestured at the room around me and then looked back at the boy I had seen party for days on end and drink more than any one human should. "Len's been good for you, and now you're getting hitched."

"Yeah, and you'll be next." Gabe raised an eyebrow at me. "Ash mentioned he never sees you anymore. You and Freya got heavy quick." I turned my head to look at Asher, who had suddenly decided he found Gabriel's guitar collection fascinating.

"Ash?" I asked. I knew I hadn't been around much lately, but I thought he understood. Asher had always been the little brother I never had, and I didn't like the thought of him talking about it to anyone but me.

"Well it's true." He shrugged. "You basically live at Fray's now." There was no malice in his voice, but I could tell some hurt was laced through it despite the smile he had pasted on his face.

"Look, I'm sorry I've been AWOL a lot, but Fire likes her space and I can't deny that I don't want to have to watch the volume because you're next door." He scowled at me and I shook my head. "I didn't mean for that to sound as shitty as it just did, I'm just saying that we have privacy at her place."

"You thought about getting another roommate?" Gabe asked as his eyes moved from Cameron to Asher. It didn't take me more than a couple of seconds to figure out what he was getting at. Asher and I had brought a three-bedroom place, so it wouldn't mean me losing my room; I couldn't deny that it was a decent idea, I just wasn't certain why we hadn't thought of it before now.

"I wouldn't trust some random to come live there so they can steal my shit and put it on one of those auction sites. No thank you!" He shook his head and picked up his beer bottle.

"What if it wasn't a random?" Gabe pushed, and I couldn't help but wonder why Cameron wasn't speaking for himself—until I took a good look at his face and saw the scowl firmly planted there.

"You know someone?" Asher asked, and it seemed as though he was quickly coming round to the idea.

"Yeah I think I do."

"Gabe leave it." Cameron sighed.

"You?" Asher asked, and Cameron's eyes moved from Gabe to Asher as his fingers fumbled with the label on his beer bottle.

"Don't worry about it man. Gabe has just been on my arse to get out of my mum and dad's. I think he's caught the meddling bug off Len."

"Honestly I'm more confused as to why we didn't think to ask you if you fancied it before man," I said as Asher turned to look at me as though asking my permission. Cameron's eyes shot up to mine and I saw that his brow was furrowed.

"Are you serious?"

"He's serious," Asher answered for me. "And I'm serious. Don't you want to get out of your mum and dad's?"

"I have been looking for a while," he admitted.

I couldn't quite get a read on what was going on inside his head which irked me to no end, but it was nothing unusual with Cameron. I had known him for almost as long as I had known Gabe and we had spent weeks at a time in the same place, but he was one of the only people I had ever encountered that I couldn't read. If Freya was the most guarded female I had ever met, Cameron was her male counterpart. It was odd to me though because he hadn't always been this way; there had been a turning point with him, and I knew it was when he had turned up in New York. I'd never seen anyone look as wrecked and defeated as he had at the time since I had looked in the bathroom mirror the night I'd tried to end it all.

"Why didn't you say something?" Asher pressed. In Asher's world, that was how things worked: if you wanted something, you asked for it.

"He's too proud," Gabe supplied.

"So are you moving in then?" Asher's eyes were alight now. "You can join one-man movie night."

"What's one-man movie night?" Cameron asked, his eyebrows furrowed slightly.

"Where I watch movies alone. I guess it would become two-man movie night then," he mused as he pushed up from his stool. "Just start moving your stuff in whenever you want."

"Simple as that?" Cameron asked.

"Yep." He nodded before sliding off his stool and heading in the direction of the pool table.

"See man, I told you." Gabe clapped Cameron on the shoulder and followed Asher. The tell-tale sound of balls dropping from inside the table filled the air and I knew it would keep them both busy for a little while.

"Are you all right with this?" Cameron asked, turning his attention to me.

"Course I am. Like I said, Cam, I don't know why we didn't think of it before. The flat was the best one we saw and it coming with three bedrooms was something we ignored in our haste to get out of the hotel and start laying some roots. Ash is right that I haven't been around much lately, and if it helps you out and it's good for him, then I have no problem. We can split the bills three ways if you want or sort it out however." For the first time in a long time I wasn't really too fussed about the details. I was normally the one who got caught up and bogged down in the small things, but this time all that mattered was helping out two friends.

"I appreciate it man."

"You're doing me a favour as well—Ash doesn't love being on his own." I laughed as Cameron moved around the counter to take the stool beside me.

"Things are really getting serious with you and Fray then?" he asked.

"They are." I nodded.

"How's she doing with that?"

"Better than I thought she would." I smiled as I turned to look at him. I knew he and Freya were close, but I hadn't anticipated what I could feel coming from him. It was an oversight on my part, and I could see that now because he acted as though she was as much a part of his family as Lennon.

"Good." He nodded as he twisted his beer bottle between his hands.

I turned my head slightly to see that Gabe and Asher were far too engaged in their game to notice us before I twisted on my stool. Cameron was not the kind of guy you tried to outsmart or hide shit from, and I had no intentions of doing either. There was no obligation on him to vet any guy Freya spent her time with, but the fact that he was putting himself in this position when I had just offered him a place to live and could quite easily retract that offer was honourable.

"Was there something you wanted to talk about?" I asked, making sure to keep my voice low.

"How much has she told you about herself Knox?" The query caught me off guard, and I knew the look on my face told him all he needed to know. "I'm going to assume from that look that she has told you nothing about herself besides the basics. It doesn't surprise me, but that makes this really fucking difficult." He scowled down at his hands and I shifted slightly.

"Just say what you need to say man," I offered, trying to make it easier on him, but he barked out a harsh laugh in response.

"You say that, but if I stick my foot in it, she will probably castrate me. Freya is fiercely protective of her past and all I know I pretty much found out by accident. You know she came to live with us after she met Len right?" I shook my head in the negative and he sighed heavily. "Well she did, and then they moved in together after that. Freya doesn't have anyone else, only us, so I feel like I need to warn you not to fuck around with her. I think I know who you are Knox, and I think I know what you are all about, but I want to put it out there anyway. I had this same conversation with Gabe even though he's my best mate because those two girls are everything to me. They're the sisters I never had, and I don't want to see either of them get hurt. I've done everything I can to take care of both of them. I had to hand Lennon over to Gabe for the most part, and I'm okay with that now because I can see how he's taken care of her." He ran his hand through his hair and shook his head. "I guess what I want to say is that out of all the men Freya has fucked around with and gotten herself tangled in, in even the most basic ways, I'm glad it's you she's chosen to go all in with. You're a good man. You're steady and loyal, and based on the fact that I've never seen you flinch even when she goes off on one, I would say you are more than equipped to handle her sass. When she decides to tell you about her past and herself, I just hope you don't mess it up like that idiot did." He gestured over my shoulder towards where I knew Gabe was standing and laughed. "Freya thinks a lot of shit about herself that isn't true, but none of us have ever been able to undo the damage that was done to her. Just do me a favour and decide if she is it for you before she tells you anything, because if you decide to leave afterwards, I have no doubt it will send her to a place none of us can retrieve her from, even if you don't leave her because of that."

I took a breath because I hadn't been prepared for any of what he had just said. Sure, I was becoming increasingly more aware that she didn't have any family. There were no pictures in her flat of anyone besides Lennon, Cameron, and Cameron's parents, Emmy and Tommy, but I hadn't pushed her on it. I knew it was because I was being selfish —I hadn't pushed her to open up because I hadn't yet mustered the courage to tell her about myself. I also knew that it needed to end. We were getting further and further into something with no real idea about the fundamentals of what made us who we were, and it was a recipe for disaster.

"I hear you man. I've avoided pushing her because I haven't had the backbone to confess my sins." I caught his eye and I knew he knew what I was referring to. The three men in this room, Calvin, Matt, and Viva were the only people on this earth who knew the truth about who I was. "I spoke to Viva the other week and she encouraged me to, but I've been terrified of changing the way she looks at me. I like her Cam; in fact, I'd go as far as to say I'm in love with her, but I haven't told her yet."

"Why not?"

"Because I can't tell her that if I haven't been honest with her. I've got her and I want to keep her."

"I think you'd both be surprised by each other's secrets, and I think you'd be more surprised by how you both are going to take the revelations. Just do me a favour and look after her. She puts on a really great show, but deep down she's broken. She was broken down in ways Len never was, and she needs someone like you to help her find the pieces." His hand clapped down heavy on my shoulder and squeezed hard before he walked away to the pool table.

My desire to have fun was well and truly gone now that I knew what I had to do. I pushed away from the counter and pulled my phone out of my pocket.

Me: Can I take you on a date tomorrow? Xx

I tapped my thumb against the screen and waited for her response.

Fire: I think I can manage that ;) Han is completely wasted so Len and I are bringing her back to Len's to sleep it off. We don't want to send her

home in this state in case that asshole comes back from his 'conference' xx

    Me: Why 'conference'? xx

    Fire: Because in my opinion he's a cheating wanker! Are you coming home with me? xx

    Me: Always x

I put my phone down on the counter and walked over to where Cameron was now playing against Asher.

"The girls are on their way back. Hannah is wasted."

"Is she okay?" Asher's cue clattered to the table as he spoke, and Cameron, Gabe, and I exchanged a look before I answered him.

"She's just drunk man."

"They probably got overexcited about Gabe and Len setting a date," Cameron said as he resumed his stance over the table and potted a solid red ball.

"They say how far out they are?" Gabe questioned as he shoved the discarded pool cue back into Asher's hand.

"Nah but I doubt they're far. I'm going to take Fire home." I caught Cameron's eye as he looked up at me. "I think we might be out of touch for the weekend. It's time for some honesty." Gabe straightened at my words and he gave me a nod of his head.

"You really think she'd do a runner?" he questioned.

"Time will tell," I said as we all heard the bang of the door upstairs and a flurry of activity. Once again, Asher dropped the cue to the table and hotfooted it up the stairs.

"He's gonna get hurt." Cameron sighed as we headed up the stairs behind him.

"And again, time will tell," I said gently as we emerged into the entryway. Asher already had Hannah scooped up in his arms and was heading for the stairs to the bedrooms with Lennon trailing behind. I caught sight of Freya as she emerged from the kitchen with a bucket and a glass of water in hand.

"We can take those," Cameron said as he relieved her of both objects and gave the glass to Gabe.

"I'm almost certain she doesn't need four of you to take care of her, she only had too much champagne," she called after them before turning to face me. Her hands landed on my hips and I bent my head to press a kiss to her crown. "She's hurting really bad," she admitted quietly.

"You think?"

"I know." She tilted her head up to face me and smiled. "I'm not even a little bit drunk."

"You girls didn't celebrate?"

"They did, but I'm not much of a champagne drinker. Besides, I know you won't have sex with me if I've been drinking." She winked and I smacked her arse instinctively.

"That's my girl," I murmured.

"You gonna take me home now or what?" she asked as her fingers trailed under the hem of my t-shirt and skated over my abs. Hearing the word *home* fall from her lips had my chest tightening. I wasn't sure I'd be able to find the right words to explain what hearing it meant to me, so I dropped a kiss on her mouth instead and turned her towards the door.

"Let's get out of here Fire girl."

chapter
ELEVEN

Knox

I scrubbed my hands over my head as I stepped inside the flat. I had come up with the bright idea as I lay beside her last night that we should do something fun today before I came clean, but with a headache now pressing behind my eyes, I was starting to wish I hadn't been such a coward.

"Okay that is it." The sound of her keys hitting the table just inside her front door jolted me into the present and my eyes swung up to meet her bottle-greens. "What is wrong with you? And don't even think about pulling that fucking confused face you've been working with all day. Your brain has been somewhere else and I want to know where."

I turned to lock the front door and jolted when something solid and sharp hit me between the shoulder blades. I looked down as the object thudded against the wooden floor and saw one of the fancy red high heels she had been wearing was now sitting on the floor by my feet.

"Did you just throw your shoe at me?" I knew it was stupid question, but I couldn't stop myself from asking it.

"Yeah I did." She nodded without remorse as I slammed the last lock into place.

"Why?"

"Because you're ignoring me and I'm tired of you pretending everything is okay when it very clearly is fucking not." She didn't yell, but I could tell she wasn't far from it. I had been trying to keep my head on straight, but I clearly hadn't given much thought to how perceptive she could be. She bent down to remove the other shoe and when she scooped it off her foot, I took a step back with my hands up in front of me.

"Are you going to tell me what is going on or just not bother? Because you know what, Knox? I can take it, all right?"

I came up short as those words flew from her mouth and finally realised why she was so furious all of a sudden. I stepped closer as she scowled at me.

"I didn't need you to take me shopping for pretty things to soften the blow. You could have just told me and not bothered with all the bullshit today has clearly been." My eyes dropped to the two small bags she had brought in with her and I felt the scowl on my face intensify.

"Is that why you didn't buy much?" I had wondered why she had been so quick walking around those shops when I had expected to spend hours sitting in dressing rooms while she tried things on. Now it was beginning to make sense.

"I'm not some fucking idiot Knox. I know a brush-off when I see one, so forgive me if I don't want any more stuff to remind me of you than I already fucking have. God I'm such an idiot." Her head tipped back and she finished her sentence while staring at the ceiling. "When you brought me home last night and fucked me until I couldn't breathe, I should have known something was going on. Jesus!"

"Stop!" I demanded as I moved towards her until my boots were touching the tips of her bare feet and my chest was pressed against hers the way it had been all those weeks ago at the bar. I swallowed against the memory of how that night had gone as I backed her up against the hallway wall. "How many times do I have to tell you I don't *fuck* you before you understand?"

"Really?" She scoffed. "That's all you have to say to what I just said? Well fuck you Knox Sutton. Fuck—"

I slammed my mouth down on hers and swallowed the rest of the sentence I didn't want to hear. I never wanted her to think I was going to be the one leaving, and the fact that she was so convinced I would told me that things were even more fucked up than I realised.

"Knox, what are you doing?" Her hands pressed against my chest and broke our kiss as I tried to move impossibly closer to her.

"Not leaving you."

The words came out gruff and barely audible, but I knew she had heard them. I moved my hand up to comb through her hair, which was curly and loose—by far my favourite way she wore it. I didn't feel as though I was rumpling her up when she was like this, and she looked more like the wild thing I knew she was when she just allowed herself to be.

"Not leaving you unless you tell me to go," I murmured as I leant down and pressed my mouth against hers, again sealing us together in one quick move. I took a second to revel in the press of her cushiony lips against mine before I let her take some of the control. I could tell she wanted to fight me, wanted to shove me off and demand I tell her what the hell was going on, so I slicked my tongue across the closed seam of her mouth and nipped her bottom lip with my teeth in that way she liked. Like magic, her mouth opened for me.

I pushed inside, twisting and turning my tongue against hers as I squeezed my eyes closed; I didn't want to leave any room in my head for the thoughts that were plaguing me. I wanted what was coming for me to fall quiet so I could revel in this moment. I only wanted to hear her gasps and throaty moans of pleasure, and I only wanted to feel the silkiness of her mouth. I only wanted to feel her soft hair and the luscious curves that were mine now. I wanted to taste her honey sweetness and smell the scent of her perfume on her skin. I wanted to focus on only her and stock up the memories just in case this turned out to be our last kiss.

I pressed us tighter together, getting my hands under the sweet curve of her round arse so I could boost her up and pull her legs around my waist. I ground my cock into the warmth of her centre as she wiggled and writhed against me while I plundered her mouth relentlessly. Her hands landed on my neck and her fingers curled tightly into my flesh, but there were no nails this time. I wanted to beg her to hurt me. I wanted to beg her to punish me, but I couldn't find the words because soon enough she would know all the reasons why I craved those things and I had no idea what she would think of me then.

The wax of her lipstick felt heavy on my lips as I broke our kiss again. I saw instantly that I had made a mess of her pretty makeup and I lifted my hands from her arse and ran my thumb over her bottom lip, trying and failing to clean up the disaster I had caused.

"Knox," she whispered, and I let my head roll forward until it was buried in the curve of her soft neck.

I squeezed my eyes closed and felt her hands move to either side of my shaved scalp. Instead of pulling my head away like I had expected her to, she simply held me and caressed the sensitive skin over the top of each ear with her fingertips.

"When you want to tell me what's going on, I'm right here." Her voice was gentle and I knew it was because I had freaked the life out of her. She had been gearing up for me to walk out on her but instead I had thrown all of me at her feet.

"I'm sorry." My voice sounded odd and I cursed myself for attempting to speak out loud right away. I felt her legs stiffen around my waist and I released the hold my pelvis had on her to let her stand down. I expected her to step away from me, but instead her hands cupped my face, her thumbs running over the short hair of my beard as she pulled my face up so I was looking at her.

"I've got no idea what is going on Knox, but you are not okay. You've been acting so strange all day and I don't like it. You need to talk to me." I felt my eyebrows rise slightly and she rolled her eyes. "I fully understand how ironic those words must sound but I mean it. You're freaking me out."

I stepped away as those words tumbled from her mouth; if I was freaking her out now, I hated to think how she was going to feel when I really got going. I had made the agreement with myself that I would be honest with her after hearing what Cameron had said. I knew she deserved my truth, and I knew I wanted her to trust me with hers in return more than anything, but there was no guarantee that once I got done telling her all the things I needed to, she wouldn't demand that I leave.

"Can you just tell me what is going on?" She was pleading now and I hated that I was doing this to her. I took her hands in mine and looked her in the eye as I spoke, willing her to hear the truth in my words.

"I'll stay forever if you let me." Her eyes widened and her lips parted as I continued. "But there are things about me you deserve to know before you make any life decisions based around me. I just need you to know that I want you more than I have ever wanted anyone and I know I will never want anyone but you from here until eternity. No woman has ever come close to making me feel the way you do just by being in the same room, and no woman has ever understood and needed the same things in the bedroom as me. You were made for me, I can feel it, and I am certain a woman like you only comes along once in every man's lifetime. God I want to keep you so bad, but that's not my choice." Her hands tightened around mine as her chest rose and fell heavily.

"I don't know what you mean by any of that Knox." I licked my lips because I couldn't recall a time before now where she had ever said my name as many times as she had tonight.

"My name isn't Knox." It was the first thing in a long list of things I needed to explain to her, and I could only pray she would let me get past this first one. The shock of what I had just said flashed across her face and her eyes narrowed.

"What do you mean that isn't your name? That's what everyone calls you."

"Only a few people know it isn't my real name." She took a step backwards, pulling out of my grasp, and I felt my stomach clench.

"So you changed your name."

"I did."

"When?"

"When I got into the band."

"Why?"

"Because I needed to be someone else. I needed to reinvent myself, and it had to start with my name."

"And your surname?"

"Legally my name is Knox Sutton, but that wasn't what I was born." She shook her head and took another step back from me. I fought the urge to reach out and grab her and shoved my hands into my pockets instead.

"I can't figure out if you've lied to me or not." I was glad she wasn't being shy about putting a voice to the thoughts in her head. I could only hope it might make this a little easier.

"I have and I haven't," I admitted. "I am Knox Sutton now. I don't even think about the name I had before because that belonged to a different person in a different time." Her slender hands lifted and dragged through her hair as she looked down at the floor. I could see that her brow was furrowed and she was having a hard time figuring out what she was supposed to say next.

"I wanted to take you out today and do something fun. I wanted the chance to build another memory with you before I had to take apart all the things you think about me and rebuild them in a way that makes more sense. I didn't want to upset you or make you anxious."

"Stop!" Her voice was hard as she held her hand up to halt the flow of words from my mouth and finally her eyes rose to meet mine. "You're going to need to go slower because I am struggling to keep up right now." I nodded my acceptance of her terms and waited for her to ask the question I could feel was on the tip of her tongue. "You're legally Knox Sutton, but what were you born…?"

"Kain Edwards."

Just the way the name sounded in the air around me made me cringe. Every connotation and whispered version of it that ricocheted inside my head was enough to make self-hatred thunder through the blood in my veins. I didn't dare look at her because I wasn't sure I could live with whatever her face might show me, but when her pretty red toes came into my line of vision and her hand planted itself in the middle of my chest, I knew I didn't have a choice.

"I don't like it," she said simply. "You're not a Kain, you're a Knox. Knox suits you." I felt my shoulders drop as I exhaled sharply and instinctively wrapped my arms around her.

"It would be my pleasure to never hear it again." Her arms wrapped around my waist and her head rested against my chest for a brief moment before she pulled back to look up at me.

"I need you to tell me the rest of it, not because I think I need to hear it, but because I think you need to say it out loud."

I felt my brows furrow at her words because I hadn't been expecting that. She smiled softly up at me and it took me a minute to register that she was using that expression for me. I had seen her use it before, but only on Lennon. Her hand moved up to caress the side of my face and I shuddered slightly at her touch.

"I've been in therapy, Knox, and I've learnt all the tricks and the ways of avoiding telling people things. Right now, you don't look like you want to avoid this anymore, even though it clearly terrifies you." She pushed up onto her tiptoes and pressed her mouth against mine briefly. "I just want you to know that I know you now. I know who you are, and I know what you have done for me."

I let her slide her hand down my arm and link her fingers through mine as I took a harsh breath and she tugged me towards her bedroom.

Freya

I didn't like anything about the way I felt right now. I didn't like the pained look on his face or the slump of his shoulders. The whole situation had my stomach twisting and turning, and I couldn't deny that my first instinct was to jump off this train and let it carry on without me, but I was beating it back. I wanted to be there for him the way he had been there for me. For once I wanted to be the strong one in this pairing, and even though I knew it was probably going to take every ounce of guts I had, I was going to see it through.

I pushed open my bedroom door and felt his arm pull taut in my grip. I turned slightly to see what was stopping him and saw that his big body was braced in the doorway and he had a wild look in his eyes that made my throat tighten. I took a breath and released his hand. I could ask him why he had stopped and why he looked terrified, but I wasn't going to; there were some things he was going to have to lead on.

I caught sight of my reflection in my mirror as I walked into my room. I looked wilder and more natural than normal, and I knew the frightened man behind me was the reason for that. For that reason alone, I would help him through this night, and I would still be standing there at the end of it.

I tugged on the hem of my t-shirt and pulled it over my head. I unhooked my bra and reached for the Acerbus t-shirt Asher had given me after I'd admitted I had never been to an Acerbus concert. My fingers had just brushed the soft cotton when his lips hit my bare shoulder and I turned slightly to see our reflection in the mirror. Knox made me look almost as tiny as Lennon and his big hands practically spanned my entire waist where they were resting just above my hips. His body was bent over mine so he could put his mouth on me and I couldn't fight the urge to push my arse back into his crotch and tilt my head to the side to give him better access. It was a natural reaction now to give myself over to him, and even though it still terrified me at times, I was over fighting it because he always made it feel so good.

"You look so beautiful," he murmured as his eyes caught mine in the mirror. I sucked in a breath as his hands skated over my belly and up to cup my breasts. The full globes were completely engulfed in his hold, and the gentle pressure he applied to the sensitive flesh had heat zinging through my body and straight to my clit. I knew that if I let him, he could derail this whole night with sex I would never forget; I also knew that for once I had to have some kind of willpower when it came to the choice between doing the right thing and chasing an orgasm. "I never want to forget the way you look right now. You are the most beautiful woman I have ever laid eyes on."

"Knox." I tried to push the breathiness out of my voice as I closed my hand on the t-shirt. I knew what he was doing because it was a tactic I had used on him more than once; he was trying to use sex as a way to avoid the bigger subject.

I stepped out of his hold and felt the loss instantly. I tugged the t-shirt on quickly so the Acerbus logo was now covering my naked body and turned to face him.

"I'm sorry," he whispered. I reached out and stroked my fingers over his cheek, and he turned his face into my palm, the hair of his beard tickling my skin.

"Don't be sorry. I know how it feels to want to avoid something. I know how to distract better than most people I have ever met." I dropped my hand and undid my jeans, peeling them down my legs. Thankfully the t-shirt was long enough that I didn't have to put trousers on. "Get comfortable." I motioned towards the bed and stepped around him.

"Maybe we shouldn't do this in your bedroom,"

"Get comfortable, Knox. I'll get us some drinks."

I slipped out of the room and down to the kitchen. I had no idea how to encourage him when I wanted to keep all my secrets, but I needed to remember that the difference was he needed to share his with me. I could see the way it was riding him and I knew we couldn't go on without acknowledging it now.

I curled my hand around the fridge door and tugged it open, retrieving two bottles of water. I squeezed my eyes closed and gave myself the best pep talk I could manage before heading back to my room. I made my way over to the bed where he was now sitting, still fully clothed, and handed him one of the water bottles. I watched him twist the cap off and gulp down a quarter of the bottle while I tried to ignore the way the sight of the plastic quivering in his hand had my heart clenching painfully. I sat down at the foot of the bed and curled my legs underneath me so I could face him.

"I know I have to tell you, I just don't know where to start." He looked down at the duvet and traced the pattern for a second before continuing. "I guess the beginning is as good a place as any right?" He peeked up at me and for the first time, he seemed younger than his age.

"What do you need me to do?" It seemed as though my question caught him off guard, so I continued. "When Lennon tried to tell Gabriel her story, it all fell to shit pretty quickly. I don't want to make the same mistake, so before we start, tell me what you need from me. Do you need me to prompt you, ask questions, or stay quiet until you've finished?"

"I have no idea." His voice was full of honesty as he answered me. "I've never told anyone all of this in one go before, especially not someone who means to me what you do. I guess I just need to get it all out, but if you need me to stop, then tell me."

"Okay." I nodded because I knew it was what he wanted to hear, but unless he was about to tell me something that really was too hard to handle, there was no way I was going to stop him.

I curled my hands around my water bottle and waited for him to continue. He swallowed hard a few times, drank a bit more water, and took a few deep breaths before he spoke again.

"I was born to a junkie prostitute. My older brother was seven when I was born. I was a product of a night with one of her customers. From what I was told, she moved away from the area they had been living in after she found out she was pregnant, and Eli thought things were going to be better when they moved. Apparently she was taking him to school in the morning and picking him up in the afternoon, and there was food in his lunchbox and dinner at night. He thought I was saving him from his old life." He took another deep breath and I tried to remain as still as I could while I wrapped my head around the fact that he had a sibling roaming around. I had no idea why I had never known he had a brother, but I didn't have long to ponder that before he continued. "It didn't last long. As soon as I was born, she wanted to get back to her drugs. Kids weren't enough for her."

"Like Danni," I said breathlessly. Even though I hadn't known the mother of my best friend, I had heard the story enough times to know that they sounded awfully similar. Lennon needing her hadn't been enough to stop her mother from shooting things into her veins either.

"Not exactly." He shook his head. "Over the years, I've wanted my story to sound better, wanted my mother's story to sound better. Danni was depressed, grieving. She had mental health issues, and she was lost. The drugs were like an escape for her, and yeah she should have fought that stuff harder to be there for her little girl, but those are strong demons to wrestle. My mother had been a junkie her whole life. She started dabbling with cannabis when she should have still been playing with dolls, and she hit harder and harder drugs as the years passed. My childhood was bleak, but my brother always did his best for me. He cooked what little food there was in the house and tucked me in at night. He told me stories about the day we would get free and he stood between me and any of my mother's clients who didn't take too kindly to two kids being in the house while they fucked her mercilessly. Time after time, he took the beatings himself." His hands shook as he dragged them over his face, and my heart ached at the sight of him stripping himself raw this way. I could only imagine what must have been happening in his head right then.

"They'd fuck her until she screamed and begged for mercy and then they'd carry on. They'd beat her senseless and she'd cry, but it didn't matter. She was a means to an end, and they knew she would let them back in the next day because she needed their money for her next fix." His shaking hands reached out for his water bottle, but I thrust mine into them instead. My fingers lingered against his skin as he looked down at it, and suddenly his hatred of the term *fucking* made horrible sense to me. I took in a shaky breath as I stroked my fingertips against his and looked up at him.

"I'm sorry you had to hear those things," I whispered as he raised the bottle to his lips and took a long pull. I couldn't imagine a young boy standing over his baby brother and shielding him from the harsh hands of an outsider who had no place in their home. I couldn't imagine being the young boy who had to watch his mother and his big brother get smacked around by strangers. The hairs on my arms were on end and I wanted nothing more than to wrap him up in my arms and promise him he didn't have to tell me any more, but he had asked me to let him finish so I steeled myself for the rest.

"I woke up one morning when I was seven and I was alone. Eli and me slept on a mattress on the floor, but when I woke up, he was gone. I assumed he was up already, but every room I went into was empty. She was passed out on the living room floor but he was gone. He was only fourteen, but he'd vanished. The next thing I knew there was knocking at the door. I was too frightened to answer it in case it was one of her clients. He'd had been teaching me how to take care of myself, but I was still scared." His eyes slid closed again and I knew he was getting lost within the memory.

"Who was at the door Knox?"

"Social services." His voice was a hoarse whisper and I felt it like a knife across my skin. "She was still unconscious when they took me out of there. It was the last time I ever saw her."

My heart ached for him and I felt that stinging behind my eyes again as I caught his hand in mine and squeezed it hard.

"I went into care. It was pretty dark, but at least I had food, right?" His attempt at humour fell flat because I couldn't see the funny side, and deep down, I knew he couldn't either. "I bounced around the system for eight years. I went from foster home to care home and back again. When I was fifteen, I landed in this care home that wasn't so bad. It was probably the best one I had been to, and when I was called to the office one day, I freaked out. I went in there thinking I was about to get my arse kicked for some infraction I hadn't realised I had made, but when I walked in, my brother was sitting there, and he sure as hell wasn't fourteen anymore. He was suited and booted and looked like he had money. I remember him getting to his feet and holding his hand out to me. I hadn't seen him in eight years, and I had no idea why he was there then. I shook his hand and took my seat, and he told me she was dead, said her body had been found in the boot of a burnt-out car. Then he told me he wanted to take me with him. It had to go through the process, obviously, but I was finally getting out. I can remember being so fucking happy, so proud that my big brother had come and saved me. Once the court put me in his care, I walked out of there like I was king of the fucking world…but it didn't last long."

I was attempting to breathe through the pressure in my chest, but I wasn't sure how much of the pain I could watch play out in him before I cracked. I had seen the effect reacting too soon had had on Lennon when Gabriel was in my shoes, and I knew I couldn't make the same mistake. I took the water bottle from his loose grip and chugged some down, pushing the lump in my throat down with it.

"He wasn't the same. He was older and bitter, really fucking bitter. It took me some time to notice because at first it was just stupid comments about me being the devil's spawn and how my father used to come into the house beat my mother, fuck her until she begged, and then beat her again before he left. He told me stories about how he was the one left to clean up her blood and get her to bed after my father was done with her. He told me all the things my father had done to him, unspeakable fucking awful things." His head dropped into his hands and I didn't even need him to clarify what he meant by that. My heart hurt and my stomach felt as though I was going to lose the contents of it any second.

"He told me I needed to earn my keep seeing as he'd taken me on when he could have left me in the system. I was young and I wanted to atone for all the bad things that had happened to him. I wanted to make things better. I told him I would do whatever he needed because he was my brother and we were a team." He barked out a harsh laugh as he tipped his head back and eyed the ceiling for a long minute. "We were never really a team, but he played along and told me that if I made it up to him, we could go back to being the brothers we had once been. He was a criminal, a loan shark, a gambler, a drug runner, a king pin. He frequented places like those bars you kept going to and by default, so did I. I was his muscle. Even when I was younger, I was big for my age, and I sure as hell didn't look like I was sixteen, so I was the one to run around delivering messages on his behalf. I was the one who went out collecting debts and anyone who couldn't pay became a casualty. I would beat people for money. I would beat people for crossing him. I inflicted pain on people who couldn't have stopped it if they'd tried. I did everything he asked of me, and I have more blood on my hands than I can cope with some days."

I fought to swallow the bile creeping up my throat as I watched him stare at his outstretched hands, the same hands that pleasured me so tirelessly and perfectly. I wanted to scream and yell and find that bastard man and make him pay for the scars he had put on his brother, but I knew Knox would never let me. I hated the powerless feeling it left me with.

"I was nothing but someone who could get their hands dirty so he didn't have to. I broke bones. I broke souls. I hurt some people so bad I wasn't sure they would ever be fixed. One thing I can say is that I never killed anyone, because that would have tied my soul to him even further. I was a child and he knew I would do anything to please him. I wanted him to love me. I wanted him to be my brother. I wanted us to be a family, and yet every day he took great pleasure in reminding me that I was my father's son, that I was good for nothing, just the way he had been."

I fought hard to keep the words that were begging to break free locked down inside of me. I wanted to tell him it was all wrong. I wanted to tell him he had only been a little boy and had done nothing to deserve the treatment his brother had given him, but it was going to have to wait.

"He met Viva when I was seventeen. She was so sweet and starry-eyed in love with him. At first he let her believe the cover he had given to the courts. He ran a respectable business to cover up his criminal one, but her father saw through it. He was a master manipulator and he had her like putty in his hands. He broke her so bad, broke the sweetness in her and forced her to replace it with hardness. He broke her relationship with her parents and exposed her to the pain and fear of the filthy world he reigned over. She married him, thought she could save him. I wasn't like him though. I wanted out more than I wanted my next breath, and she saw it. Viva got me a job in a music shop owned by the father of a guy she had been to college with. The guy, Darren, was in a band, and when his drummer left him high and dry, he asked me to go on tour with him. I didn't want to leave Viva alone but she forced me, told me it was my chance and I had to take it. I was gone for ten months and when I came back, things had changed; he was sullen and moody and no longer had the world at his fingertips. Viva was different too. She was hurting and I hated it, but when Darren gave my name to Calvin because he was forming Acerbus, she made me swear I would go. I'd been gone two months when I got the call from Viva saying he had been found drowned in a hotel bath."

I gasped out loud and immediately slammed my hand over my mouth as his head shot up. His black eyes were swimming with unshed tears when they met my own, but I wasn't sure who he was crying for.

"I came home and we turned off his life support together. I went to see her parents before I went back to the States, begged them to look after her. I told them about him, and luckily her father heard me. Once I knew she was safe back with them, I left."

I watched him as he drank more water. Seeing him sitting on my bed in my room in all his muscled, beautiful glory, no one would have ever guessed he had been through and survived so much pain and torture. I had believed I knew what fucked up looked like, but I was beginning to see I knew nothing.

"I'd been back a month when I decided it was too much."

I felt the tear slide down my cheek as I realised what that meant. I had heard one other person in my life use that phrase before, and it hurt so bad that I had to press one hand to my chest to make sure it hadn't torn a hole right through the middle of me. I reached out with my free hand and wrapped it around his, not caring if he hated me touching him because I knew I was going to need to remind myself that he was still there, that he was still alive and vibrant and taking over my whole life in ways I could never have dreamt of.

"I'd always self-harmed. It was my way of coping, and when Viva came into our lives, it wasn't so easy to hide it. I ended up going out and using any woman I could find as an outlet. I used the cutting and the sex as a form of punishment for all the things I had done. I didn't deserve good things, so I only let myself have them if they were wrapped in pain. I fucked countless, nameless women. I did all kinds of fucked up shit."

Tears were dripping steadily down my cheeks now, but he hadn't noticed because his eyes were trained on the point where our skin touched.

"I cut my wrists and got into a bath. Viva was back where she belonged and I was tired of fighting, tired of the pain. Gabe kicked the door in and dragged me out. I'd been in hospital two days when Viva came bursting into the room, wide eyed and screaming. She slapped me so hard Gabe jumped out of his seat to drag her away, and then she crumpled to the floor. She was pregnant and frightened, and she didn't want me to be gone as well." I swiped tears from my face as his words echoed around us. "I vowed there and then to break the cycle. I got my shit straight and I was there when Kaleb was born. I promised I would be better for him and I think I have. I hope I have." He finally tipped his head so he could look at me as he finished, and I knew what he could see. My carefully applied makeup was now running in rivulets down my face, and I was probably swollen and blotchy. "Fire." His voice sounded pained, but I didn't let him say any more. I launched myself at him, sending the water bottle cascading to the floor as he fell backwards onto my bed.

The sob I had been fighting surged through me. I let it overtake and consume my body as I tried to get a grip on him. I needed to touch him, to feel him. I needed to show him how much it hurt me to hear what he had gone through, and I needed him to hold me and show me again that it hadn't broken him.

"I'm so sorry I had to tell you any of that."

"Shhhh." I sobbed into him. "Just shush please." He huffed out a breath and curled his arms around my back, holding me to him. I cried for his pain and I cried for my own. I cried for how fucked up we were and how the universe probably didn't believe we stood a chance.

"I'm so sorry," he whispered against the crown of my head as my sobs subsided. When I calmed down, I sat up and stared down at him, running my fingertips over his face.

"I hate that you ever had to go through that. I hate that those things are inside your brain and I can't undo them. No one can undo them, but you're not that person, Knox. You're not him, and you are not the person he forced you to be. You are kind and patient and caring. You get me and you handle me and you don't lose your temper. You're strong and you're solid, and you're so fucking resilient in a way the rest of us could only hope to be. I can't put it all into words, but just no. Just don't ever think that's who you are." He pushed himself up to sitting and clasped my face in his hands.

"Do you mean that?" His eyes were begging, and I nodded as more tears dripped down my cheeks. I hadn't cried this much in years, but now that the dam was wide open, I couldn't seem to stop it. "Jesus, I didn't want to make you cry." His thumbs swiped at the falling tears but he wasn't fast enough.

"I hurt for you, Knox. I hurt for you and for me and for all the things people have done to us." I collapsed against him as my body shook from the force of my crying. I wasn't lying; it was the purest pain I had felt in so long, and I couldn't help but wonder how on earth we were meant to survive with all the scars others had left on us.

"I was so frightened I was going to lose you," he whispered against my ear. "One day when you want to tell me your truths, I'll hold you so tight, and I promise when all of us is out in the open, I'll help you pick up your pieces the way you're helping me pick up mine."

I shuddered against him and he held me tighter as I let my eyes drift closed. One day I wanted to be able to show him who I had been, but the thought of reliving it and knowing it was all my fault terrified me. I couldn't be certain he would hold me when he knew. Knox had been a victim of circumstance, but I had been the master of mine.

chapter TWELVE

Freya

"Fire." Knox's fist thudded against the door, his voice loud enough for me to hear over the sounds of Bowie as I stared at my reflection in the mirror.

I ignored him and tugged on the khaki-coloured midi dress and twisted to the side to study my reflection in the mirror. It was annoying me that none of the clothes I had tried on seemed to look the way they used to when I wore them. I wasn't sure if it was my anxiety that was making me hate all of them or if they really did make me look fat. I had applied, removed, and reapplied no less than three different makeup looks and had pinned and unpinned my hair more times than I could count, but I still wasn't happy.

"Fire." His voice was harder now and I knew he was getting impatient. I had implored him to wait for me in the living room, promising I wouldn't make us late, but I knew I was fast running out of time. "I'm coming in."

"No don't," I squeaked as I grabbed the hem of my dress again in order to tug it over my head. My room looked like a bomb had gone off in it and I really didn't want him to see the evidence of all my crazy.

It had been a few weeks since he had shared all of himself with me and I had found out he was a brother-in-law and an uncle. As soon as he had told Viva I knew everything, she had been on him to bring me to dinner, and I had no doubt he now thought I was stalling deliberately. I saw the bedroom door open from the corner of my eye and then his big frame appeared in the reflection of my mirror.

"What's going on in here? Your entire wardrobe is on the floor." I scowled at him as I pulled the dress the rest of the way over my head and tossed it onto the bed to join the other discarded items.

"No it isn't. See." I motioned at the wardrobe in front of me; it was still at least half full. "There are still clothes in there."

"What was wrong with any of these outfits?" he asked as he reached over and hit the off button on my speakers.

"They made me look fat." I reached inside the wardrobe and clasped my fingers around a coat hanger as he made his way across the room towards me.

"You are not fat," he said gently as he skimmed his hand over my rib cage and round to my stomach. I felt my muscles tense under his touch and he shook his head at me.

"As if you'd tell me if I was," I grumbled as I held up a blue and white flowing maxi dress that had been sitting in my wardrobe since Lennon had insisted the colour was pretty on me.

"Can you look at me please?" His voice was calm, but there was an undercurrent of the tone he only ever used on me in bed as he turned me in his arms to face him. "You are not fat. You are the most beautiful woman I have ever laid eyes on. Viva, Matt, and Kaleb are excited to meet you because I have never brought a woman home before so they know I am not messing around. They want to meet *you*, Fire, not some random façade you pull from your bag of tricks in order to get through tonight. I don't want to take a version of you to dinner that I don't know, so if you really don't want to do this, you need to tell me right now so I can call and cancel." His onyx gaze was searing into me and I let my eyes slide closed as my forehead thudded against his chest.

"I'm just nervous," I admitted, even though saying it out loud felt like I was stabbing myself with something sharp and pointy. I hated admitting weakness more than anything, but he always seemed to be able to pull the admissions out of me effortlessly.

"I know you are, beautiful." His hands skimmed over my bare back. "But I promise you this will all be fine. They're my family. I want you to meet them, I want them to meet you, and they will love you."

I winced as he said the *L* word because no matter how much Lennon reassured me that it was the best thing to hear, I still wasn't on that page. It wasn't that I couldn't feel myself falling further into him, especially after all he had shared with me, but I knew I needed to hold back. I couldn't hear him say that word or say it myself until there were no secrets between us. If he noticed my reaction, he was kind enough not to draw attention to it as he brushed his lips against mine before letting me go in favour of turning his attention to my jumble of clothes.

"I think you should wear this one," he said, holding up my red sleeveless midi dress. "Red and green are my favourite colours on you." He handed it over to me and tipped my chin up so I was facing him. "I'll be waiting in the car. If you aren't in the passenger seat in five minutes, I am coming up to get you and will take you there in whatever you are or aren't wearing." His eyebrow cocked as though he was challenging me to argue with him but I simply dipped my chin.

"I'll be ready."

"Good." He pressed a hard kiss to the top of my head and left the bedroom.

I looked down at the material in my hands and quickly pulled it over my head. It was a dress I had worn a few times around him, and I could only guess he had considered it his favourite for a little while. I was also grateful that out of all the outfits scattered around, this was probably the loosest fitting. I ran a brush through my hair again, slicked on a coat of lip gloss, grabbed my bag, and exited the flat before I could cause myself any more trouble.

I made my way down the stairs, the heels of my shoes clicking against the concrete, and wondered—for what felt like the hundredth time lately—how long I could go on living there. I was starting to feel as though I had outgrown the place, and with Lennon gone, I didn't have anything to tie me to it. We'd had some good times, but now she was making memories somewhere new and I was beginning to want that too.

I shoved open the security door in time to see Knox climb out the driver's side of the car. I didn't need to have a watch to know my five minutes was probably up and he was about to make good on his threat to come up and haul me out. I let the door go behind me as I made my way down the walkway to where he had come to a halt.

"No need to go all caveman on me." I smirked up at him, trying my best to leave my nerves behind me. I could see how much it meant to him and I didn't want to go on making it difficult when it was clearly a very big first for him.

"I didn't think you were all that averse to a bit of caveman action these days." He winked as he circled his arms around my waist and cupped my arse in his big hands.

"Public," I warned him.

"Since when do you care about that?" He chuckled as he bent forward and pressed his open mouth to the skin of my neck. I let the sensations wash through me for a second as he kissed his way up to my jaw.

"I know what you're doing," I murmured breathlessly; even though it had been two months since I had first gone to bed with him, every time felt like the first time.

"What am I doing?" The vibrations of his words bounced through my throat, sending little jolts of heat and tingles to all the good places.

"You're distracting me."

"Is it working?"

"It always works." I grasped the sides of his head and tugged him away. "But unless you want us to be late, you need to quit."

"Fire—" I pressed my fingertips against his lips to halt the flow of words and smiled at him; I wasn't sure I wanted to hear what he was going to say.

"Let's get going. I don't want to make a really bad first impression." I turned on my heel and made my way to the car.

Knox closed the car door behind him once he slipped inside and automatically revved the engine before pulling out of the space. I had gotten used to the way he drove over the last few weeks considering he drove us everywhere, and I was more comfortable with his skills now than I had been at first. I didn't feel the need to grip the door handle or have my eyes pinging from him to the road every ten seconds, which made riding with him a hell of a lot more relaxing.

"Tell me about Kaleb again." I wasn't going to admit it out loud, but I had a feeling I was more terrified of meeting his six-year-old nephew than I was of meeting Viva. I knew she meant a lot to him and that he considered her a sister, but his nephew was a part of him, however diluted that part might be, and I had never really been around children all that much. I had no idea what they liked to talk about or what they liked to do, and it was making me anxious. I didn't know what I could possibly have in common with a six-year-old, but I was going to have to make conversation with the little boy at some point.

"He's a really good kid." It was the same answer I had gotten from him every time I asked, and I was starting to feel as though there was more to it than he was letting on.

"You always say that Knox, but I don't know what that means. That doesn't tell me what he likes to do or what he likes to talk about. It doesn't tell me about his temperament or whether there are any sore topics for him." I reached out to skim my fingers over his wrist as his face tightened. "What is it?"

"He's a good kid, but he has some problems."

"Problems?"

"Yeah." He sighed. "He has some difficulties."

"What kind of difficulties?" I pushed because this was really information he should have given me before now.

"He's dyslexic."

"Okay," I said slowly while I waited for him to continue. When he didn't, I turned to face him properly. "And? Lots of people are dyslexic, Knox. Like, *lots*." I emphasised the last word because I felt like I needed him to hear it.

"He gets bullied pretty bad because of it and it hits him hard. You'll see when you meet him that he's a sensitive kid. Viva and Matt do all they can and I help wherever I can, but I'm not exactly the sharpest tool in the box myself."

"Well I call bullshit on that one. You're one of the smartest people I know."

"Fire—"

"No," I interrupted. "You are, and I'm sure Kaleb is too. So maybe he finds it a little more difficult than other kids, but that doesn't mean there's anything wrong with him, and it sure as hell didn't mean you had to hide that from me."

"I wasn't hiding it."

"You were Knox," I said as the car rolled to a stop in front of a neat little house with flowers in the front garden and a small built-on garage. "Are we here?" I asked as he pulled up the handbrake.

"We are." He nodded.

I took a deep breath as I tried to persuade my nerves not to show back up now. The front door swung open and a small black-haired boy came barrelling out of the house. He was dressed in jeans and a black button-up shirt, and I found myself smiling. I knew Knox and his brother had only shared a mother, but there was no denying that this little boy had taken the genes they both shared as his own. Knox squeezed my hand just once before hopping out and rounding the hood of the car to bend down and ruffle the bouncing little boy's hair. I could tell he was trying to get a good look in the car as Knox bent down and spoke to him. I was about to reach for the door handle when Knox's hand came down on the windscreen. I knew without even seeing him that he was telling me not to open the door. I opted to unbuckle my belt instead and the door swung open from the outside. I was met by the beaming face of the little boy and his eyes immediately stole my breath; they were exact replicas of his uncle's.

"My name is Kaleb." His voice was gentle and I smiled at him. "I'm here to take you into my house." He pushed his little shoulders back as he held his hand out to me. I slipped mine into it and let him help me down. Once I was clear of the door, he slammed it shut and I turned to Knox.

"Humour him," he murmured in my ear. I smiled as Kaleb appeared in front of me.

"If you would like to follow me, Miss Freya." It took all my might not to laugh at just how cute he was, but I knew he wouldn't understand if I did so I forced it away and fixed my eyes on his.

"It's a pleasure to meet you, Kaleb. Your uncle has told me a lot about you." His little eyes went wide as they darted from me to Knox. I racked my brain to find something he had told me about him over the last few weeks, and I recalled a night last month where Knox had had him round to stay at his place and they had played video games. "He told me you're really good at computer games." I could only pray I had gotten that right; when Kaleb's eyes lit up, I knew I had. I felt Knox squeeze my elbow as we followed Kaleb up the pathway.

"Did you really say that Uncle K?"

"Course I did, champ. You know you're good at them all, so quit fishing for compliments," he teased, and Kaleb wrinkled his nose.

"I don't like fishing. When Dad took me, it was gross."

"Kaleb." A female voice floated down the hallway. "I hope you aren't harassing Uncle K's guest."

"No way Mum. Miss Freya is super cool, she even knows about all my computer games."

A dark-haired, very pregnant woman appeared in the doorway, and I was surprised by how pretty and young she was. I had no idea what I had been expecting, but this had not been it. She was dressed in a loose flowery dress, but her baby bump was still very prominent. A tea towel was tossed over her shoulder and her long hair was pulled back in a braid.

"And that is the way to my son's heart." She smiled as she made her way across to me and kissed my cheek. "It's lovely to finally meet you Freya. I thought this one was going to try to keep you all to himself forever." She tugged the tea towel from her shoulder and whipped it in the direction of Knox's stomach. He stepped forward and tugged her against him, pressing a kiss to the top of her head before running a hand over her bump.

"How's the small one cooking?"

"Just fine." She smiled up at him before turning back to me. "So Freya, I hope you like Mexican food because that's the order of the day in this house."

"I love it, thank you."

"Miss Freya, will you come with me?" Kaleb tugged gently on my hand and I looked down at him. "I want to show you my village that I'm building."

"Sure." I smiled even though I was almost certain I would have been better off staying with the adults.

"When Freya has had enough, you have to let her leave, Kaleb." Viva's voice trailed after us as I followed him into the back room.

"You can sit there." He pointed at a black leather sofa and I perched on the edge, watching him set up the game. "I can show you how to play if you like," he offered as he sat down beside me. "I taught Uncle K, Uncle Ash, and Cameron when I stayed last month."

"Wow, so I'd be learning from the master then?" His giggle filled the room and I felt my shoulders relax. Maybe this wouldn't be so bad after all.

"You forgot to mention the part where she was absolutely bloody stunning." Viva rounded on me as soon as Freya and Kaleb were out of earshot. I had wanted to follow after them because I could see she was overwhelmed, but I knew I had to give it a minute.

"Did I?"

"Yes. I look like a slob in comparison."

"Not you as well." I groaned as I followed her into the kitchen. The glass door to the back room was shut, but I could see Freya's orange hair peeking over the top of the sofa and the flashes from the computer game. I had no idea how she had remembered what Kaleb's favourite pastime was, but I was grateful. It had endeared my nephew to her instantly, and that made my life easier. I wanted her to feel comfortable and at ease with my family, and I wanted them to feel the same way with her.

"What's that supposed to mean?"

"It means I spent the afternoon locked out of the bedroom while she tried on every piece of clothing she owns and then declared that she was fat. I'm tired of you women in my life always having such a warped bloody view of yourselves. You look lovely and she looks beautiful."

"They're women, K—what else do you expect from them?" I turned at the sound of Matt's voice as he walked into the kitchen.

"All right, man?" I held my hand out to him and he pulled me in to slap his hand on my back a few times. I liked Matt; I had since the first day we met. I wasn't sure what it was about him; it could have been his stability, his loyalty, and his lack of judgment, or maybe it was the way he treated my nephew and the woman I considered my sister as though they were something to cherish. Whatever it was, it had always helped us to get along.

"It's good to see you. Where's the lady friend?" He rubbed his hands together and the look on his face could not have been construed as anything other than gleeful.

"What's that face for?"

"I'm just curious to see who you finally decided to bring home. I mean, she must be something pretty bloody special," he said as he moved around me and wrapped an arm around Viva's shoulder, pulling her into him almost instinctively. I had been envious plenty of times in the past watching the easy and effortless way they were with each other, but tonight I didn't feel any of it because I knew that once my nephew was done hogging her, I had exactly the same thing going for me.

"She's stunning Matt. I think I have a girl crush." Viva giggled and I rolled my eyes as Matt laughed long and loud. When they had both finished, I shook my head.

"I'm going to go rescue her from your son and bring her in here." I took off before I had even finished my sentence and headed for the back room. As I neared the door, I slowed down because I could hear them talking and was curious as to what they had found to converse over.

"So how long have you been playing this one?" she asked, her voice gentler than I had ever heard it as she peered at the screen in front of them.

"Well, since Uncle K came home. We started it together, but he tells me I should go on playing even when he's busy."

"I see. Do you have to do your homework before your mum lets you play?"

"Always." He nodded. "So sometimes I don't get to play because it can take a long time."

"I used to have the same problem when I was at school."

"You did?"

"I wasn't very great at reading." I felt my eyebrows rise at the sound of those words from her mouth. "And I wasn't allowed to do anything fun until I'd finished all my work. It used to take me hours sometimes."

"Did your mummy help you? My mummy helps me and sometimes it makes it go faster."

"You're a lucky boy to have a mummy who helps you, and when you're older, if you practice really hard, you can be anything you want to be, trust me."

"I don't know," he said quietly. "The other kids tell me I won't be able to do anything because I'm stupid." I clenched my hands into fists at the sound of those words. Viva and Matt had both assured me they had spoken to the school about the bullying, but it didn't sound to me as though it had stopped.

"Well other kids suck." I fought the urge to laugh because only Freya would have the balls to be so blunt with a kid. "Kids when I went to school were pretty rubbish as well, but that doesn't mean anything. I have the best friends in the whole world now and they definitely don't suck. Sometimes when you get older things just get better, Kaleb. You just put the work in now so you can climb the ladder all the way to the top." There was silence for a moment except for the pinging of the computer game, and I was about to step inside and make my presence known when I heard Kaleb's soft voice speak again.

"You really think if I practice, it will be better?"

"I know it will Kaleb. I have a really good job now and no one can ever take that away from me. I practiced really hard and I made it, so that means you can too."

"Do you think you might be able to help me?"

"Of course I could, if that was okay with your mummy."

"Cool, and by the way Miss Freya, you can call me Kale. That's what my friends call me." I stepped into the back room as silence fell again and both of their heads swung in my direction. There was no way I was going to bring up the fact that I had just been listening to their private conversation, so I opened with the original reason I had come back there.

"Hey champ, any chance I can steal my girl away for a minute? Your dad really wants to meet her."

"Sure Uncle K. See you in a minute Miss Freya." He spoke without taking his eyes off the screen. Freya pushed off the sofa and walked over to me.

"Is that true or did you think I needed rescuing, because I was actually doing all right."

"It's true. Matt doesn't believe you're real." She laughed as I linked my fingers through hers and tugged her in the direction of the kitchen.

"And why would he think that?"

"I told you I've never brought a woman here before; he thinks I made you up." I pushed open the kitchen door without knocking and immediately regretted it when I got an eyeful of Matt and Viva getting steamy over the fajitas. "My eyes," I groaned as Freya burst out laughing beside me. I very rarely got to hear her laugh so comfortably, and it caught my attention as Viva and Matt both joined in.

"As if you don't do worse than that to me at home." Freya smirked as she smacked me across the chest.

"You must be Freya. I'm Matt," he said as he held his hand out to her and she shook it.

"It's a pleasure to meet you." His eyes found mine over the top of her head and I could see the approval in them without her even having to utter more than a few words. I hadn't realised until that moment that his approval meant something to me as well.

"I like this one K." Viva's voice travelled across the room to me. "I like even more that you waited until now to bring a girl home, because I don't think I ever would have liked another one the way I like Freya."

I had no idea how they had all come to that conclusion so quickly, but I wasn't going to argue with it. I caught the flush in Freya's cheeks at Viva's words and tugged her towards me, she wound her arm around my waist and rested her head on my chest as the conversation ebbed and flowed around us. I was surprised when it became clear that she was going to be an active participant in our evening considering how nervous she had been, and I was even more glad I had told her all about my past so that when the discussion briefly turned that way, I could still breathe easy.

It wasn't unusual for me to be the quiet, brooding one at dinner, but tonight it was more than that. I was content for the first time in my life, and I finally understood what it felt like to have all the pieces of me in one place. As I looked around the room and listened to them laughing, I could see what my future looked like. I knew I needed to get Freya to be as open and honest with me as I had been with her so the rest of our lives could finally begin. I had hoped me coming clean would spur her on to letting go as well, but so far she hadn't said a thing. I could only hope that after spending time with the people who mattered to me and seeing the family we had cobbled together, she could find it in her to trust me with her past.

"I can help wash up," she said as she pushed away from the table we were still sitting at. Matt and Kaleb had disappeared into the garden to look at something a few minutes before, which left me, Viva, and Freya.

"You're a guest."

"I'm really good at washing up—Knox can attest to that." She shot me a grin over her shoulder as I sat back in my seat.

"I can actually. I cook, she cleans."

"How domestic," Viva teased as she gathered up the cutlery from the table. I expected Freya to bristle at the use of the word, but once again, she surprised me.

"It is actually, though I don't know how much longer it will last." The cutlery Viva had been holding clattered into the sink as she turned her head to look between the both of us. "Oh shit, no, I didn't mean it like that."

"How did you mean it?" I questioned as I willed my heart to quit thudding against my ribcage.

"I've been thinking about moving out of the flat. I figured I would just crash at a hotel or somewhere until I can find somewhere I really want to live. I'm tired of not having a lift that works and of reporting the light bulb in the front entrance." She shrugged as she turned back to the sink and Viva shot me a dark look, motioning with her head that I needed to speak up.

"Why would you need to crash at a hotel when I have a place to live?"

"Because we've been in this for five minutes and that is far too soon to be moving in together." Her tone told me she really did not want to be having this conversation there, but I couldn't stop myself from pressing now that I had started.

"If you want to leave that flat, you can come stay with me until you figure out where you want to go next."

"Knox." Her tone was a warning now as I pushed up from my seat and made my way over to the sink.

"No, you need to hear me on this one Fire. If you want to get out of that rundown block, I am all for that, believe me. The thought of you being there alone worries me sick most of the time. If you need a place to stay while you figure out your next move, or even a place to stay until we figure out our next move, then that will be with me. No arguments." She opened her mouth to do exactly that, but we were interrupted by Kaleb bounding back into the room.

"Miss Freya," he said, excitement colouring his voice. She turned out of my hold and smiled down at my nephew despite the fact that a few seconds before she had been glaring daggers at me. "I have a present for you." I had no idea where the kid had managed to get her a present from, but as I looked over at Matt and Viva, I saw them both smiling. It wasn't often that Kaleb took to people the way he had Freya tonight, and I couldn't help but feel it had a lot to do with the secret she had shared with him that she hadn't even shared with me.

"For me?" she asked as she bent down.

"Yep." He nodded proudly as he brought his left arm around from where it had been hiding behind his back. Clutched in his hand was a roughly tied bunch of little white flowers. I looked between him and Freya when she didn't respond instantly and saw that her face was frozen and pale. "They're for you," he said as he thrust them towards her a little bit more insistently. I looked up at Viva, who seemed to have just noticed what I had.

"Hey Kale, why don't you come wrap them in some cellophane so Freya can get them home safely?" she said gently. I saw his face fall as he looked from the little bunch of flowers back to Freya.

"You don't like them." His voice was no longer excited, instead sounding dejected, and I was about to speak when she suddenly dropped hard to her knees and reached for the gift.

"They're my favourite flower Kaleb." Her voice was shaky and full of emotion, but he didn't seem to notice as his face broke into a beaming smile. When he relinquished the flowers to her, she brought them up to her face and inhaled so deeply I was afraid for her safety. Her fingers danced over the petals for a minute before she looked back up at him. "I haven't smelt these in a really long time."

"If they're your favourites then you should get to smell them all the time Miss Freya. Uncle K, you need to buy her flowers, and make sure you get her favourites or she might like me better." He laughed as he looked up at me and I tried to school my face away from the concern I knew was etched there.

"Yeah, all right big man, you're more of a gentleman than I could ever hope to be." He puffed out his chest before turning to Matt.

226

"Nice one Dad." He held out his fist for Matt to bump and he did so before scooping him up.

"You've shown your uncle up, so now you can say goodnight and get in that bath." Matt laughed as he tossed Kaleb over his shoulder. His little face peeked back up to yell a goodnight as he disappeared out of the room with Viva gliding silently after them.

I crouched down beside Freya as soon as they were gone and found that her gaze was transfixed on the flowers in her hand and silent tears were tracking down her face. I reached out for her and she toppled into me, taking us both fully to the floor. I held her shaking body against mine and noticed that she had kept the flowers out of harm's way.

"What do those flowers mean to you?"

"Everything." Her voice sounded strangled and it took everything in me not to demand that she tell me right then what that was supposed to mean. Instead I climbed to my feet and took her up with me. I swiped away her tears and kissed her quivering lips.

"Let's go home." She didn't protest as I guided her out of the house and down the driveway. She didn't argue as I helped her into the car or as I buckled her seatbelt, and she didn't take her eyes off the flowers as I climbed into the truck beside her. "When you're ready, we can talk." I needed her to hear that because the days of keeping secrets needed to be far behind us now. I needed to understand the woman I wanted to spend the rest of my life with, and there could be no more putting it off.

I looked down at my phone as it vibrated in the door and pulled it out.

Viva: Take care of her K. I don't know what those flowers mean but what she was feeling was deep.

Don't push her. You have to let her come to you with this one. I know how hard that is going to be for you but I really need you to trust me x

Me: I'll take her home and I'll take care of her tonight but I need to know who she is Veev x

Viva: And you will, but if you push too hard you could lose her for good. Don't make that mistake when you don't need to x

I looked down at my phone for a long minute before shutting off the screen and dropping it back into the door. I could understand what Viva was saying and I could practically feel her pleading through the phone, but I wasn't sure this was something I would be able to turn a blind eye to. I glanced across at the woman curled in on herself in my passenger seat and resigned myself to having to try, because losing her wasn't an option.

chapter
THIRTEEN

Knox

I stared up at the dark ceiling as I ran through the events of the night in my mind. Freya had barely spoken since we left Viva's and I had allowed her the silence in the car, but by the time we walked through her front door, I'd had enough, and all of Viva's warnings had fled my mind. I had pushed her to explain the flowers to me and she had snapped. She'd tried to send me away completely, but when I'd refused to go, she had slammed her bedroom door in my face. That brought me to where I was, lying on her sofa, staring up at the ceiling and wondering how the fuck I was going to make this better.

I'd had plans for us tonight; they had formulated in my mind as we had dinner. I'd wanted to make love to her for the first time in my life. I'd wanted to lay her beautiful body out on her bed with no games and none of the toys she had become so used to. I hadn't wanted to tease her or play with her. I hadn't wanted to deny her orgasms until she screamed for mercy. I'd wanted to give her everything. I had wanted to give her all of me. I had planned to pleasure her in every way I knew and then sink myself slowly into her tight, warm heat and have her cradle me there as I pushed and pulled my body in and out of hers as slowly as I could without either of us losing our minds. I had wanted to make love to her the way they did in books and movies. I had wanted to give her the fairy tale she had never had, but I'd fucked it up before it had even begun.

I shifted onto my side because now even the ceiling was pissing me off. I was too big for this sofa and I didn't even almost fit, but it was the best I could have. It didn't feel right to sleep in Lennon's room even though she didn't live there anymore, so I was stuck with this or going home, and there was no way I was leaving in case she needed me in the night.

I shoved my hand beneath my cheek and wondered why I hadn't been able to keep a lid on my temper just for the night. I knew I had shown her parts of me I wasn't proud of before, but tonight should not have been one of those nights. I should have had the patience she always claimed I had. I should have listened to what Viva had told me and I should have let her bury her face in my chest and hide from whatever her reality was because she trusted me. I should never have let her down.

"Knox."

I twisted so hard at the sound of her voice that I almost fell to the floor. I pushed myself up to sitting and looked at where she was hovering, half in the passage and half out. She was bathed in moonlight from the front room window and I could tell she had been crying even from across the room. Instant self-loathing slid through my veins because I could have been holding her while she cried if I hadn't been such a wanker.

"Fire." Her name escaped my lips on a harsh whisper and she leant her head against the door frame, her eyes dropping to her bare feet.

"I spoke to Lennon." I felt my brow furrow as I cocked my head to the side.

"Lennon?"

"Yeah." She sounded far away and I hated it. I pushed off the sofa and padded over to where she was hovering so I could try to read her face better. "She told me what I told her all those months ago when she didn't want to tell Gabriel the truth about herself." Her green eyes shifted upwards to meet mine and the pain that was held in the depths was enough to cut through me. "You deserve to know, especially after what you told me."

"We don't have to do this right now. I was a bastard tonight and I know that, but you're—" Her fingers pressed against my mouth and she shook her head.

"I'm afraid if I don't do it now, I never will. I don't want you to know any of this. I don't want to tell you the story, Knox, but Lennon is right—if I don't, I will lose you anyway, so it's a chance I'm going to have to take."

"You're not going to lose me." I said the words with every shred of conviction I possessed because there was no way anything she had to tell me was going to be any worse than what I had shared with her almost a month ago. Freya had cried with me that night when I had expected her to run, and there was no scenario I could fathom where I wouldn't repay her the same way. I loved the woman standing in front of me and nothing she could possibly have gone through was ever going to change that.

I reached out and stroked the side of her face as Cameron's words echoed through my mind. I didn't yet know the extent to which she had been screwed up by someone or something, but he had warned me that it was even deeper than the way that Lennon had been.

"You can't promise me that."

"I can." I stepped closer so all she could see was me. "I can tell you that, Fire, because you are the only woman I have ever wanted to spend my time with. You are the only woman I have ever looked at and known I need. It wasn't even a conscious thought process the first time I ever met you; it was a fundamental truth. I knew I needed you in my life and I knew that once I got you, I was going to do everything I could to keep you." I pushed my hands into her hair and hers instinctively curled around my wrists the way I was becoming so used to. "I'm not going to walk out of that door because something bad happened in your life. I'm not going to turn my back on you because you're broken because I'm fucking broken too and when I showed you my scattered pieces, you helped me start to pick them back up. I'm promising you here and now that when you tell me all the things you need to, I will still be standing here. I will still be holding your hand, and I will be whatever you need me to be. I just need you to trust me."

Those big green eyes blinked up at me for a minute, and tears slid from the corners of each one and touched my thumbs.

"The difference between our stories is that you were a victim of circumstance and I was the master of mine." I frowned at her because I didn't have the first idea what that was supposed to mean. "Living room." She pointed behind me and I couldn't help but notice that she was already drawing differences between the two of us. Freya had all but forced me to tell her my story in the comfort of her bedroom, and yet she wanted to tell me hers in a neutral room.

I shook my head at her request and shifted my hands from her hair, twining my fingers with hers.

"I have a better idea." I tugged on her hand and had her follow me down the hallway to the bathroom. Once I stepped inside, I reached out to twist the taps and picked up the nearest bottle of bath stuff that smelt a lot like she always did.

"What are you doing?"

"Running us a bath," I said without looking over my shoulder at her. "Then you are going to tell me all the things you need to."

"I don't want a bath." I rolled my eyes before turning to face her.

"Just humour me, beautiful, because there is no way I am doing this in the living room, and you don't seem to want to do it in your bedroom, so the bathroom is my compromise."

"We won't both fit." I wasn't sure I could argue with her there because the bath wasn't exactly huge, but I knew my sheer determination was going to make it work.

"We'll be fine." I hooked my thumbs into the waistband of my boxers and pushed them down my legs. I eyed her clothes and crossed my arms over my chest while I waited for her to catch up. She slowly tugged off the t-shirt she had pulled on and shimmied out of her knickers while I tested the temperature of the water.

I climbed in first because it seemed like the better option, and then I held my hand out to her.

"There's not enough room."

"There's plenty," I said as I grasped her hand and tugged her towards me. "It's a visual representation of how there will be no more secrets between us once this is over. Climb in Fire. Just follow me, all right?" I desperately wanted her to understand the meaning behind my words, and when she hesitantly lifted one leg to climb in, I knew I had her.

I sat down in the water, willing it not to slosh over the sides, and when I was settled, I tugged her down onto my lap and settled her in, allowing her to face away from me for the time being. I grabbed a washcloth, dipped it into the warm, fragrant water, and slicked it over her arms. She was silent for a long while and I knew better than to push her as I wiped every bare inch of skin I could. When she sighed long and hard, I knew the moment I had been waiting for was coming. I took a breath to steady myself because I knew I was going to have to let her finish the whole story no matter how much it hurt me, and I knew it would because there was no way I was going to be able to listen to her pain and not feel it for myself.

"I'm twenty-four by the way. I'm not the same age as Lennon, even though I always let everyone believe I am." She twisted in my arms and looked up at me, and I knew she didn't miss the look on my face. "What?"

"I couldn't care less how old you are. I know who you are, and that's what I want. Twenty-four or thirty-four, it makes no difference to me." I stroked my hand through her hair as she nestled her head back underneath my chin and her nails traced the pattern of the Polynesian tattoo I had as a left sleeve and half chest piece.

"I was sixteen when it happened." I braced myself as best as I could without tipping her off and waited for her to carry on. "I'd been sixteen for three months." Her fingers curled and her nails dug into my chest slightly as I shifted her body so that her face was closer to my neck. "It was supposed to be a good weekend. There weren't many good ones in the Anson household, so we kind of went at it full throttle. We planned it for weeks. We were going to drive down to the coast and I was going to win and then we were going to have dinner at the fish and chip shop on the pier. We were going to get ice creams and candy floss and spend the night at a little bed and breakfast I'd found. The next day we were supposed to go to the arcade. I'd been saving up so we had enough to play on the machines as well as go on the rides, and then we were going to come home. That was the plan…" Her voice trailed off as I wrapped my arms tighter around her. "It was all in the plan, and if we had just stuck to the plan, it would never have gone so wrong. It never would have happened Knox. It never would have happened if things hadn't changed." Her fist beat down on my chest in time with her words and I grasped her wrist in my hand.

"Tell me what happened, beautiful girl. Just tell me."

Freya

Knox's voice was the closest I had ever heard to begging as he clasped my wrist in his hand and held it steady against the thumping beat of his heart. I could never get close enough to that sound but I would always try because whenever I pressed my ear to it, I found that my demons fell silent for a minute. All the things I was about to tell him had never touched me when I could hear his heart beating steady beneath my ear and I craved that now, but it was too hard to move in this bath with both of us. I settled for flattening my palm against it and willing his strength to seep into me.

"My dad was the best man I ever met before you." My voice wobbled and another tear slid down my cheek. Lennon hadn't been joking when she'd warned me that this would be like ripping my own heart out, and for once I was glad she hadn't sugar-coated it. I wanted to scream out loud because of the pressure building in my chest.

"What was he called?"

"Jeremy. Jeremy Anson. He was a good man and he loved us. He loved us so much. He was busy though. He was in business and he sometimes had to go away. I hated it and I would always count down the days until he came home. I think he knew that because when I was older, he started to go away less. It felt like he was at home every day all of a sudden and I liked it." I took a breath as my fingers shook against his skin. I knew he hadn't missed it either, but I was thankful he hadn't grabbed them. "He was the one that told me I could be whatever I wanted to be. It was him who encouraged me to go out and find something I loved, and he said that when I found it, I should come tell him so he could make it mine."

I looked up at him as tears trickled down my face and I could see that he was trying his hardest to mask whatever he was feeling right then.

"I went out and found it. I loved to dance, but not the kind of dancing she wanted her daughter to do. She put me in ballet when he was in Dubai for work when I was little and I was so bad at it. The teacher had this cane and if you didn't get the moves just right, she would smack your ankles with it. I used to cry so bad when I came home from lessons and when Daddy came home, he told me I never had to go back again."

"Are you talking about your mother?" I nodded my head against his chest because I hadn't called Adrienne my mother in a very long time. "Fucking heartless bitch. What did she do?"

"She said it was my own fault." I hiccupped as he swore loudly before apologising. "She hated me. She never wanted me. She told me so many times when Daddy was gone that she wished she had just gotten rid of me when she had the chance. She had never wanted children but she wanted to keep Daddy so she just got on with it. That was what she said, that she got on with it." His big hand cupped the back of my head and I could feel how hard he was trying not to react to what I was saying. "I had more nannies than I could count because she never let them stay for very long; she didn't want me to get attached to them."

"Fucking hell, Fire." He moaned and I stroked my fingertips over his skin to soothe him.

"When I was six, I found these magazines for a boarding school, and when I asked Daddy about them, he got really mad. I heard them yelling and shouting and I found out later that he told her there was no way in hell I was going to boarding school. Sometimes I wish I had," I admitted. "If I'd gone, none of it would have happened." I couldn't fight the sob threatening to burst from me as I let that thought settle in my mind. I had wished it on countless nights, but hearing myself say it out loud in Knox's arms somehow seemed to hurt more.

"So you didn't go to boarding school." His voice was strained now and I shook my head.

"A little while after that she fell down the stairs. Now that I'm older, I can see that she did it on purpose because I was getting all the attention. After the boarding school drama, Daddy didn't even want to speak to her, but when she fell, he rushed her to the hospital. I stayed with our neighbour. She gave me toffees and let me sleep in her spare bed with her daughter's teddy. When they came back, Daddy sat me down and told me I was a big girl now because I was going to be a big sister. I was excited and Daddy told me she would be mine. I wanted her so badly." I shuddered and felt him shift so he could reach the warm tap. I didn't have the heart to tell him it wouldn't make any difference because the cold was deep inside of me.

"A sister?" he asked gently.

"She came a little while later and she was perfect. She was blonde and had chubby cheeks and little tiny hands that grabbed onto my finger when I talked to her. I always tried to take care of her, especially when Daddy was gone. She was so tiny and we had new nannies all the time and they never knew how to take care of her properly. They didn't know that her favourite song was 'Silent Night' and they didn't know that she liked it if you rubbed her tummy in circles or that she only liked to sleep with her pink bunny and not the blue one. They always got it wrong and it made me so mad."

"How old were you?"

"I was seven when she was born. I took care of her as well as I could, but I wasn't very good at reading her bedtime stories. I'd never been very good with reading and no one ever helped me. The nannies would try but then she would send them away and tell me I was thick and stupid and that I was no daughter of hers if I couldn't even read a sentence." I winced as her cold, high-pitched voice echoed around inside my brain and Knox's arms closed around me impossibly tighter.

"Are you dyslexic?" His voice sounded pained and I knew he was thinking he had offended me by not telling me about Kaleb. I tipped my head up to look at him and skimmed my fingertips over his jaw.

"No." I shook my head and took a deep breath. "Mine was more of a pressure and fear thing, and lack of help, I suppose, but it didn't stop other kids from picking on me the way they pick on Kaleb. It didn't stop everyone from looking at me like I was thick. When Daddy stopped working away, it was him who helped me with my reading, and that was when he told me I could be whatever I wanted to be."

"The same way you told Kale tonight." His voice was barely a mumble as I pushed away from his chest and looked up at him.

"You heard that?"

"I was coming to get you and I heard you two talking. Thank you for giving him something the rest of us can't because we can't relate. We can tell him he's capable of anything, but he knows we haven't had the same troubles." He cupped my face in his hands and rested his forehead against my own.

"I only told him the truth Knox." I turned my face away from his and settled back down against his body.

"Well I thank you for that."

I let those words sink into my skin as I tried to dig up the energy to get to the next part. There would be no stopping for other conversations once I started. There would be no coming up for air, and there would be no deviating. I was about to splay myself wide open, and I prayed to God he could keep the promise he had so effortlessly made me.

"I took up street dancing. There were no words involved and it wasn't like ballet. There was nothing complicated about it. I could feel the beat of the music; it was like an instinct. I went to classes and she hated it. She didn't think any daughter of hers should be gyrating that way. It was my thing though, and I knew I couldn't let her take it away from me the way she had taken so many other things I had no control over. I threw myself into it and I was good. I won competitions and when I sat down with my teacher at fifteen, I told her I didn't want to be a performer. She was surprised because that was the ambition of every other girl in my class. I wanted something that would last longer, and I wanted to help other people like me. I wanted to be a teacher. She told me most teachers started off as dancers and segued into it as their bodies got older and they had established some sort of platform in the industry. I could hear what she was saying, but all I knew was that I wanted to teach, so she helped me. She helped me find competitions that would have important people at them and she helped me practice for them. I'd done a couple before the big one came up. There were going to be dancers from all over the United Kingdom at this big convention on the coast and if I did well in it, there would be all kinds of exposure. That was our weekend, just me, Dad, and Jasmyn."

I felt his body shift beneath me as the name I had just said out loud suddenly seemed to register with him. My mind flashed back to earlier tonight when I'd almost had a breakdown on Viva's kitchen floor. I hadn't seen or smelt a jasmine flower in years, and seeing them in Kaleb's outstretched hand had levelled me.

"The flowers," he whispered.

"I didn't mean to freak out, but it's been so long. I never thought I would hold one again."

"Were they your favourite flower before she was born?" he asked gently.

"No." I shook my head as I wiped at my cheeks with my hands. My body was starting to prune and I knew we should probably get out, but I couldn't bring myself to move. Instead I pressed my face farther into him and wished that the next bit wouldn't rip me to pieces. "I won first place. Jassy was so excited and so was Dad. We went straight to the fish and chip shop from the contest and Dad told everyone we were celebrating. He kept telling everyone how his baby had won first place and that I was going to be a star." I squeezed my eyes shut as the memory played out behind my eyelids. I swallowed hard and tried my best to go on. "Then she rang, said she was ill and that she needed him. She asked him to come home so he could take her to the hospital. What could he do Knox? He couldn't tell her no. He just shook his head at me and Jassy and told us how sorry he was. He paid the bill and we left. We didn't get ice cream or the bed and breakfast and we never made it to the arcade."

"Fire girl." His hands skimmed up and down my back as he held me even closer to him before finally making the decision I had been putting off. He scooped me into his arms and carried me out of the bath, stopping to grab a towel and dry us both off before picking me back up and carrying me to my bedroom. I didn't bother to fight him because I knew it wouldn't change anything no matter where I did this.

I tried to get some control over my breathing as he climbed into bed and pulled me so I was lying across his chest, my ear pressed to his heart. He smoothed my hair away from my face and whispered for me to go on.

"We got in the car and I was disappointed, so was Jassy. I knew he felt bad but I couldn't stop myself. I was mad at her for ruining everything just the way she always did. When we got onto the motorway, Dad put the radio on and found the song I had danced to at the contest, and just like that, he broke our sulking. The song was on repeat, Jassy and me were dancing, and even Dad was singing along. Then out of nowhere a car veered in front of ours. I screamed, Dad yelled. I felt him slam the brakes and then Jassy screamed but it wasn't enough. Our car somehow flipped over the top of the other car and then it was flying, at least that was what it felt like. I can't even explain how it feels to be in the air when you're strapped into a car. I was so terrified. I was panicking. We were all screaming and

Dad just kept saying how much he loved us and how sorry he was. I grabbed Jassy's hand and I screamed that I loved him and I made her say it too even though she was almost choking with fear. For a split second you get to acknowledge that you're probably going to die. Dad got there first and then I did, but I don't know that Jassy ever fully realised. I like to hope she didn't." Sobs bubbled up my throat, battling for space against the hiccups that were never ending. "When the car finally hit the ground, the song stopped playing and the only sound was the horn blaring. I yelled at Dad. I yelled for him to tell us he was okay, but he never answered. Jassy was screaming and crying and I knew I had to be strong for her. I talked to her. I told her stories about what we would do when we got home. I told her that when I was old enough, she could come live with me. I sung to her. I told her jokes. I held her hand. I held her hand so tight, but it wasn't enough. It wasn't enough." I banged my fist against his chest again but this time he didn't stop me. He didn't grab my wrist and hold me still; he just let me pound on him as the sobs rattled through me.

"What happened then, beautiful? When did you get out?"

"I don't know." I slumped against him as all the fight went out of me. "Jassy was gone and once she was gone, there was nothing stopping me from joining both of them. The last thing I remember was that she was smiling. I'd just told a really bad joke and she was laughing, and then she wasn't anymore."

"Jesus," he hissed.

"I woke up in hospital six weeks later. There was no one there when I woke up. She had washed her hands of me by then." I pushed up to sitting and looked down at my hands. "I went to Willow for PTSD or some shit, I don't even know. They were kind to me there, but I just wanted to be gone. I never actively tried to end my life, but I didn't live, not for a long time. I was meant to be leaving but Pippa, the lady who owns Willow, told me she had a new girl coming and asked me to help settle her in seeing as I'd been there so long. I owed her so much and I agreed. That was when I met Len, she was the new girl. I wanted to look after her, wanted to protect her, so I threw myself into it. She became my reason and my rock. I was going to go my own way when she was due to leave, but she asked me to move in with her. She didn't want to be without me and I didn't want to be without her, so I agreed. I was shocked as hell that Emmy and Tommy wanted me, and I swore I wouldn't be a burden. They were so good to me, and then we found this place, and well, you know the rest." I hurried through the remainder of my story because I just wanted it to be over now. I stared down at my hands as I waited for him to react, and I saw him push himself up so he could meet me eye for eye.

"What about their funerals? Your dad and Jasmyn." I had hoped that by me speaking so fast, he wouldn't pick up on that, but I should have known better. "Fire?"

"She had them while I was in the coma."

"Sorry?"

"You heard me Knox. She did it while I was unconscious and she pretty much buried me as well that day."

"How did you... I mean, what did you..."

"When I was nineteen, I went with Len to Danni's grave, and when I got back, I found her number online and called her office. I asked to speak to her and when she came on the phone she was the same old Adrienne." I swallowed hard. "She hated me from birth, Knox, and the words she said to me that day on the phone were the first I knew to be true." I twisted away from him but he caught me around the waist and tugged me down on the bed, looming over me. I shifted to try to get away and he caught my face in one hand.

"What could she possibly have ever said to you that was the truth? What could she have said to make her actions okay? Tell me, because I really want to hear this."

The words tore from my throat as I stared into his eyes. "She told me it was my fault, that I was a murderer. She told me if it wasn't for me, they wouldn't have been in the car or on the motorway and then she told me—" My voice broke. "She told me she would never tell me where they rested so I couldn't trouble them in death the way I had in life."

A sob burst through me as a growl emanated from him. It was full of pure rage and anger, and for a fleeting second, I saw the hardened look of the man that night at the bar before it shifted out and was replaced with startlingly clear black. His body fell beside me and he instantly pulled me against him and spoke in my ear.

"She was wrong. She was more wrong than I can ever fucking explain, but I know you can't hear that so I want to make you a promise right here and now." I tried to look up at him but he held my head into his neck and all I could do was absorb his words. "I will spend every day for the rest of my life showing you that it was a lie. You are fierce, you are strong, you are independent and beautiful, and you were put on this earth for me. You are everything I could ever want and all I will ever need. What happened was a tragic, horrible fucking accident that had nothing to do with you. I need you to understand that you are worth so much more than she ever let you believe because you are it for me. I love you." My throat seized at those three words, the ones I had been so avidly avoiding. "I know you don't want to hear that right now and I don't expect you to say it back, but I need you to know. I need you to feel that I love you because I want to help you put your pieces back together. We fucking deserve this. We deserve to be happy after what they put us through, and you are the only one who has ever made me feel this way."

I wrenched my head out of his grip and looked into his black eyes as he bit down on his bottom lip.

"Fire—" He started to speak, but I slammed my mouth down on his and halted the words. I tasted my tears in our kiss and I knew he was the only person who stood a damn chance at helping me come out of the other side of the fog I had been living in. I pulled away and watched him for a long minute.

"Make love to me Knox." It was a shaky request, but I saw the emotion in his eyes change.

I had warned him once before that I might not always be able to say the words he needed to hear, but I would always do my best to show him.

chapter FOURTEEN

Knox

I pushed open the door of the truck and jumped down onto the tarmac of Gabriel and Lennon's brand new driveway. I had no idea what issue they had taken with the gravel that had been there previously, but I wasn't about to get into a discussion of the pros and cons with either one of them. Transforming this house into the place they wanted to live had turned them both into housezillas, and I knew better than to get into the middle of it.

It had been nearly three weeks since Freya had finally bared her soul to me, and I hadn't been able to get Lennon alone to talk to her about any of it, which was something I planned to rectify today. I had swung by the office in the hopes of catching her there, but Hannah had very quietly informed me that Lennon had taken the day off and that Freya had gone out for lunch. I was glad she felt the need to tell me what my girl was up to, but it was unnecessary considering I already knew she had flaked out on her longstanding lunch arrangements with Cameron so much lately, the guilt was starting to eat at her. She had told me that morning she planned to rectify that today, which was the only reason I had gone to the office in the first place.

I jogged up the front steps and pressed my thumb down on the doorbell. I heard the sound echo through the cavernous interior and then Lennon's voice as it floated towards the door. It swung inwards not two seconds later and I smiled at her. Her blonde hair, which was getting longer now, was pulled haphazardly up in some sort of clip, her t-shirt had once belonged to her fiancé, and there was paint spattered all over it, her leggings, and her face.

"Hey you, what are you doing all the way over here? I thought you guys were at the studio all day."

"I left them to it. They were starting to make me want to smack their heads in with one of the stock guitars." Her mouth popped open before her laugh hit me full force.

"Yeah, Gabe is being a super huge pain in the arse these days."

"You think?"

"I know." She rolled her eyes as she stepped back to let me in and closed the door behind me. "That's the reason he thinks I'm at work right now when in fact I am here, painting alone."

"I feel like there's a story behind that," I said as I trailed behind her into the kitchen. Lennon was ever the consummate host even when I was barging in on her while she was in the middle of painting. I propped myself up on one of the barstools and watched as she pulled two glasses down from the cupboard over the sink and proceeded to fill them up with ice and water from the fancy gadget on the front of the fridge. She handed one over to me and leant against the counter.

"There's always a story where Gabe is concerned. The short of it is that we do not agree on methods of decorating, and instead of me hitting him with a hammer or some other decorating implement, I choose to ignore him and do things when he is out of my way." She smiled and I laughed.

"So that is how he got the surprise man cave?" I arched an eyebrow at her as I made sure to put *surprise* in air quotes.

"You're damn straight it is, and he was full of all the gratitude in the world, so I considered it a win for everyone."

"So you're playing games with him, are you little girl?"

"Always." She winked. "But only when I know we both win. Anyway"—she narrowed her eyes on me a little as she tapped her paint-splattered fingernails against her glass—"you didn't come here to discuss my decorating habits or why I'm sneaking around behind my fiancé's back in an effort to get this house under control before my wedding, so why did you come?"

"I'm not allowed to swing by and see one of my favourite women?" I feigned hurt as I pressed my hand against my chest. I had always gotten along well with Lennon from the very first night we met, and I liked to consider her my friend as much as she was Gabe's fiancée or Freya's makeshift sister.

"Of course you can, but you don't ever do anything on a whim, Knox Sutton, so I know there is more to this than you are letting on."

I briefly looked down at the glass clasped between my hands and then back up at her. I knew I had to bite the bullet and pray it didn't come back to bite me on the arse. I could only assume Lennon knew everything Freya had told me, and I could only hope she wouldn't be offended on her friend's behalf that I was considering discussing it with her.

"I wanted to ask you about Freya's mother." I studied her features and saw the shock flash across them before something else settled. I held my breath, praying the next words out of her mouth wouldn't be her chewing me out. She took a sip of her water and then her eyes fluttered closed.

"Did she tell you everything?" The words were barely more than a whisper.

"As far as I know, but she was fairly vague about her mother."

"She's evil, Knox," she said as her eyes flashed open again; the blue was frosty, and that was how I knew she was being serious. "The woman is Satan personified. I hate her and I've never met her. I think if I did, I'd have to do some damage for all the shit she has done and all the ways she ever made Freya feel inadequate. There's only one other person on this planet I have hated as much, and thankfully she is already dead."

I knew who she was talking about without her having to elaborate, and if Lennon felt as strongly about Freya's mother as she had about the woman who had singlehandedly gone about wrecking her and Gabe's lives, I knew my feelings were not totally unfounded.

"She had her father and her sister buried before Freya even woke up from the coma that car accident put her in." I pushed the words out through gritted teeth because reliving even a little of what Freya had sobbed all over me made me want to commit worse acts than I ever had during my brother's reign of terror.

"And she told her it was her fault they were dead and that she wouldn't be allowed to trouble them in death the way she had in life." She finished the thought for me as her hand moved across the counter to rest over the top of my shaking fist.

My nostrils flared as the fury coursing through me took hold. I needed to get a grip on it, but hearing Lennon say those words again had cut me to the core.

"I know how you feel, if it's any consolation. I understand what it's like to hurt for the person you love."

My head snapped back and my eyes met her crystal blue ones as a soft smile graced her face.

"Yes, it's that obvious that you are in love with her, and no she hasn't told me that you've already said it or that she didn't say it back, I just know her." She shrugged and straightened up. "For what it's worth, she loves you too, but she hasn't said those words a whole lot in her life. She's barely ever had them said to her, so I don't suppose for one second she knows what to do when a man like you lays them at her feet. Freya has spent years of her life believing she should be alone, believing she doesn't deserve the same things the rest of us do, and it's all because of her mother. You're changing that piece by piece, and I for one couldn't be happier about it. Freya will get there. She will catch up to you in the end because she will come to see that losing you is not an option."

"She'll never lose me."

"I'm glad."

I squeezed her slender fingers before pulling back; once again I had been sidetracked from my original aim.

"Do you have any idea where their graves could be? Did Freya ever mention where she grew up or what places she went as a kid?" Lennon shook her head and I already knew I wasn't going to like the answer.

"I looked everywhere she could think of Knox. I was obsessed for a while until she lost the plot with me one day. It's a fruitless exercise because there is no way she let them rest anywhere Freya would ever think to find them."

"Fuck!" I cursed as I slammed my fist down on the countertop.

"I know how that feels too."

"I wanted to find them, Len. I need to fucking find them because I want to give her something. She never had the chance to grieve for them properly, never had the chance to lay flowers down for them or have somewhere she could go to speak to them."

I ran my hand harshly over my face as she stepped around the counter to wrap her arms around me. Her head rested on my shoulder for a minute as I considered the fact that I would never be able to give Freya the one thing she would want above everything else. When she suddenly jerked upright, I twisted around to steady her, but the look on her face gave me pause.

"You might not be able to give her the exact place, but that doesn't mean you can't give her something." My brows furrowed as I tried to keep up with what she was saying. "You can give her a place she can go to remember them. You can give her the kind of place where she can talk to them. I mean, okay, so you can't give it to her right now because you live in a flat and so does she, but you can give it to her one day when you two have a house of your own." Her eyes glittered back at me and the smile fighting for its place on her face was undeniable.

"Len, I have no idea what you're talking about." I reached out to grab hold of her so she would stop bouncing on her tiptoes and held her still. "Go through it slowly for me." The smile got impossibly bigger and her eyes wider before she spoke.

"Okay, I mean that one day when you two have a garden, you can make her her own place that she can go. It doesn't have to be much, just a pond, a bench, or a flower bush, some place she can go to outside where she can be quiet and feel them around her. I know it isn't the same as the final place they rest, but there is no guarantee either of them even have a place like that. There is no guarantee that Adrienne didn't have them cremated and keep them with her. We all just assumed there was a grave she could go to, but maybe there isn't, so instead of a grave, you give her a memorial."

My eyes widened as the words she was saying finally started to seep into my brain. My hands moved from gripping her arms to tugging her towards me so I could hug her.

"You, Lennon Walsh, are a bloody genius. Has anyone ever told you that?"

"Once or twice." She giggled. "It will be all hers, Knox, and she can do whatever she needs to with it. It might take a little while, but in the end you'll be able to give that to her." Her hand cupped my cheek and Gabe's voice echoed around the kitchen.

"Am I interrupting?" I couldn't get a read on the tone of his voice, but there was no way I was going to let him get carried away with himself and start thinking all kinds of crazy things.

"Only my gratitude for your fiancée's pure genius," I said as I looked up at him and saw his eyebrow raised.

"Freya told Knox all her secrets and he wanted to do something for her that is impossible. I was helping him find another option." She bounded over to him and pushed up on her tiptoes to kiss his cheek.

"You're supposed to be at work." He frowned down at her and she tossed a look over her shoulder that told me I should probably make tracks if I didn't want to get involved in their domestic dramas.

"And that is my cue to head out." I stood up and walked across the room, kissed Lennon on the cheek, and when I saw the face Gabriel was pulling, gave him a slap on the back of the neck that had him jolting forward. Before he could say a word, I shoved my finger in his face. "Do not be a fucking jackass Delaney. I know you are a jealous little shit, but your bride-to-be only hid her true whereabouts today because you don't let her do the things she needs to do to make this place your home. You need to remove your nose from her business and let her do her thing. Also, never look at me like I'm here getting cosy with your lady. I have my own woman now and I intend to keep her. Don't be a tool."

I heard Lennon laugh as I headed for the front door. I slammed it closed behind me and walked down to my truck. Lennon had given me plenty of things to think about during our brief conversation, and I knew she was right. I couldn't bring back pieces of Freya's past, and I could see what she meant about it not being the best thing anyway. I wanted us to start afresh without ghosts clinging to our backs, and giving her something brand new was definitely the only way to do that.

Freya

I pushed open the heavy metal door of the warehouse and stepped inside. Johnny was the only one to look up from the table he was in the midst of varnishing. I smiled as he put down his tools, pulled the mask from his mouth, and walked across the room towards me.

"It's good to see you, Freya. You haven't been around much lately."

"I know," I admitted as I glanced around the room. "Things have changed in here a little bit." I tipped my chin in the direction of the two boys I didn't know who were busy sawing planks of wood.

"Well you know how it is when things take off. There was too much work for me, Cam, and Arlo to do all on our own so we had to recruit."

"They look young."

"They are," he agreed as he turned his attention back to me. "They're also bloody talented. They put me to shame with some of their concepts."

"Good." I smiled. "Someone needs to keep you old men on your toes, don't they."

"Cheeky cow," he grumbled. "Cam nipped out about a half hour ago to get you guys lunch. Go on back to his office, he shouldn't be long."

"Thanks Johnny." I smiled before heading in the direction of Cameron's office. I had been in this warehouse before it looked anything like it did right now. It was me who had trawled around a ton of different spaces with Cameron looking for the perfect one, and I liked what he had done with it. Now, instead of it being a blank space, there were work stations and a ton of machinery. Even though I didn't have the first clue what any of it did, it looked impressive. It had been Cameron's dream in life to own his own furniture company, and I loved that he had made it so successful.

I picked my way across the room towards Cameron's work space. It had been one of his requirements when we had been looking at units; he needed to be alone to work. He had wanted to get a space for Johnny as well, but he had been insistent that he preferred being in the hustle and bustle of the main room. Johnny was sociable and liked to bounce his ideas off his colleagues while Cameron liked to work in solitude. I respected that because I was the same.

I pushed open the door to the office and stepped inside. The room was neat and the desk was clear, which was unlike Cameron; he was normally messier than I was. Out of the three of us, Lennon was always the one going around picking things up and putting them back in their correct place. I had lived a lifetime of having things in proper places, and as an adult I made a conscious effort not to care about it more than I had to.

"Admiring my handiwork?" He laughed from behind me. I didn't bother to turn around as I ran my fingertip across his desk and held it up to him—there was a layer of dust now coating my skin.

"You forgot to dust."

"God Johnny was right, you are on form today." He laughed as he walked past me and put the bag he had been carrying down on the coffee table. I recognised that little white bag and my eyes lit up as I stared at it. I was starving. I'd been starving for days, and Lennon assured me that was what happened when you became content with the life you had. I had no idea what it was, but nothing had ever looked better than that little white bag full of a bunch of foil containers. "Earth to Freya." I jumped at the sound of Cameron's voice and looked up at him.

"What?"

"When you're quite done drooling, I said here's your plate." He thrust the white china disk at me and I grabbed it from him.

"I'm sorry, I'm just starving."

"Skip breakfast?" he asked as he pulled containers from the bag and put them down on the desk.

"No." I shrugged as I sat down beside him on the sofa and tugged the containers marked with an F towards me. Cameron and I shared a love of Indian food that didn't interest Lennon one bit, and when we had discovered the little Indian shop around the corner from this unit, it had been the last selling point. Cameron had put in an offer the same day.

"Oh, are you doing that whole content person thing?" He quirked an eyebrow as he dumped rice onto his plate.

"I didn't even know it was a thing, but you and Len both seem to so I'm just going to say yes and use that as my excuse for being a greedy cow." I laughed as I upended my container of rice and then reached for the part I loved the most. I wasn't necessarily someone who enjoyed a whole lot of spice—unlike Cameron, who was already pouring his vindaloo onto his rice while digging a forkful of it into his mouth—so tikka was enough for me, and the tikka from this specific restaurant was unlike any I had ever had before.

I pulled off the lid and as the smell hit my nose, I felt my stomach turn. I frowned down at the food as I let it spill onto my rice anyway.

"You okay?" Cameron asked from beside me, his fork paused halfway to his mouth.

"I'm fine." I shook my head as my stomach twisted again.

"You don't look fine. You look ill."

"Does this smell different to you?" It was the only explanation I had for my reaction. I picked the plate up from my lap and held it towards him.

"No." He shook his head. "Smells just as weak as it always does."

I stuck my tongue out at him in reaction and picked up my fork. I scooped up as much as I could and shoved it into my mouth, hoping I was just being an idiot. When the food hit my tongue, though, my stomach clenched hard and I retched.

"Jesus Fray, do not puke on the floor!" Cameron exclaimed as he grabbed the plate from my lap and chucked it onto the coffee table. The next thing I knew his bin was between my knees and I released the food from my mouth into it. "Are you okay?" he asked.

I looked up at him and saw concern etched into his features, but the small movement proved too much for my stomach. I shook my head and pushed up from the chair. My hand flew up to cover my mouth as I bolted into the toilet that was just off of his office. I slammed and locked the door behind me, muffling his protests and questions. There was no way on earth I wanted an audience while I tossed my cookies.

I shoved the toilet seat up and lost the fight with myself. Everything I had eaten that morning and every sip of water I had probably ever had hit the bottom of his toilet bowl. I could feel the sweat beading on my forehead as my stomach protested wildly, clenching and releasing as I crouched down on the floor as best I could in my skirt.

I had no idea how long I was in there, but I knew that at some point Cameron's yells had stopped and I was grateful for that. I flushed the chain and let the toilet seat bang down before pushing up and walking over to the sink. I looked at myself in the mirror and cringed at the sight. My mascara and eyeliner were a total write-off, and most of it had run in rivers down my cheeks. I grabbed some toilet paper and ran it under the tap to clean up as much of the mess as I could then ran my fingers through my hair as I unlocked the door.

I was surprised to see Cameron sitting on the sofa when I came back out, and I noticed that the offending food was nowhere to be seen so I supposed that explained his eventual silence. I slid down into the seat next to him on shaky legs and looked up at him.

"That was disgusting. I wholeheartedly apologise that I just subjected you to that. Do you have any mints?"

"I don't think you need mints Fray." His face was deadly serious and it had me frowning in response.

"Oh no, believe me, I really do." I reached for my handbag and tugged open the zip; there had to be something in there. At that point I would have taken a Murray mint over the rank taste in my mouth.

"How long have you been feeling sick?" I rolled my eyes before turning to look at him.

"I'm fine, it was just the food Cam."

"I didn't ask what caused it, I asked how long."

"It comes and goes." I shrugged. "In case you haven't noticed or Lennon hasn't been giving you updates, things have been changing pretty fast in my world."

"How long?"

"A few weeks." I sighed as I finally got my hands on a long forgotten packet of Polos that were crumbled at the bottom of my bag. I popped one into my mouth and fought the urge to gag because Cameron's eyes were focused on me a little too hard.

"How much weight have you put on?"

"Excuse me!"

"It's a fair question Freya. You said you've been hungry, so naturally you would have put weight on if you've been eating more."

"I don't know what the hell you're getting at, Cam."

"I think you know exactly what I'm getting at, Freya." His icy blue eyes burnt into me and I fought the urge to fidget beneath his stare. "This is for you." He held out a plastic bag and I frowned down at it as I noticed the logo.

"No way!" I shook my head, pushing it back towards him. "There is no chance…" My voice trailed off as my mind flashed back through the weeks. I swallowed hard as that night in the car played out in glorious technicolour.

"Are you sure about that?"

"Cameron." I bit down on my lip. "No, I can't be, okay, I just can't. I'm not."

"Freya,"

"No, no, no!" I could feel the panic rising through my body, choking me hard as I shoved my hands out towards him. "No. I can't be anyone's mother. I'm not pregnant. I'm not fucking pregnant Cameron!"

"Jesus Freya!" he exclaimed as he caught my flailing arms in his hands.

"No Cam, just no!" A sob escaped me without me giving it permission, and I frowned as the sound burst in the air around me. I took my eye off the ball for a second and it gave him enough leverage to tug me against him. His arms wrapped around me and his lips pressed to the top of my head. "No, no, no." I mumbled the word over and over against him and felt his hands skim up and down my spine.

"Saying no won't change it if you are Freya." I knew he was right, but I couldn't seem to make my mind understand that. I squeezed my eyes closed as I trembled hard against him.

"I wouldn't even know where to start and Knox...god, Knox." I moaned against him. "We've been together for five minutes. We can't be parents. It's not right. It's not... I don't even know if he wants kids. I don't know if I want kids." My words were starting to jumble together now as a slideshow of Knox playing with Kaleb and stroking Viva's bump flashed through my mind. Kids had never been on my agenda, and I had never stopped to find out if they were on his. "This can't be happening Cam."

"I think it is happening Fray." He pushed me away from him so he could clasp my face in his hands. I looked up and noticed the concern on his face had morphed into something else. There were shadows in his eyes that I wasn't used to and his features looked pained. "I'm going to tell you something, but you have to promise not to lose it, okay?"

"Cameron—"

"No, you have to promise Freya."

I wanted to shake my head but he was holding my face too tight, and suddenly I realised why he had done that. Instead I nodded as best as I could and watched as his chin dipped and his eyes fell away from mine as he spoke.

"I was almost a father." My eyes widened involuntarily because this was news to me; now I understood why he had forced me to promise I wouldn't lose it. "We hadn't been together for very long." His eyes flickered up to mine and the torture shining back at me now felt physically painful. "I was young. I was working at that old furniture place, living with Mum and Dad, riding a motorbike and boxing. That was all I was back then, but when I met her, I knew she was different. She was something." His voice quivered slightly and I felt it right in the heart of me. "I fell in love with her pretty fucking fast, and when we found out she was pregnant, I couldn't have been any happier if I'd tried. I wanted to shout it from the rooftops. It didn't matter who I was or what we did or didn't have, Fray. What mattered to both of us was the baby. I hadn't told anyone about us at the time and only her best friend knew." I wanted to ask him why. I wanted to demand answers from him, but I knew I couldn't. "We had it all in our hands for two days." My chest tightened as his face contorted harder. "We were at dinner planning how we were going to tell everyone and she went to the bathroom. I waited fifteen minutes before I started to wonder where she had gotten to, and then my phone rang. I looked down and saw her name. I answered it and everything fell apart. I can't even explain how quickly I went from having it all to having nothing, but it happened."

"Cameron." My voice was shaking almost as badly as his as he shook his head. His eyes were glassy with unshed tears and I wanted to tell him it was okay to cry, but he spoke first.

"What I'm trying to say to you is that if you are pregnant, it's going to be the best thing that ever happens to you and Knox. It doesn't matter if you've been together for five years or five days, what matters is the life growing inside of you. I know Knox and I know he is the kind of man who will see it for the blessing it is, so if that is what you are worried about, it's off the table. As for what kind of mother you will make, if it's worth anything, I think you will make a damn good one. You sure as hell took care of Len when the rest of us couldn't."

My chin trembled and I couldn't stop the tears from sliding down my face at his words. He pressed the plastic bag into my hand and kissed my forehead.

"Go do that test and then come back out here knowing you will rock this the way you rock everything you do."

I swallowed hard as I stood up, the box clutched in my hand. I took a step forward on shaky legs and then turned back to him. I wrapped my arms around his neck and rested my cheek on the back of his head.

"I wish I'd known," I whispered.

"You always wanted to know why I ran off to New York, Fray. Now you do." I blinked slowly and took a shuddering breath.

"I won't tell anyone, I swear." I held my pinky out and he hooked his around it.

"Stop stalling Anson. Go pee on that stick." His attempt at humour was raw, but I wasn't going to point it out to him. Instead I took a deep breath, pushed my shoulders back, and took the few steps to the bathroom. Things were going to change one way or the other once I was inside, but I knew I couldn't hide from this the way I had hidden from so many things in my life.

I closed and locked the door behind me and looked at myself in the mirror. I didn't look any different than I had a few minutes ago, but I knew that in another three, I possibly wouldn't even recognise myself. I ran my fingertips over my cheek and closed my eyes.

"Daddy, Jassy." I whispered their names and they echoed back at me. "Whatever happens next, promise me you'll help me make this okay, please." It was a useless plea, but it felt like a blanket of warmth surrounded me now. I opened my eyes and pulled the box from the bag. There was no use stalling anymore.

chapter FIFTEEN

Freya

I looked down at my phone and reread Cameron's text as I pushed open the door that led back to the gym changing rooms. The words shone back at me and I knew without having to ask exactly what he was summoning me to talk about.

"Whoa there."

I gasped as I walked straight into a hard body and my eyes shot up to find Mac, the owner of the gym, looking down at me.

"I am so sorry. I didn't see you there," I said as I took a step back from where I was pressed against him.

"No harm little girl." His smile made his eyes twinkle and I found myself smiling back at him. "You looking for our boy?"

"I am." I nodded as I held my phone up. "He summoned me." He barked out a laugh and stepped around me to carry on out to the main gym.

"I've taped him up so he's all yours for a few minutes."

"Thank you," I called after him as he walked away. I took a deep breath and made my way further down the corridor. As I pushed open the door I knew Cameron would be behind, I covered my eyes with my hand.

"I'm dressed Fray." He laughed.

"Forgive me if I don't want to see your bits and pieces." I smiled as I looked up at where he was stretching against the benches. "What's up anyway?"

"You know what's up." His voice was gentle but his blue eyes were stormy as they caught mine.

"I haven't told him yet." I knew I couldn't let him make me feel bad for that because I wanted to tell Knox, I just needed to get my own head around it first.

"Freya." Cameron sounded exasperated as he tossed his head back, his eyes on the ceiling. "Did you not hear a word I told you the other day? You don't have any guarantees."

"I know and I did hear you, but I also don't want to throw it at him and run and rock in the corner. I want to get used to the idea first."

"You will never be used to it until you start living it as your reality, I promise you. You can't prepare for this like it's one of your meetings. This is life, it is real, and it's living inside you right now." He moved closer to me as he spoke and I could tell he was itching to put his hand against my stomach to drive his point home, but he resisted.

"I know it's living inside me Cameron."

"But do you? Because it looks an awful lot like you are still in denial."

"Don't!" My voice was louder than I had anticipated and it bounced off the walls. "I will do it my way and in my time, okay? It's my life and my choice."

"Just remember that you are not the only one lying now, Fray. I don't like lying to him after everything." I shook my head as I crossed my arms over my middle because his words made my stomach churn.

"Don't pull that on me. I wasn't going to tell you what it said but you practically tackled me for a stick of plastic I had pissed on, so don't get all shitty now about me making you keep secrets."

"I'm not being shitty, and I didn't tackle you." He stepped closer to me and caught my biceps in his big hands, forcing me to stay where I was. "You looked like you were going to pass out and I wanted to know if I needed to get you to hospital or just sit you down."

"You have no say in how I choose to handle this." I poured as much conviction as possible into my voice as I poked my finger into the centre of his barrel chest. "It's my choice. All of this is my choice."

"He has a fucking right to know Freya. He has as much right as you do and you damn well know it."

"No!" I yelled back as I yanked myself free from his hold. "It is my body and I decide what I do with it! You just need to keep your mouth shut." My voice sounded shrill as it echoed, punctuated only by the sound of the changing room door slamming shut behind us. I twisted on the spot as Cameron's eyes went wide in his face and found Lennon standing with her back to the door, her head cocked to one side as she appraised both of us.

"What are you two fighting about?"

"It depends how much you heard," I said honestly as I jammed my elbow into Cameron's rib cage in a silent plea for him to keep his mouth shut.

"Why don't you just tell me?" My nostrils flared at her words.

"Freya—" Cameron started to speak so I rounded on him.

"Shut up!" I hissed before turning away from him. "I'm just going to head back out. Good luck up there Cameron," I called over my shoulder as I reached for the door, but I didn't get the chance to open it before Lennon's hand came down on top of mine.

"You aren't going anywhere until you tell me what is going on between the two of you." My eyes went wide in my face as I turned my head towards her. I could hardly process the words she had just said so I was grateful when Cameron spoke up.

"What the fuck Len?"

"I heard you both. I heard you saying it was your body and that he needs to keep his mouth shut so I'm going to ask you both one more time before I rain fucking Satan's hellfire down on both of you. Are you fucking around?"

I blinked and looked at Cameron because I wasn't even sure how to answer that question. Of course the obvious thing to do would be deny it—on no fucking planet would that ever be the case—but the fact that she was even asking it had my brain doing somersaults. I had always thought she understood that I viewed him as a brother.

"Of course we aren't Len. Are you crazy? Freya will you please fucking say something." He growled in my direction. "I don't much like being accused of fucking the woman I consider my sister, and I really hate the fact that my own flesh and blood thinks I would betray a friend that way. Your input right now would be helpful."

"Freya?" She turned her big blue eyes on me and I could see the pleading in them.

"You think I'd do that?" The words tripped off my tongue because it was the only thing I could think of. I had believed she knew me better than I knew myself, but if she thought for even one second that I would cheat on Knox, I was clearly mistaken.

"I don't want to think it, but I heard you both and I don't know what the hell else that could mean."

I blinked a couple more times before the words I had been trying to keep to myself fell from my mouth.

"I'm pregnant."

A heavy blanket of silence fell over the room at my declaration and all I could hear was the thumping of my heart in my ears as I looked at her stunned face.

"I'm pregnant and I haven't told Knox. Cam was lecturing me about keeping it a secret." Her eyes swung from me to Cameron and he nodded just once before she looked back at me.

"Fucking hell." She breathed. "You're actually pregnant? Like with a baby pregnant?"

"There aren't any other ways you can be pregnant Len." I sighed, suddenly feeling exhausted as I leant my shoulder against the doorframe. The last four days had been a mess. I had thrown myself into work and avoided Knox at all costs. I hated myself for it, but I just didn't know how to deal with this. I hadn't been prepared to ever find myself in this situation, let alone so quickly. With everything still so new and fragile between the two of us, I was scared this would be our tipping point. I had gotten so used to having him by my side, I knew I couldn't stand to be without him, and I had absolutely no idea where this was all going to leave me.

"Fucking hell." Lennon breathed again as she sunk down on one of the wooden benches.

"You said that Len," Cameron said as he sat down opposite. "She found out on Wednesday when she threw up at the warehouse."

"Wednesday!" she exclaimed, her head swinging around so she could pin me with her eyes.

"She's trying to get her head around it," Cameron continued. "And she seems to think the best way to do it is to block everybody else out—me, you, and Knox included. It's not working though, is it Fray, because you look fucking exhausted." I let my head roll forward on my shoulders and stared down at my toes.

"I don't know what I'm supposed to do," I finally admitted out loud. It suddenly felt as though I could breathe a little easier. Lennon squeaked and then her toes came into my line of vision and her arms closed around me.

"You should have told me. We could have talked this all out by now."

"That's just it Len," I said as I stepped out of her hold. "This isn't something we can talk out. This is my problem." Her eyes widened and she frowned before she spoke again.

"I don't want to call your baby a problem so I'm just going to say this is something you need to talk out with Knox. This is part of him as well and you can't just shut him out. He is out there right now completely oblivious to the fact that you are carrying his child. Do you think that's fair?" My head snapped back to look at her. "I'm sorry if you don't want to hear this, Freya, but right now you are being selfish and stupid. That's not a good combination on anyone, least of all you."

"You don't understand."

"I understand plenty. I understand he is a good man who is in love with you. I understand that he wants to lay the world at your feet, and if you expect me to be as good as you were and keep my nose out of it, you are sadly mistaken. Knox loves you Freya. Why the hell are you tearing yourself apart over this? I'm so tired of people thinking they have to fight their wars alone."

"What do you mean Len?" Cameron asked, but even before she answered, I knew what she was going to say. There was only one thing she could have meant by that.

"Hannah handed in her resignation after I left last night. Max said she tried to talk her out of it but she couldn't." I ran my hands through my hair and blew out a breath.

"God, I knew this was going to happen." I sighed as I looked between them both. "She was upset and confused at Derail. We were talking in the bathroom and then she ran and hid in a toilet stall. I was hoping she would come to one of us before she took a leap."

"Well she didn't." Lennon sighed. "And then I went and made it worse."

"What did you do?" Cameron asked.

"I reacted out loud to Max's text and Ash went off the deep end and charged out of the house. Han hasn't been answering her phone and neither was Ash, but he just rolled in here ten minutes ago. From the state of him, I can only assume it ended really badly. Ash is drunk as hell. Gabe and Knox are trying to talk to him and get some sense out of him, but he's not exactly cooperating. It's all such a mess."

"She told me she's expected to make it work with that arsehole, that they're a perfect match." I made sure to put *perfect* in air quotes because Ross and Hannah were more like chalk and cheese than perfection. "This isn't her. This is so fucked up."

"Ash is so upset." Lennon shook her head as the door swung open beneath my hand and Mac's son Rob poked his head in.

"When you three are finished with your mothers' meeting, the fight is starting in five." Cameron nodded at him as he disappeared back through the door and then turned to us.

"Are you two going to be okay?" he asked gently.

"We'll be fine. Go." I nodded at him.

"Yeah she's right, you need to go," Lennon said. "We'll be there in a minute." Cameron pressed a hard kiss to the top of each of our heads and exited the room.

"I'm sorry I yelled at you," Lennon said as soon as the door closed behind him. "I don't really think you two would do that, but after what I heard, I just couldn't think what it could be. I didn't expect you to be…" Her voice trailed off as she stepped closer to me and clasped my hand in hers. "Talk to me Fray."

I tried to blink away the moisture in my eyes as I looked at her but failed miserably and a single tear trailed down my cheek. She sighed as she reached up and brushed it away.

"I want to help but you need to speak to me."

"I'm terrified," I whispered. "I'm so frightened of being pregnant. I'm frightened of having a baby. I'm terrified of what Knox will think and what he will say." I gulped as she squeezed my hand tighter.

"I can tell you everything will be okay but I know you won't believe me, so instead I'm going to say that whatever happens, you will always have me, you and this little baby. I will do anything and everything that you need."

I swallowed hard once more before tilting my chin up. I knew I couldn't stay in there crying all night, no matter how much I wanted to, so I would need to summon up the game face I had perfected over the years, the same one I hadn't had to use in the weeks since Knox had been with me. I couldn't give this all up; I needed more time. I needed a better setting.

"You're right." I nodded. "I know you are, and we have one boy out there hurting something fierce and another who is about to step in the ring. That is what matters tonight."

"You matter as well," she insisted.

"Tomorrow." I nodded at her and settled it with myself.

"Tomorrow."

Knox

I caught Asher's flailing body and did exactly what I should have the moment he came stumbling into the gym—I

273

manhandled him across the room as he moaned and cussed until I could shove us both out of the front doors.

"Get the fuck off me! Get off me." He thrashed wildly as I pushed him around the corner and out of full view of the car park then finally released him. He took a few shaky steps before rounding on me. "Why the fuck did you shove me out here? I'm here for the fight. I want to watch Cameron make that motherfucker eat mat!"

"You're drunk off your arse and while I don't have the first idea how you got this trashed so fast, I do know you are not staying here like this."

"And what are you going to do about it Knox? You gonna drive me home and tuck me up in bed like a good little boy?" He threw his head back, his dark hair wild and loose around his face as he barked a harsh laugh into the night. "You can fuck off if you think I'm going to disappear and stop embarrassing you."

"Just tell me what the fuck happened."

"What's the point?" he grumbled as he walked away. "I thought drinking a bottle of tequila had made me feel better but clearly that's embarrassing to someone who prides himself on being a fucking saint."

I bristled at the insult because not once had I accused him of embarrassing me, but knew I couldn't take the bait right now. Asher wanted me to fight with him to make himself feel better, but in reality, that was the last thing he needed. I had seen the look on his face as he stumbled through the doors and the pain still swimming in his eyes told me all I needed to know. In this moment, it didn't matter that we had all known he was bound to get hurt in the end; he was hurting, and he needed me more than he probably ever had before. I wanted to be there for him the way he had been there for the rest of us, I just wasn't sure how I was supposed to get through to him in this state.

"I know you're hurting man," I started as gently as I could. "But I promise you this is not the answer, because in the morning it's just going to give you one more problem."

"It's always the same with you Knox. Don't do this, don't drink that, don't use alcohol to numb the pain that feels as though it's ripping a hole right through your middle, but I tell you what," he yelled as he shoved his hands hard into my shoulders, causing me to stumble backwards. "It fucking does start to work until you start lecturing and then it all goes to hell."

"It doesn't work man. Alcohol is a depressant."

"Alcohol is a depressant," he mimicked as he paced away.

"Jesus Ash." I sighed as I scrubbed my hands over my shorn hair. "Just tell me what the fuck happened when you went round there! I want to help."

"You wanna know what happened?"

"Asher!" I warned.

"Fine!" he roared. "I went round there, I got to the front fucking door, and I rang the bell." I stepped a little closer to him as he yanked his hands through his hair. "And I heard them. I heard him telling her it was just that fucking freak, just that fucking no good, tattooed, thick as shit piece of scum she'd been wasting her time being friends with. I heard him say she'd always had a habit of picking up waifs and strays and that it was about time to put an end to it once and for all."

Anger bubbled in the pit of my stomach and my hands curled into fists as those words echoed in the air around us.

"Hannah wouldn't have—" I started to speak because there was no way I could believe Hannah had been the other side of that conversation, but Asher didn't let me continue.

"You don't have the first fucking idea how I feel right now because your girl is in there." His shoulders slumped and he turned towards the building, but not before I saw the way the light glistened off his tear-glazed eyes. "So just fucking don't Knox. Just don't."

"Asher—" I tried again as I stepped forward. My boots crunched the gravel beneath my feet as the most gut-wrenching, pain-ridden noise I had ever heard escaped him. My own heart twisted at the sound and I instinctively reached out to grasp his shoulder. As soon as I touched him, his body lurched and then spun, his fist shooting out and connecting hard with my jaw. I stumbled from the shock but managed to regain my footing in time to see his face contort even further.

"Fuck!" he roared, and I heard birds rustle in the trees as the sound went on and on. I didn't move. I don't think I even breathed as my chest tightened. The pain he was feeling was real and tangible, and there was no avoiding it as it poured out of his mouth and smothered everything, including me. I wanted to tell him it was going to be okay, but as his eyes met mine, I knew he wouldn't hear it.

"Ash—" I didn't get the chance to finish that sentence because he turned away from me and broke into a run. I let my head fall back against the concrete wall of the gym because there would be no use in me going after him. Asher wouldn't want to be found for a while.

I rubbed at my now-sore jaw as I tugged open the door and stepped back inside the gym. My eyes immediately landed on the ring and I could see that the fight was well and truly under way. I dodged the people crowded around to revel in the violence and made my way back to our table. Lennon was on her feet, hands clasped beneath her chin and bouncing on her toes as she yelled instructions to Cameron, who probably couldn't hear a word she was saying. Gabe was beside her, his hands in his pockets, no doubt to stop himself from reaching for her in her agitated state. When his eyes found mine, all I could do was shake my head.

"He hit you?" Gabe asked as he nodded towards my jaw, which was clicking every time I moved it.

"Harder than I assumed he'd be able to."

"Asher doesn't fight," Lennon interrupted.

"No, he doesn't." I dipped my head as I stepped a little closer.

"Where is he Knox?" she asked as she craned her neck to look around me.

"He ran off right after he socked me. I don't think we'll be seeing him for a while."

"Oh god." Lennon moaned and I hated seeing the pain move across her features as she turned frightened eyes to Gabe. "We have to go after him, we have to find him. He can't be on his own."

"He'll be okay baby," he reassured her, despite the fact that I wasn't sure he even believed it. "Men and women work really differently in these situations."

"No! What if he gets hurt? He was drunk and clearly not thinking straight. How can we just stand here and let him be on his own?" Her eyes swung back to mine and I shrugged because I knew the last thing he would want was a larger audience; me seeing him that way had been bad enough.

"He's going to go to one of two places Len, the flat or home to his parents."

"Then we have to call his parents."

"Baby stop!" Gabe's voice was harder than it normally was when he spoke to her as he turned her chin so she was facing him. I knew they were about to get into a long discussion, and the only thing I wanted to know was where my girl was.

"Where is she?" I asked before I lost their attention completely.

"Bar." He tipped his head in the direction of the makeshift bar that had been set up in the farthest corner and I nodded before heading in that direction.

I weaved through the hordes of people with my focus solely on finding and holding her. It felt as though I hadn't seen her in months, and I hated the way I was suddenly resenting the job she seemed to love so much. She had been working herself stupid the last few days and I hadn't been able to snatch more than a couple minutes on the phone with her.

I missed her. I missed her laugh. I missed the way she rolled her eyes at me. I missed her strength and her wit and I missed her body. If the night had taught me anything, it was that I needed to make every second count. I needed to show her we were in this for the long haul, that I wanted to start making the kind of plans with her that Gabe was making with Lennon. It hadn't been lost on me these last few days that if we lived together, I would be able to see her regardless of how much work she had. I would be able to drag her away from her laptop at some ungodly hour and take her to bed and relax her the best way I knew how, and I wanted nothing more than to be able to put those plans into action. I wanted a life with the only woman who spoke to my demons as much as my heart, and I wanted it to start yesterday.

My stomach dropped as I my eyes travelled over the sea of people at the bar. That fire orange hair was unmistakable in the sea of blondes and brunettes, and the fact that she was pressed up against the bar with some slick fucker making googly eyes at her made me want to wade right in and rip him limb from limb. My spine stiffened and every muscle pulled taut as I watched them for a minute. I knew I shouldn't go off the deep end and cause a scene like the one all those weeks ago in that dive bar, but watching her laugh at something he said was enough to tip me over the edge.

I hated the way he was looking at her, and something about the whole setup made my skin pull tight across my bones. She looked comfortable with him; they looked intimate, and to any outsider, they looked like a matched set. He was fitted out in a suit that looked as though it cost more than I would ever want to drop on an item of clothing, and his hair was slicked back in the way all the models wore it. Freya was done up to the nines in a strawberry-red blouse with a bow at the neck and a pair of leather-look trousers. I had no clue why the universe was being such a twisted son of a bitch, but I couldn't lose her. I didn't want to end up the way Gabe had or the way Asher was right now. The pain I had felt second hand from him was enough to bring me to my knees, but losing her would be what ended me. That thought was the only one playing on repeat in my mind as I made my way to where she was standing. When those bottle-green eyes lifted to meet mine, I felt my abdomen contract harshly at the way the arsehole took a step closer to her.

"Knox," she said breathily.

"Who the fuck are you?" I barked at the jackass who was now holding out a glass for her to take.

"Dale, who are you?" I felt the ache in my jaw intensify as I ground my back teeth together at the cocky way he asked it.

"I'm her boyfriend, so I suggest you take your wandering fucking eyes and your drinks and fuck off."

"Knox what the hell are you doing?" she exclaimed as she shoved at my chest, pushing me away from them both slightly. "You need to calm the hell down right now." She growled at me before turning back to the suit. "I apologise on his behalf, tonight has been—"

"You don't speak for me; I can speak for myself."

"And right now that is what I am most afraid of. You need to go sit down right now."

My spine stiffened as I looked down at her, and all manner of unbidden thoughts began to riot in my mind over just how quickly she wanted to get rid of me. I tried to breathe through them but failed miserably when words started to tumble out of my mouth.

"Is that what you want? You want me to fuck off, is that it? Because you could have just said so."

"I have no idea what the hell you are talking about right now!" she yelled back as the bell behind me dinged and the crowd erupted into cheers. The fight was clearly over, but mine was just beginning.

"You know damn well what I am talking about!" I yelled as I slammed my fist down on the bar behind her. She flinched but regained her composure quickly.

"You are being a jackass. You need to back off. Go sit down!"

"So that you can go back to talking to Dale here?" I was being an arsehole and even though I could acknowledge it, I couldn't seem to stop. I had believed I was walking over here to make sure I kept her, but now every word from my mouth seemed to be pushing her away.

"Are you serious?" she screamed, and it felt as though she'd slapped me. "He's my fucking client!" I rolled back onto the soles of my feet and looked between the two of them.

"So that's where you've been the last few days is it? Working with him? All those late nights and missed calls, were they all because you were with him?"

Freya's face contorted into something I didn't even recognise, and her chest quivered beneath the material of her top. I wanted to take it back the instant the words were out of my mouth. I wanted to tell her I was sorry and beg for her forgiveness, but the suit started talking before I had the chance.

"Listen mate—"

"I suggest you fuck off," I growled at him without taking my eyes off Freya, but I caught him flash her an apologetic look before turning tail and walking away.

"I cannot believe you just did that." She shook her head before turning her back on me to retrieve the glass from where he had discarded it on the bar top.

"Are you fucking him?" I ground the words out and they felt like acid on my tongue, but I needed her to tell me she wasn't. I needed to hear her tell me I was being an idiot and that she would never do that to me, because I felt adrift. I had no idea how I had made it to this point so quickly, but I needed her to grab hold of the wheel to stop me from running us right off the tracks.

"Fuck you!" she screamed as she spun on the spot and tossed the warm liquid from the glass in her hand straight in my face. I blinked as it stung my eyes and opened them to find her face pushed into mine. "First you embarrass me in front of Dale by acting like a Neanderthal, and then you have the fucking audacity to accuse me of cheating on you. Fuck you Knox. You don't get to accuse me of shit." She sucked in a breath and I opened my mouth to speak, to beg forgiveness for yet another idiotic move, but she beat me to it. "It's nice to know how you see me though. It's nice to know that no matter how much of myself I share with you or how hard I try to be better, you will always see me as the girl who is willing to drop her knickers for any man who shows her a little bit of attention."

"Fire I—" I reached out for her, my fingertips grazing the bare skin of her arm before she yanked her body away from me as though my touch had burnt her.

"No!" she yelled. "You don't get to touch me. You never get to touch me again!" Her voice broke on the last word and I saw a single tear escape from the corner of her eye. The sight of that one glistening drop of water as it rolled over her cheekbone had my heart stopping in my chest as she shoved past me and disappeared into the crowd. I hadn't realised we had drawn as much attention as we clearly had until Lennon's voice screeched over the top of the light hum of conversation.

"What did you do to her?" she demanded as she shoved me square in the chest.

"I fucked up," I said as I stumbled backwards.

"I promised her you wouldn't hurt her." She spun on her heel as the words echoed around me and ran for the exit. I put one foot in front of the other and prepared myself to follow when Gabe's hand landed heavy on my shoulder.

"I have to go…" I gestured in the direction the two girls had gone, but he shook his head.

"Right now you will make this worse than it already is. What you're going to do is let Til handle Freya, and you're going to sit your ass down and tell me what the fucking hell just happened." I couldn't have argued with him if I'd wanted to because I knew I had just watched my heart run out that door. I hadn't wanted to lose her to someone else, but I had brought it about by my own hand instead.

"I can't lose her man. I can't fucking lose her. She's everything."

"After all that, I'm not sure that's your call right now. Tomorrow I'll help you however I can, but tonight, no." He shook his head and grabbed my shoulder. "Tonight we leave her with my girl and we straighten your head out."

chapter
SIXTEEN

Freya

I needed to tell Lennon she had missed a spot on the ceiling when she had been decorating, but the thought of crawling out of bed seemed harder than it should have. I shifted my head on the pillow so my eyes were fixed on the closed curtains of the window instead, and I tried to feel anything other than the soul-deep ache I was sure was slowly suffocating me.

I hadn't been prepared for any of this. I had watched Lennon go through this pain and I had helped her in all the ways I could, but now when feeling it for myself I wasn't even sure how she hadn't banished me forever when I had been sticking my nose in. I hadn't had the first clue what it felt like to be here, and now that I did, I knew all the tequila, pretty dresses, and ice cream in the world could never help.

I'd only made it into the car park before I broke down. I had been leant against the wall when Lennon found me, her face murderous and her hands shaking as she pulled me against her and all but dragged me to her car. I hadn't even questioned her as she drove us away, and when I realised she was bringing me to her house instead of back to the flat, I was grateful. I didn't want anything near me that reminded me of Knox.

I let her help me take off my makeup and loan me a t-shirt and a pair of shorts to wear to bed. When she curled up underneath the duvet beside me, I hadn't sent her away, but that was last night and this morning was different. I knew I needed to get up and try to figure out how I was going to sort this mess out; I couldn't put her and Gabriel in the middle any more than they already were, but I just couldn't seem to muster up the energy. There was a dull throbbing pain that had been present in my brain all night, and it seemed to be getting worse, not better. My eyes hurt and my lips were dry, and all I wanted to do was curl up in a ball and hide away from it all. I had known all along that he would have the power to level me, but I hadn't been prepared for just how desperately alone it would make me feel.

"Knock knock."

Lennon was standing in the now-open bedroom door with a mug in one hand and a plate in the other. The sight of food made me feel physically sick and there was a lump in my throat the size of a boulder that had been there since those words fell out of his mouth. I had never imagined he would accuse me of something like that. I had made him so many silent promises and been under the illusion that I had shown him just what he meant to me on countless occasions, but clearly all my efforts had been pointless because he hadn't even given me a chance to explain.

"I brought you tea and toast. I googled what you could have and I figured coffee was right out the window." She settled herself on top of the duvet, put the plate down next to me, and held the mug out for me to take. "This is a really stupid question, but did you sleep at all?"

I busied myself with taking a long sip of the tea I really didn't want before I answered.

"No."

"I guessed you wouldn't have. Did you hear from him?" Her eyes skipped over to my phone, which was lying motionless on the bedside table. I had given up checking it at about four o'clock that morning because there had been nothing from him—no apology, no take-backs, just silence.

"Not a sound." I put the mug down on the table and tugged the duvet up a little higher. It was June so there was no real reason for me to even have a duvet, but Lennon was kind enough not to mention the fact I was basically creating a personal sauna. Her head dipped and she nudged the plate towards me.

"Try to eat something Fray. I know you don't want to and I know you feel sick as hell, but you need to eat."

"I'm not hungry Len."

"I know you think you're not hungry but—"

"I said I'm not hungry Len. It's not that I think I'm not hungry, I'm just not hungry," I snapped and her chin dipped before she carried on speaking.

"Look, I know, okay. I've been there. The thought of doing anything at all is painful, and I'm not asking for you to get up or get dressed or to do anything besides eat some toast."

"Lennon…" I sighed as I shoved my hands through my hair and looked up at the ceiling.

"Freya please, it's not just about you anymore." She was almost pleading now, and I couldn't take hearing those words from her mouth. I moved my eyes away from her and they settled on her dodgy ceiling again.

"You missed a spot when you were painting, right there." I pointed up at the slightly darker patch and refused to look at her.

"I'll get on that," she said quietly.

"Good. Where's Gabriel?" It was the question I dreaded asking but needed answering. I was almost certain I hadn't heard him come home the night before, but I supposed there was always a possibility he could quietly get into his own house.

"He didn't come home last night."

"Fuck!" I exclaimed as I sat forward, my fingers tugging at my hair. "This is exactly what I was trying to avoid. I didn't want anyone to feel as though they had to pick sides and I told him that."

I tossed the duvet off and climbed out of bed. My body felt weak from the hours I had spent crying and going over every single detail of the past months in my mind, but I forced it away. I clenched my hands at my sides and started to pace. I caught sight of Lennon's eyebrows lowering slightly, but she didn't say anything or make any move to have me sit back down.

"I've been such a fucking idiot, such a huge fucking idiot! It was inevitable you guys would get pulled into this when it went bad. Knox just made everything seem so fucking easy and before I even knew what was happening, I was falling down the rabbit hole and he was catching me." I dragged my hands down my face, causing the stinging flesh around my eyes to crack and send little arrows of pain zinging through me. "For the first time in so long I wanted to believe things would be okay. I wanted to believe I could have all the things you'd always told me I could. I was changing my whole life and I was okay with it. I was okay with us. I was more than okay with us. I thought..." My voice broke and I pressed my fist to my mouth, trying to cough without throwing up all over her beige carpet.

"Come sit down Fray, have a drink." Her voice was soft as she patted the bed in front of her. I shook my head in the negative and carried on with my rant.

"I thought he was it Len. I thought we had finally made it and then this week happened and now it's all so beyond fucked up. I don't know what to do. I don't know how I'm supposed to deal with any of this." This time when my voice broke, the tears slipped down my cheeks along with it. I was powerless to stop them and I was suffocating under the weight on my chest

"That's why you have us." She tugged on my hand and pulled me back down onto the bed. "That's why you thinking you would ever be able to keep any of us out of this is crazy. None of us are taking sides. All we want is what is best for both of you." She pushed my hair away from my sweaty face and cupped my cheek in her hand. "Gabe called me last night when you were in the shower and told me he wasn't coming home. I know exactly where he is and exactly what he is doing." Her smile was gentle when I looked back at her.

"What is he doing?" My voice was rough from the tears that were still falling down my cheeks.

"Trying to figure out what the hell went wrong in Knox's brain last night. I don't know what happened and I don't know why he said any of the things he did, but I do know there is no possible way he meant any of them. We have all seen the way he is with you. I've watched him watching you when you aren't looking. It's beautiful and it's fragile and you're both so bloody hot-headed it's like holding a match to a fuse most of the time, but this thing between you is so worth it."

"He accused me of cheating on him, Len, not half an hour after you accused me of the same thing. That has to say something about me, doesn't it?"

"I was waiting for that," she said as she moved the plate of uneaten toast off the bed and propped herself up on the pillows next to me. "I was being an idiot last night; it was probably one of the stupidest things that has ever come out of my mouth, and I am sorrier than you will ever know that I asked it out loud. I don't even know why I did except that my head was all over the place with Hannah and Asher. Can you forgive me?" I nodded and she reached for my hand, twining our fingers together. "I don't know what happened with Knox and I know I can't speak for him, but maybe it was something similar, maybe that was his moment of idiocy the way it was mine. I've never known him to be insecure but—"

"I have," I admitted as memories of the night he had told me all about his life flashed through my mind. "He thought he was going to lose me once before and it frightened me to see how soft his underbelly is despite the fact that no one was attacking him. Last night, for some reason, he saw Dale as a threat…" My voice trailed off because I just couldn't quite get my head around it.

"Oh." She sighed.

"But this isn't just about us anymore and I know he doesn't know that, but last night frightened me." I fixed my eyes on that spot on the ceiling once more as I gave voice to the thoughts that had been swirling in my brain. "Let's just say that deep down that is what he thinks of me and this whole time he's been masking it."

"Hypothetically right?" she asked.

"Yeah. Hypothetically, say he still thinks I'm that girl I was all those months ago and that what he's been saying he feels for me isn't enough to keep those thoughts at bay…where does that leave me? I'm carrying his baby, but if he thinks I'm a whore that's going to mean DNA tests, and if he can't be with me, it means shared custody and visitation. How can I bring a baby into that? Life is shit enough without all of that added on top, and this baby is innocent. It has no idea how fucked up its parents really are. This baby didn't ask for any of our shit, so how can I inflict it on it?"

"Can I just say that I think this hypothetical game really sucks and I don't want to play it?"

"You can say it, but I'm going to ask you to anyway." I sighed as her grip tightened on my hand and she rolled onto her side to face me.

"Fine. Hypothetically, if he thinks any of those things, I will castrate him with my bare hands. I mean, I won't even bother with a knife, I'll just rip the bloody thing right off." She made a yanking motion in the air with her hand and I couldn't fight the quirking of my lips.

"Be serious," I moaned.

"I was being serious, but okay, if he thinks any of those things, he's the worst kind of idiot, and I never had

Knox pegged as one of those. I'm not going to touch on the DNA test part because that goes hand in hand with the castration, and as for inflicting you two on that baby, I think it could do far worse." I rolled onto my side at that and found her blue eyes gazing back at me, open and honest. "I know what a fucked up parent is. We all do, Fray, and yeah, you two might be a little nuts sometimes, but you would never make a child feel the way you were made to feel. Do you think he would? Deep down inside, do you think he would ever do anything to make your child's life unhappy?" I shook my head as she stared back at me. "I think you two need to work on yourselves and your relationship, but I don't think you will ever have to worry about the love that is waiting for this little baby when it makes its way into the world." She reached out and gently rested her hand against my still flat belly.

"There's nothing to feel yet," I whispered as more tears slid from the corners of my eyes.

"Only my niece or nephew." Her own smile was watery as she kept her eyes on my stomach. "We will all be behind you two while you figure this out, and if you need someone to lean on, you know I will be there, any minute of any hour of any day, because this is what everything has been about. We're growing up and we are getting the things we always deserved."

"Do you think we can fix what happened last night?" I asked as I rested my hand over the top of hers.

"I do." She nodded. "I might need to apologise for shoving him." My eyes widened at those words and she let out a soft laugh. "I mean I'll apologise if it hurt, but I won't say sorry for doing it, because he deserved a lot worse."

"I can't believe you shoved him. I'm surprised you didn't get hurt—he's the equivalent of a brick wall."

"You should know by now that I will do anything for you Freya Anson." She winked. "Getting back to the question though, I do think it's fixable. I think last night was a horrible mess, but you two will be able to straighten your shit out if you just talk."

"I'm really proud of you," I said almost to myself, but I knew she had heard me when her blonde eyebrows rose slightly. "I'm proud of what you've become and all the things you've achieved, and I'm so happy you got your fairy tale."

"And you'll get yours," she said with more conviction than I felt. "You two just need to talk this out. Trust me Fray, he loves you, and last night was just a moment of madness."

"It hurt though," I murmured, and her face softened further.

"I know it did, it would have hurt anyone, but I know what all of this has meant to you. Just promise me you will talk to him. Tell him about the baby and let him grovel at your feet, because he will put himself there, I promise you."

"How can you be so certain?" I asked as I rolled back until my eyes were on the ceiling again.

"Because it's how those men are made. He'll be here soon, and then all this will just be a bad memory."

I allowed her words to wrap around me and keep me warm for a minute before those niggling self-doubts I had been wrestling with found their way back into my mind.

"What if he doesn't want a baby Len?" She sighed heavily and I could feel her shaking her head, but none of them could know for certain if this was how he saw his future.

"Knox could make things picture perfect, but when you hold that little baby in your arms for the first time, with or without him, I know your whole world will become unrecognisable. You will do anything and everything to give that baby the life we didn't have. You are going to be happy no matter what happens with Knox because you'll be holding a piece of yourself in your arms. I will always call myself your sister, but I don't share your blood. I don't share your DNA but that baby does, and you'll be connected with a piece of you again. While all of that is going on, I'll be standing in that hospital room so fucking proud I don't think I'll even be able to see straight, and I'll have my I-told-you-so look on my face."

"Can you promise me something?" I asked after a few moments of silence had passed.

"That depends on what it is."

"If I do this and I'm not good at it, promise me you'll step in." I held my breath as I waited for her to answer, but I didn't have to wait long before she was bolting upright and looking down at me.

"Freya no—"

"Just hear me out," I begged as I sat up so we were face to face. "If he walks away and I'm useless, then I need you to promise me you will step in. I need you to promise me that whatever happens, this baby will have somewhere safe that it can call home. I need to know that."

"I could never take your baby," she whispered, her voice broken by the tears welling in her eyes.

"It's not taking when I'm asking for your promise Len. I just need to know…I need to know that even if I'm a failure, this baby will never have to bear the brunt of it. Please just promise me—I wouldn't trust anyone else."

"Freya look at me," she demanded as she caught my face between her hands. "I'll always help you, but I will never, ever take. That has to be enough for you. You can live here with the baby if that is what you need to do, but you will always be the only mama it ever knows. Let that be enough if it ever comes to it, please."

"I want him to want this." My body shook as another sob ran through me, and she caught me up in her arms and cradled my head against her shoulder.

"He will Fray," she whispered. "All this hurting will be over soon."

Knox

"Are you sure you're ready for this?" Gabe turned to look at me as I pulled the truck onto his driveway and yanked up the handbrake.

"I've been ready to do this since last night. You're the only reason I stayed away as long as I did."

"She needed time, man. She needed to process the shitty things you said to each other, and she needed to do it without you in her ear." He quirked an eyebrow at me as I rubbed my sweaty hands on my jeans. I knew I would have a fight on my hands once I got inside, and there was no sense in starting one with him just to prove a point.

"You were right and I get it, but now I want to go inside and see my girl."

"You and me both." He shoved open the car door at the same time as me and I followed him up to his front door. His key was hovering over the top lock when it swung open from the inside and Lennon appeared. Her blonde hair was tied back and she was wearing what I could only assume was a pair of pyjamas. "Til." He breathed her name as though they had been apart for years, not just one night, and he leant down to press a kiss to her lips. I saw her fingers skim across his chest before her blue eyes found mine and she pulled away from him.

"I need to talk to Knox." Her voice brokered no argument as he pressed another, gentler kiss to the top of her head and disappeared into the house. I was about to take a step towards her when she pulled the door to behind her and came out onto the front step.

"Len—"

"Before you speak, let me just make a couple things really clear to you." I nodded my acceptance of her terms because I knew trying to speak over the top of her was going to cause me more trouble in the long term. "I like you, I always have, and when she told me she had finally given in to the thing between you both, I couldn't have been any happier if I'd tried. I have always liked you for her, you couldn't have been a better match if I had picked you from a magazine, but last night was a joke."

"Last night was a shit show."

"It was more than that."

"I fucked up Len and I'm sorry, all right. I know I shouldn't have done it, but I can't turn back the clock. All I can do is try to move forward and make it right." I could only hope that was going to be enough for everyone involved, because it was all I had. I could wish all I wanted that the previous night had never happened, but it was done and gone now, and I couldn't alter it.

"It's not going to be as easy as clicking your fingers Knox. You fucked up bad last night. I can't even begin to wrap my head around it, but I will tell you something, and you need to listen really good." Her finger poked the centre of my chest as she went toe to toe with me. "I didn't like the side of you I saw last night, and if that's the man you are and this whole other persona I believed in and trusted is a lie, you need to turn around and walk away. I will not let you or anyone else hurt her ever again, and you better believe I will wake the demons from hell to make your life as painful as possible if you ever pull a fucked up stunt like that ever again." I felt my eyes widen as her words hit me with the force of knives. "I'm not saying you two aren't allowed to fight or argue like normal people, but when you go as low as you did last night, you've gone too far. I will always protect her."

"What you saw last night…that's not the man I truly am. You know me, the real me."

"I really hope so, because she deserves the man I thought I knew, not the one you became last night." I swallowed hard as she spun on her heel and walked back into the house. I had taken my eye off the ball by not realising she would have it in for me today, and now I knew I had more than one person to make things up to.

"I'm going to fix this, Len. I'm going to make this all right again."

"You'd better," she said as her hand landed on the kitchen door. "She's upstairs, second bedroom on the right." She pushed the door open and slipped inside before I managed to work up the courage to walk up the stairs.

I had gone over and over what I wanted to say all night. I hadn't slept for a second because I needed every bit of thinking time I could get my hands on. I needed to be ready for anything, because chances were I was going to have an almighty fight on my hands to get my girl to see that I was truly sorry.

I lifted my hand and knocked as gently as I could against the piece of wood now separating us.

"Yeah." She sounded weary and her voice was rough from what I could only assume was crying.

I took another deep breath, cracked my neck as though I was about to walk into the ring, and pushed down on the handle. As the door swung inwards, my breath caught somewhere between my chest and my mouth at the sight of her. She had never looked smaller or more fragile than she did sitting with her knees to her chest against the headboard of one of the enormous beds Gabe and Lennon had brought to kit the place out. I wanted to reach for her and pull her into my arms, but I knew better than to start off with something as domineering as that.

I padded across the floor and stopped as I reached the bed. I smoothed the duvet out slightly and took a seat on the edge, never once taking my eyes off her. I had no idea what to say now that I was sitting in front of her and those big green eyes of hers were looking back at me filled with pain and fear. Every carefully planned sentence and well-thought-through explanation for my behaviour fled from my brain because all I could see was her.

"You really hurt me last night." Her voice was full of pain as she murmured the words into the space between us, and there was no denying how true those words were when I heard her say them. "You hurt me worse than anyone has hurt me in a long time, and I gave you that power Knox. I allowed you in past the walls and the armour I put up to protect myself. I allowed you to slip under them and get to the heart of me, and last night you used that against me." Her hands clasped on top of her knees as her voice wobbled, and I squeezed my eyes shut at the sound of her words. When I opened them again, her bottom lip was trembling and trapped between her teeth.

"I abused the power you gave me in a way I promised you I wouldn't. I couldn't be any sorrier for that if I tried. I wanted to come last night, but Gabe was right when he told me I couldn't. I needed to calm down and get my head back on straight because you deserve so much more than what I gave you. I'm supposed to show you I love and respect you. I'm supposed to treat you the way I promised I would, and last night I broke that. I'm here now, though, because I love you and I couldn't stay away any longer. You probably need more time, but I just can't give you that. I need to be here and take whatever you want to throw at me because I deserve it all and more. I'm ready to get down on my knees for you and I will do it without blinking."

Her eyes fluttered closed and her hand lifted to wipe the tears from her cheeks before I continued.

"I don't want to be the man you saw last night. I watched those things happen to Viva day in and day out, and it broke pieces of her she never got back. I watched the light go out in her eyes as he took the power she gave him and used it against her. I watched him break her and I refuse to do that to you. You are everything, Fire. You are the most beautiful, vibrant, strongest, most vulnerable woman I know, and you deserve the world at your feet, not me behaving like a brain-dead caveman. I had no reason to doubt you or accuse you last night, and I hold my hands up to that. Everything that happened was in my head. I saw him standing there looking the way he did and you looked so pretty and polished together, and I don't even have a good enough reason for my behaviour because I just snapped."

"I don't want him Knox. I never wanted him."

"I know." I sighed as I ran my hands over my scalp. "Last night was about me. It was about all the ways I don't believe I deserve you. I was an idiot because just the fact that you stay with me should prove that I do." I blew out a harsh breath as I turned my head to look at her again. "I know now that the only way to not hurt you again the way I did last night is to fix myself."

"I don't understand." Her voice was shaky and there was lingering confusion in her eyes as she stared at me.

"What happened last night was about all the ways I have hidden and covered up my past in the vain hope that it will go away. I can tell you that I'm sorry and that I will do whatever it takes to get you to see that I am, but those are just words, and words are easily forgotten or manipulated." I tugged my phone from my pocket and opened the text Viva had sent me after our long phone call before handing my phone to her. I hated the way her hands shook as she took it. "Words are one thing, but showing you is something different. I will apologise to you every night if you need me to. I will get down on my hands and knees and beg. I will buy you anything and take you anywhere, but while I'm doing all of those superficial things, I'm going to be doing this as well so that we never have to suffer a night like last night ever again."

"What is this?" she asked as she held the phone back out for me to take. I clasped my fingers around the plastic and her hand as I shifted my body closer to her.

"He's a therapist. He's the guy who got Viva back on her feet. I called her at three o'clock this morning when I couldn't stand the sound of my own brain anymore. I told her what I did and that I was afraid of what I could become. She knows losing you isn't an option for me and when she was done flipping out on me, she told me I had to be serious about this. When I came off the phone, she sent me his number and told me to sort it out once and for all. I know I need to do something to truly break this cycle or I risk losing you forever—if I haven't already." I couldn't read her face as the words tumbled from my mouth, and it felt as though something was coming loose inside me. I needed a clue as to what she was thinking because without her, this would all fall apart. "If baring all the dirty, ugly parts of me to a shrink is what I need to do to give us the life we deserve, then I'm going to go all in. Without you, I won't work."

I kept my hand wrapped tightly around hers as I watched the words I had said filter through. I could practically hear the wheels turning in her mind as she processed what this all meant.

"You're going to go to a therapist because of me," she said finally, her eyes not wavering from mine as she spoke.

"Not because of you. I'm going so we have the chance we deserve."

"You'd do that for us?" She swallowed.

"I would do anything for us, Fire girl. I will do anything to make this up to you. I want us forever and I will fix the broken parts of me to do it. I hate that I made you cry." I moved closer and cradled her face in my hands as I gently pressed my lips to her forehead. "I love you and I'm sorry." I shifted my head until our noses were touching and I was breathing in the air she was breathing out.

"I'm sorry too," she whispered, and I felt my brows furrow as she pulled herself away from me and looked down at her hands. "I have been keeping something from you, Knox."

I bit down on my tongue to stop myself from interrupting her and watched as she twisted the fabric of the t-shirt she was wearing between her fingers.

"I just didn't know how to tell you. I didn't know what you were going to say and I was so frightened that I just avoided you and kept my mouth shut. I didn't know what else to do and I'm sorry. I can't go back and change it, but I can't let you take the whole blame for last night when I played my part as well." Her eyes came up to meet mine and I could almost feel the apprehension that was swirling in them settle around me like a heavy cloak. I swallowed hard past the dryness of my throat and reached out for her hand.

"Whatever it is, we will work it out together. Not having you isn't an option for me. I can't live the rest of my nights like last night, so we will figure this out together." I knew I was making promises I didn't understand and it probably wasn't my smartest move, but knowing I couldn't live without her was a hell of a driving force. Her slender fingers clenched tighter around mine as though she thought I might disappear, and as her mouth opened and she whispered out those words, I was glad she was holding on to me so tightly. I needed something to tether me to this moment and to this earth because those words were ones I had never expected to hear.

"Say that again," I said, my voice hoarse as I forced it up my throat.

"I said I'm pregnant. I don't know if—"

I swallowed whatever else she was about to say when I crashed my mouth into hers and took everything she had to give. I kissed her until her arms wound their way around my neck. I kissed her until she went soft and pliant beneath my hands, and I kissed her until my body was cradled between her knees.

"I think that means you're happy." She half giggled as tears slipped from her eyes faster than I could catch them with my thumbs.

"I never thought I would see the day a woman told me those words, Fire girl, especially not a woman like you. I can't explain how I feel right now." I bent my head again so I could take her lips more gently this time, making sure to keep my eyes on hers the whole time. "Talk to me beautiful, tell me what is going on in that pretty head of yours."

"I'm scared Knox."

"And that's why you have me, and I'm not going anywhere, not again. I'm going to be by your side, holding your hand until the last breath leaves my lungs." Her chest rose sharply and I knew she was fighting a sob as I ghosted my lips over her cheek and towards her ear. "I'll be the one who stays up with you at night and talks through every fear you have. I'll be the one who comes to every appointment, every scan, every antenatal class, and every baby shop. I'll be the one who holds your hand when you bring our life into the world, and I won't even moan if you punch me." She giggled in my ear and I pulled back so I could see her face, my fingers tangling in her hair. "I'm going to love you through all of this and beyond that, and as for this little baby"—I shifted to my side and splayed my hand across her belly—"this is the greatest gift anyone has ever given me, and you're the only one I would ever want to share it with."

"I was so scared for no reason." I could hear the pain in her voice as she spoke.

"You didn't know this was my dream because I never wanted to force it on you, beautiful." I laid my head next to hers as my thumb stroked the soft skin of her stomach. "But this is the life I always dreamt of."

"I love you." My heart thudded hard at the sound of the words I had longed to hear falling from her mouth. My lips pressed against her cheek as a certainty I had never felt before settled around me. For the first time in forever, I knew things were exactly the way they were meant to be.

"I love you more, Fire girl," I whispered as I tugged her body against mine and held her tighter than I even knew I could.

Epilogue

Knox

As I made my way back up the stairs, I could hear the soft sounds of "Silent Night" emanating from behind the half-closed door of the nursery. I already knew what I would find when I pushed open the door and I wasn't disappointed as I leant against the doorframe. I had told Freya to get some rest, but as usual, she hadn't listened to a word I said. She was sitting in the rocking chair by the window, our precious pink bundle nestled in the cradle of her arms as they both watched the light dusting of snow that was starting to cover our garden.

Us agreeing on a house we both liked had happened quicker than I'd thought it would, and I was so glad I had put in an offer well above the asking price to ensure we got it. It had been a no-brainer that we would check out the place that had gone up for sale just ten minutes from Lennon and Gabe, and the minute we'd walked through the front door, I had known it was going to be ours. It wasn't as big as theirs but it was everything we needed, and it had meant we could ensure that the nursery was ready for our new arrival.

It was a good thing it had been so fast, really, because Ivylin Jasmyn Anson-Sutton had decided she couldn't possibly wait until the New Year to make her big arrival— she'd come kicking and screaming into the world almost four weeks early and completely perfect.

I had been the one to freak out when Freya woke me in the middle of the night to assure me she hadn't pissed the bed. All along we had been planning for Freya to panic, but neither of us had given much thought to how hard it was going to hit me. She had been calm and had breathed through labour pains I was almost certain would have levelled me while yelling instructions at me until I managed to bundle her into the car and get her to the hospital. As soon as we'd arrived, we'd been whisked into a room, and the midwife had announced with a raised eyebrow that I clearly had a woman with a high pain threshold on my hands because she was already eight centimetres dilated.

I would have liked to have been able to say I remembered everything from that declaration on, but honestly it was all a blur of Freya's face contorted in pain and the way her mouth had looked as she clamped her lips together and stuck her teeth into them to prevent herself from screaming the entire ward down. I had held her hand the way I had promised I would, and by the time Ivylin's first cries broke through the hum of conversation in the room, I had lost feeling in most of my fingers. Every shred of discomfort evaporated the moment I looked down and saw her beautiful face staring back at me. Her tiny hands were clenched into fists, and even though she was earlier than we would have liked, her face was scrunched up and her legs were kicking out as what could only have been described as a battle cry tore from her lips.

Freya's body had gone stiff beneath my hands as our little girl was whisked away to where the neonatal team were waiting for her, and I had been left to whisper in her ear that everything was going to be okay. I had expected her to be taken away from us and put into an incubator where we couldn't get our hands on her, but instead she was wrapped in a towel and placed on Freya's chest. She was perfect and exactly the little warrior I had expected Freya to bring into the world.

"This was your Auntie Jasmyn's favourite song when she was a tiny baby, Ivylin." Freya's soft voice broke through my memories as I watched her rock our daughter gently in her arms. "Mummy used to sing this to her when she couldn't sleep or when she got sad, and now Mummy can sing it to you too if you'd like her to. I can't sing as good as your Auntie Leni, but I will always do my best for you baby girl."

I watched her slender fingers lift and stroke over that soft baby face I had sat up the past few nights staring at. Having read all the books in publication on what to expect when having a baby and what the best things to do for them were, she had set her heart on breastfeeding, but it had become apparent very quickly that it was not going to work for either of my girls. With tears in her eyes and frustration on her face, she had buried her head into my chest and begged me to help her. As soon as those words escaped her mouth, I had left her in the capable hands of Viva, Emmy, and Lennon and had taken myself to the nearest shop to stock up on all things baby-feeding related. One breast pump, a steriliser, and far too many bottles later, I had finally managed to make both my girls smile, even if one was only due to milk drunkenness. I couldn't deny that part of me was glad it meant I could take night feeds, because I had come to realise there was little better in life than being able to peer down at my daughter's face in the dead of night and have her look up at me like she had the first clue who I was.

"Mummy loves you so much already, baby Ivy. I never knew I would love you so much it hurt. I'm going to take the best care of you that I can. I'm sorry your first Christmas isn't a better one, but I promise Daddy and I will make up for it next year. You were just a little too impatient for us to catch up with you."

Freya had cried about that to me two nights ago, and I hated the way she was beating herself up over the smallest things. The midwives at the hospital, the health visitor who had been round yesterday, Emmy, and Viva had all assured me it was completely normal, but I couldn't stop myself from resenting the fact that I couldn't take those worries and hurts from her so she could simply enjoy the first few days of our daughter's life.

"You already take the best care of her Fire girl," I said softly as I pushed off the door frame and made my way across the room.

"How long have you been standing there?" she asked as I pressed a kiss to her temple and then to the forehead of our baby girl, who was wide awake and staring up at us with wide green eyes. They were already heading in the direction of being the same colour as her mother's, but the hair on her head was dark like mine.

I stroked my finger over her tiny little fist as I wrapped my hand around the back of Freya's neck, bringing both my girls into the protective circle I had made for them.

"Dance with me," I whispered as the song started to play from the beginning again. I didn't give Freya a chance to argue as I helped her up from the chair, and to my surprise, she didn't question me as I swayed the three of us from side to side.

"She's so easy to love Knox. She's so beautiful." I was becoming more accustomed to Freya's tears these days, but it didn't make it hurt any less to see them, even if they were happy tears.

"No tears on Christmas Day beautiful," I warned her as I pressed a hard kiss to her mouth. It had been a few months since I had had her the way I was used to. I knew it would probably be a few more before we could get that back, but that didn't mean my desire for her had dampened at all. If anything, I wanted her more fiercely than I ever had. I loved this woman more than ever before, and every day that passed I knew it was going to consume me more. She was everything I had ever wanted, and now we were living our own version of a dream.

"Hey Ivy girl," I said gently as I looked down at her. "Are you going to tell Mummy she's silly for thinking this isn't the best Christmas ever?" She blinked up at me and her tiny fist waved in the air. "See, even she thinks you're being daft."

"I just want her life to be perfect. I want her to have everything, always."

"And she will," I assured her, because I knew there was no other way Ivylin's life was going to look with all of us in it.

"Sugar," Freya exclaimed as she caught sight of the clock on the wall. "We need to get ready to go, Gabriel and Leni are expecting us. Can you hold her while I go get something that doesn't have baby sick on it to wear?"

"We don't have to go you know. We could just stay here the three of us," I said as I took Ivylin from her arms. "I can rustle us up some dinner and we can watch a movie in bed with our baby girl."

"No!" she said as she pressed her hand to the centre of my chest.

"You're exhausted and you only gave birth three days ago. Everyone will understand."

"I will live, Knox, but she will never get a first Christmas again. Being with her family today is the best we can do for her. We are going." She pushed onto her tiptoes and kissed my mouth before heading out of the nursery.

I made my way over to the speakers and turned them off before looking down at Ivylin. She looked so small and fragile lying in my arms, and I knew I would always do anything in my power to protect her.

"You keep a mean secret baby girl. You didn't give your mama one clue about the surprise we have in store for her." I kissed her sweet-smelling head as she gurgled. "Merry Christmas Ivylin. Daddy loves you more than he knew he could."

"I'm ready," Freya said as I stepped out into the hallway. Her hair was scooped up on top of her head in a way it never would have been before, but she had never looked more beautiful to me.

"Good, because I have a surprise for you."

"A surprise?" she asked as I led us down the stairs.

"Yep, right through there." I nodded in the direction of the closed kitchen doors and saw her eyebrows furrow as she stepped forward and pressed down on the door handle.

I couldn't fight the smile on my face as Lennon appeared in the now-open doorway. Her cheeks were pink and she was wearing an awful Christmas jumper with a gingerbread woman in a tutu stitched on the front.

"Merry Christmas," she squealed before turning and hollering back into the kitchen. "Shut the damn doors now it's freezing in here."

"What is going on?" Freya asked as she looked between the two of us. "What are you doing here?"

"We all agreed with Knox when he said he thought we should bring Christmas to you and Ivylin." She smiled over Freya's shoulder at me as she pulled her into a hug. "We have everything under control in here, and all you need to do is relax."

"We?" Freya looked back at me.

"Everyone is here for us." I smiled at her as her eyes began to shine again.

"What do you mean when you say everyone? Is Hannah…" There was a note of hope in her voice that made me instantly regret my choice of words, and I knew she could tell when her smile dropped a little bit.

"I know you miss her," I said softly as I pressed a kiss to the top of her head. "We all miss her, but everyone else is here."

"Even Ash?" she asked.

"Even Ash." I nodded, and that was all it took for her to turn on her heel and disappear into the mayhem of our kitchen and dining room. I shifted my attention to Lennon as she stepped further into the hallway.

"Everything is ready for your girls Mr Sutton." She smiled as she pressed a kiss to her goddaughter's forehead.

"Thank you for helping me with all this Len."

"It's been our pleasure." She looked up at me. "How are you doing?"

"Better than ever." I winked at her and she squeezed my arm before turning her attention back to Ivylin.

"Can I have a cuddle now? I feel like I've been waiting down here for hours."

"You can." I laughed as I handed Ivylin over to her and she nuzzled her soft cheek with her nose. "You know you look damn good with a baby Mrs Delaney," I said as she kissed the chubby cheek that was closest to her. It wasn't lost on me that while she giggled, she didn't actually say anything. I decided not to press it for the moment and instead opted to follow the path Freya had taken into the room. I found her instantly, her hands pressed against her once-again tear-stained cheeks. "Are you happy?" I whispered in her ear as I caught her around the waist and shifted her body into mine.

"More than I have ever been in my life. The best thing I ever did was let you love me, Knox Sutton. Look at what we have."

I didn't need to take my eyes off her as I answered because I was already looking at the woman who had given me everything I could ever have dreamt of and more. "I'm looking at it, Fire girl. I'm always looking at it."

acknowledgements

I'd like to start once again by thanking you, the awesome person reading this. I never thought I would make it to the point where other people wanted to read the words I had furiously scribbled but here we are on book two and this ride has been the best one I have ever taken a chance on. I will always be grateful for being given the chance to share these little pieces of myself with you. I hope you've enjoyed yourselves so far!!

Secondly I'd like to say a huge thank you to Caitlin (Editing by C.Marie), my wonderfully patient and seriously amazing editor. I know that my babies are in safe hands as soon as I send them to you. You make my words sound so much better every single time!!

Thirdly I'd like to give a huge shout out and hugs to Marisa-Rose Shor of Cover Me Darling. You are my amazing!! I know you've probably heard me say that a ton of times but I truly mean it. I don't know what I would do without you!! I wait with baited breath for my proofs because I know that no matter how I imagine them you will always blow my mind and this book was no exception. Thank you for everything!!

Now on to the women in my life who stopped me from giving up on this dream, the women who talk me through the ups and downs and who root for me endlessly.

Mama, you are the best! I honestly don't know what else to say besides that. Thank you for loving my words, for loving my characters and for loving and believing in me enough to put up with reading them 10,000 times before anyone else gets to see them. Love you forever.

To my favourite baby sister ;) Yes I know you're my only one but I thought you'd appreciate that!! Thank you once again for the hours of brainstorming, for the plot rearranging and for being a highlighter warrior. Thank you for believing in me and these characters and for the beautiful image on the front of this book. You're pretty damn awesome dude. Love you always.

Dani, you've been with me on this journey since pretty much the beginning and I can't thank you enough. Your support has been unwavering and you've been an awesome friend throughout all of this. Here's to lots more stories, lots more tears and a billion more strawberry daiquiris that will have you spilling all your secrets haha!!

And finally Tricia, thank you again for allowing me to put my words in front of you and for finding time to fall in love with these guys!! Your encouragement has been awesome!! Here's to the next one!!

about the author

I love to hear from readers so if you would like to find out more about myself and any of my upcoming projects please come and join me in any of the avenues below.

Facebook: Author M.C.Payne
Twitter: @MCPayneAuthor
Instagram: author.mcpayne
Email: author.mcpayne@gmail.com
Goodreads: M.C. Payne

Made in the USA
Columbia, SC
26 April 2017